PRAISE FOR COMMON

"*Common* is a well-told tale of true sacrificial friendship with a dash of sweet romance and a sprinkling of fairy tale magic. Teens and adults alike will enjoy this engaging coming-of-age fantasy."

— Carrie Anne Noble, award-winning author of *The Mermaid's Sister*

~

"*Common* pulls readers into a fantasy world of forbidden attraction, unforeseeable twists, and memorable characters. Plan on staying up all night reading—you won't be able to put it down!"

— Sara Baysinger, author of the Black Tiger Series

~

"*Common* is a lovely coming-of-age story with a sweet romance that will have you holding your breath in anticipation."

— Julie Hall, USA Today Best-Selling author of the Life After Series

~

"Engaging and intriguing! Laurie Lucking's *Common* pulled me in and kept me riveted from beginning to end. I look forward to seeing what she comes up with next!"

— Katie Clark, author of the Enslaved Series

~

"*Common* deserves every point on each of its sparkling five stars. I truly loved it, regardless of the fact that it's a lot more romance-heavy than I normally read. The book taught me a lesson about expanding my boundaries, and that a great story is simply a great story and can be thoroughly enjoyed regardless of whether or not it's squarely set in your favorite genre. I feel silly for ever being so picky!

If you're looking for a relaxing, heartwarming story you can dive into headfirst, I highly recommend that you grab a copy of *Common*. You won't regret it!"

—Jamie Foley, author of the Sentinel Trilogy

~

"Laurie Lucking's *Common* quenches a spot in my heart that craves fairy-tale romances. With a dashing prince and a fearless heroine, you'll find yourself turning pages late into the night, unable to put this sterling debut down."

—Lucette Nel, author of *The Widow's Captive*

~

"'Common' chambermaid Leah Wellstone is shy, loyal, and brave—and relatable—a refreshing change from the better-than-everyone-at-everything warrior heroines. The romance between Leah and Prince Rafe is delightful, and the ending perfect for lovers of fairy tales—or for anyone who enjoys a good romance. I look forward to reading more from Laurie Lucking."

—Elizabeth Jane Kitchens, author of *The Rose and the Wand*

~

"*Common* is a new fairy tale, full of wonderful characters and a storyworld that pulls the reader in. Exploring the themes of loyalty, faith, and self-worth, Ms. Lucking's debut novel shares Leah's struggle to save the royal family and her friend Rafe against insurmountable odds. Carve out some time for this delightful story— once you start reading, you won't be able to stop until it's over!"

—J.M. Hackman, author of *Spark*

~

"Lucking is an amazing fantasy writer! Anyone who enjoys a bit of romance in their books will enjoy this well-written story of courage and triumph. It's nice to have a story with an HEA. Those are a scarce thing nowadays. I truly enjoyed this story and cannot wait to read more from Ms. Lucking in the future. Five stars from me!"

—Deanna Fugett, author of *Ending Fear*

~

"A shy servant girl, a handsome prince, a forbidden love, an evil sorcerer. Pair that with a group of mystic nuns and what could go wrong? This debut novel from Laurie Lucking has all these things and more! If you love a Cinderella tale with a bit of dark magic, *Common* is the story for you."

—Pam Halter, award-winning author of "Tick Tock" in *Realmscapes*

~

"Although *Common* contains all the staples readers of romance novels love, it is not just another Cinderella story. Filled with surprises that make readers eager to discover what comes next, *Common* is a fairy-tale romance unlike any other."

—Lauricia Matuska, author of *The Healer's Rune*

~

"Are you looking for a young adult fantasy with memorable characters, bold adventures, and a sweet romance? Laurie Lucking's delightful debut, *Common*, ticks all of these boxes and more. Get ready to be won over by plucky heroine, Leah, as she adapts to challenging circumstances and falls in love unexpectedly along the way."

—Jebraun Clifford, winner of ACFW's 2016 Genesis and 2015 First Impressions contests, Young Adult Category

~

"This book was a fun, romantic, and exciting read that sped time up. I'm hooked and can't wait to read what Laurie Lucking writes next."

—Sarah Armstrong-Garner, author of *Sinking*

~

"Gripping and beautifully written, *Common* is an adventure in friendship and real love. The ending had me so enthralled, I feared my reader-heart would be ripped in two. I couldn't put it down! Highly recommend it."

—Desiree Williams, author of *Illusionary*

Common

Tales of the Mystics
Book One

TALES OF THE MYSTICS
BOOK ONE

LAURIE LUCKING

Love2ReadLove2Write Publishing, LLC
Indianapolis, Indiana

ALSO BY LAURIE LUCKING

Common

Tales of the Mystics, Book One

Coming Soon:

Traitor

Tales of the Mystics, Book Two

Scarred

Tales of the Mystics, Book Three

To my husband,
my very own Prince Charming

CHAPTER 1

*J*rolled my shoulders and stretched my cramped fingers, sore from a long day of scrubbing floors. Guilt pricked my conscience as I passed the bedchamber I shared with Ma. I knew I should spend the evening helping her finish Lady Turington's new gown, and I would, unless...

I bit my lip to suppress a grin as I peeked out the window at the end of the corridor. There, across the moonlit gardens, a candle flickered in the farthest window of the North Wing. At last! It had been weeks since I'd seen Rafe.

Promising myself I would assist Ma tomorrow, I headed back toward the center of the palace. Fellow servants clustered in the halls, commiserating or discussing the latest gossip before they retired for the evening. I strode through with my head lowered, eager to avoid being drawn into conversation.

I glanced into every shadowed corner as I neared the closet, my footsteps whispering across the marble floor. Once certain I was free from observers, I eased the door open and slipped inside.

Rafe looked up from his thick textbook, one corner of his

mouth quirking into a smile. "There you are, Leah! I was beginning to worry you wouldn't be able to come."

I planted my hands on my hips and squared my shoulders in my best impression of Clara, our head housekeeper. "Always so impatient. Recall that some of us have work to finish before we're able to do as we like for the evening." I scrunched my nose at him before crouching down to grasp the handle of a fallen mop. Batting away the wisp of dust disturbed by my movements, I propped it in the corner amid an assortment of cobwebby brooms and dustpans.

He scoffed. "If you think my days don't feel like work, you're sorely mistaken. The royal party from Upper Flynn extended their visit by almost a full week. Every moment not claimed by my tutor has been filled with stuffy banquets and theatre engagements."

"Sounds dreadful." I tugged at the fraying sleeve of my dress and settled onto one of the upright wooden barrels lining the far wall.

"Believe me, it was. To make matters worse, they kept trying to push their king's whiny niece at me." His face twisted into a scowl. "Not a chance."

I ducked my head to hide a smile. Though I knew I would never be considered a suitable partner for my childhood friend, I couldn't help feeling relieved every time one of his parents' matchmaking schemes failed. "Ah, no wonder they stayed so long."

"Practically an eternity." He leaned his head back, digging his fingers into his unruly dark hair. "How good it feels to be free at last."

"You certainly have an odd definition of free." I glanced around the confines of the abandoned broom closet that had been my sanctuary from the moment I discovered it as a child. Rafe—or Prince Raphael, as I should've been addressing him —had stumbled in several years later while attempting to evade his governess. We had shared this secret reprieve from the constraints of our daily lives ever since.

"You know what I mean. This is the only room in the palace not crawling with guards and nobles. But now that the Upper Flynnites have finally taken their leave, I'm sure my parents will want to keep me out of their sight as much as possible. I ought to be able to get away a few more times this week."

My spirits lifted at the prospect of spending so much time with Rafe after his prolonged absence, only to sink again. "I'm not sure I'll be able to join you."

He gave me a puzzled frown.

"Ma's hands are giving her trouble, so I've been helping her catch up with her sewing." I ran a finger over the callus developing on my thumb. "And Purge Week starts tomorrow."

"Tomorrow?" Rafe's eyebrows flicked upward as he straightened. "I suppose it is nearly mid-spring. Thanks for the warning—I'd best avoid Mother at all costs. The chaos of Purge Week drives her to distraction."

Twice a year—once in the spring, again in the fall—the majority of the servants were relieved of their usual duties to empty Dorendyn Castle of every rug, drape, and tapestry to give them an airing. In truth, the process rarely took a full week, but nonetheless, the nickname Purge the Castle Week held.

He fixed me with a stern gaze. "Make sure they don't work you too hard."

As though I had any control over my workload. I fought the urge to roll my eyes as I bent to retrieve the novel I'd stored on an adjoining barrel. The king and queen had passed a decree many years before forbidding anyone in the serving class from learning to read, but Rafe taught me in the privacy of this closet and kept me supplied with new books.

Rafe turned through several pages in his textbook before

he flipped it shut again. "Didn't you say you were born under the last spring moon?"

"Yes." I set my open book on my lap.

"Then you'll be sixteen soon, right?" He leaned forward and glanced out the window at the waning gibbous.

"In about a month."

"You must be planning a celebration of some kind. You'll be reaching your Maturity!"

I shrugged, smoothing my apron. "Servants don't generally celebrate birthdays." We had little enough time, and nothing to celebrate with. "Ma always remembers and tries to sneak me something special from the kitchen. I doubt this year will be any different."

"I can't believe that." Rafe stared at me as though I'd sprouted an extra head. "Why, my parents even pretended to care about my sixteenth birthday last year. They threw a big banquet filled with people I don't like, and Father made a speech about how important this time was in my preparations to become king one day."

My laugh held an edge of cynicism. "I guess while sixteen may be critical in the development of a future king, it's not particularly noteworthy in the life of one who spends her days with a bucket and sponge."

"It's noteworthy to me." He rubbed his fingers across his jawline, as though plotting something.

I returned to my book, reassuring myself that Rafe could hardly turn my birthday into an embarrassing spectacle when we only ever saw each other in a broom closet.

Several days later, I expended the last of my energy striking a wicker rod against a rug from the entrance hall. I stifled a cough as dust floated around me, glinting in the sunlight.

Our head housekeeper kept turning to watch me while she

directed the placement of a set of curtains over a tree limb, making the skin on the back of my neck bristle. When the aching muscles in my arms succumbed to trembling, I let my beater fall. I glanced back as I massaged my wrist and saw Clara approaching. Cringing at the prospect of a reprimand, I took a deep, shuddering breath and braced myself to raise the beater again.

She put out a hand to stop me. "Please, take a break, child. You've earned it."

"Thank you." My arms crumpled to my sides in relief, but my posture remained tense.

"I only came over to compliment you on your fine work."

I clenched my jaw to prevent it from falling open. "Oh, I —" I glanced at the rug I'd been beating, unable to detect a quantifiable improvement.

She smiled, following my gaze. "Not just today. I've had my eye on you for some time, Leah. I admire your work ethic. You're serious, not engaging in the tomfoolery of your peers. I appreciate that."

I transferred the beater to my other hand and shifted my weight. "Thank you."

"I somehow doubt you'll remain a chambermaid all your life. It would be a waste of your talent. Maybe I'll even have the opportunity to train you to take my position one day." She tweaked my chin. "Now, I'll let you get back to it."

"Yes, thank you." I winced as she marched away to bark orders at other servants. My inability to utter anything resembling a coherent thought could hardly have bolstered her confidence. How could she envision *me* as head housekeeper? Even if I could muster the assurance to dole out commands, no one would follow them.

A cursory lunch was served outside when the church bells tolled at midday. I took my food to a shady patch of grass under the outstretched arms of a grevel tree.

Gretchen plopped down beside me, balancing her bread

and cheese on her skirt. The ends of her straight, tawny hair brushed the grass as she took a swig from her waterskin. "I'm absolutely certain the number of tapestries in this place doubles every year. Where do they find the wall space?"

I swallowed the bite of cheese in my mouth, savoring its smoky flavor. "I guess it takes a long time to fill every bit of wall in a palace this size. And a lot of tapestries."

Gretchen giggled. The freckles on her nose and cheeks always proliferated during Purge Week. "Too true. I saw Clara speaking with you earlier. Any trouble?"

"No, in fact she said I'm doing well. She thinks I may have it in me to be head housekeeper someday." I tore a tough piece of crust off my roll. "I, of course, do not agree."

"You? Head housekeeper?" Gretchen's eyebrows lifted. "You're responsible enough, certainly, but you'd have to raise your voice much louder than a church mouse in order to be effective. Quite a compliment, though."

"I guess. You'd be better at it. Perhaps I should send her your way."

"Me? If I were in charge, I'd be pilfering the tapestries so we wouldn't have to clean the blasted things anymore."

My laugh was cut short by the approach of Sam and Ned. I clutched a handful of grass, resisting the impulse to run for cover in the gardens flanking the open lawn.

"Could that be a smile lighting up your face, Red? I didn't think you were capable of such a thing."

As the only red-haired resident of the palace, I'd been teased for as long as I could remember. These two were the worst offenders, with Sam always taking the lead.

"Who could be, with you louts around?" Gretchen slid her fingers around her discarded rod and took a swing at Ned's legs.

"Hey!" He bent to snatch up my beater as Gretchen darted away with a squeal.

I groaned inwardly as Sam took her seat.

"I bet I could make you smile more often, Red, if you'd give me a chance."

I ignored him, hoping he would grow bored and leave.

Sam shifted his gaze to where Gretchen and Ned were chasing each other around the field. "If only Ned and I had carpet beaters, too, we could take you on. Ladies versus gentlemen."

"There certainly wouldn't be any gentlemen involved," I muttered.

"Aw, now, that's not fair." He leaned over until his arm brushed mine. "Just give me another one of those smiles, Red, and I'll show you what a gentleman I can be."

I edged away, digging my fingers into the soil. If only the ground would swallow me whole and put an end to my misery.

"What would you say to such a challenge?" he pressed.

"It doesn't sound appealing in the least. I'm glad Clara had the foresight to deprive you and Ned of such weapons."

"It only doesn't appeal to you because you wouldn't stand a chance against me." He jabbed me with his elbow. "And we'd be capital beaters, you must admit. But, alas, they just can't manage without us around the stables. Too important, you know. Those horses won't take care of themselves."

"I wager they'd be willing to give it a try if it meant they'd be spared the company of you lot."

Sam threw back his head and laughed. "Atta girl, Red!"

I flinched as he clapped me on the back.

"There might be some fire in you yet. Always seemed like there should be, with that head of hair."

Much to my relief, the others returned. Ned's shoulders sagged as he dropped my rod at my feet. "Let's go."

Sam jumped up but turned back to me. "Until we meet again, my pet." He patted my head before scurrying to catch up with Ned.

"Better luck next time," Gretchen called after them. Once they were out of earshot, she lay back with a satisfied smile.

"You know, I think Purge Weeks are my favorite times of the year."

I nearly choked on the morsel of bread I'd just popped into my mouth. "Purge Weeks are the worst! You were just saying so yourself."

She shrugged.

"Sometimes I can't understand you. It makes me wonder how we manage to be friends."

"Now that's an easy one." She sat up on her elbows. "You keep me sensible, or at least you try to. And without me, I'm not sure you'd have any fun at all."

"Yes, that must be it."

A bell clanged in the distance, prompting us both to rise and brush off our skirts. Time to get back to work.

I collapsed onto a barrel in the closet that evening, grateful Ma had insisted I take a break from sewing to celebrate the conclusion of Purge Week. My hands throbbed in protest as I picked up *One Hundred Days at Sea*, releasing a faint scent of buckram and wood pulp. Shifting to where I could rest against the wall, I placed the book on my lap and gingerly flipped to the page I'd marked.

I'd only progressed a few paragraphs when Rafe burst through the door and shoved it closed in his typical, careless fashion. It was a wonder our secret hideout hadn't been discovered years ago.

"Good evening. I've brought some new books for you at last." He deposited three volumes into a pile in the corner, keeping one tucked under his arm. He peered past my shoulder. "Looks like you haven't finished that one yet, though. Good. How are you liking it?"

I twisted around to regard him in the dim light. "It

certainly is exciting, but I'll admit I don't enjoy nautical adventures quite as much as you do."

Rafe chuckled. "I can't say I'm surprised. But living at sea…it sounds so liberating, doesn't it?"

"Being stuck on a boat all the time? Hardly."

"Ugh, you just have no sense of imagination. A boat could take you so many more interesting places than a horse and carriage."

"Yes, and provide so many more sea creatures the opportunity to enjoy you as a snack."

Rafe shook his head, settling against the wall with his long legs practically stretching across the length of the room. He opened the textbook he'd hung on to with a sigh. "If I were a sailor, there's no chance I'd be stuck reading tomes of ancient Trellan history."

"If you were a sailor, you'd forever smell of dead fish."

He stuck out his tongue at me, but his mirth disappeared when I failed to respond. "What's got you in such a bad humor?"

I pushed my braid off my shoulder and shrank further behind my book.

Rafe's frown deepened. "They're not still giving you a hard time about your hair, are they? That should've gotten old ages ago."

"Apparently not."

He balled his hands into fists. "How I long to box their ears for you."

"Please don't. Though I do appreciate the thought." I leaned my head against the cool wall. "When I was little, I often wished I had a protective older brother or sister to convince them to stop giving me a hard time." A thought struck me as I returned my gaze to Rafe. "Do you—?" I cut myself short.

"Do I what?"

I picked at the dirt crusted under one of my fingernails. "Never mind."

"Nonsense." He sat up straighter. "You can ask me anything."

"Fine." I drew an uneven breath. "I was wondering if you knew why you don't have any siblings. Both your parents are still around, after all, and I'd think they would've been eager for more children."

Rafe's laugh had a grim undertone. "Yes, it would've given my parents great comfort if they could've provided a few backup heirs to the throne. But I'm sure you've heard the story."

I chewed the inside of my cheek. Many whispered accounts were passed around of the king and queen's betrayal of a powerful sorcerer who cursed them in retribution, leaving them barren. "Well, yes. But you don't really believe it, do you?"

He spread his hands across the smooth cover of his text-book. "I tried asking them once and was sent to bed without supper. So, true or not, it seems to be a sore subject. It's probably nonsense, but they issued their Edict Against the Practice of Magic shortly after I was born, so you never know."

"I suppose." I'd heard of the edict but never questioned its origin. The thought of the king and queen associating with a genuine sorcerer sent trails of goosebumps up my arms. "Do you think the edict truly drove them all out of Imperia?"

"My parents would swear to it, but I sometimes wonder..." Rafe's brows knit, darkening his eyes. "Do you remember that odd business with the Emperor of Delunia? My father seemed on the verge of securing his most powerful ally yet, and then the emperor just took off without a word. Everyone said his behavior was odd, as though he couldn't recall why he'd come to Imperia in the first place."

I wrapped my arms around my waist, hoping to contain my

shiver. "Maybe a health condition arose, or he had a history of such confusion."

"Perhaps." He raised a shoulder in an unconvinced half-shrug. "I sometimes think instead of driving the sorcerers out of Imperia, my parents only succeeded in forcing them into hiding. And provoking their anger."

A knot formed in my stomach. "But surely you've nothing to fear. The sorcerer who supposedly cursed your parents must've been the first one eliminated after they passed their edict."

Rafe's chest rose and fell before he answered. "Apparently you never reached the end of the tale. They say he was never found."

CHAPTER 2

$\mathcal{M}$y eyes were still adjusting to the dim interior of our chamber while Ma bustled about, already dressed. She rushed to my side as I crawled out from under the heavy woolen blanket.

"Good morning, dear. Happy birthday!" She wrapped me in a hug. "My little girl has reached her Maturity. How the years have flown by." She stood back, placing her hands on my shoulders. "I couldn't be more proud of the young woman you've become."

I basked in the warm glow radiating from her face. "Thank you, Ma."

Releasing me, she knelt and rummaged beneath the bed.

I bent over the side of the mattress, curious what she might be looking for. "Can I help you find something?"

"Oh, no." She winced and grabbed the headboard to pull herself up. Her other hand held something wrapped in pieces of discarded fabric.

She countered my worried frown with a smile. "These old bones aren't limber enough for such acrobatics this early in the morning." Dropping onto the edge of the bed, she offered the

parcel to me. "It's not much, but I couldn't let such an important occasion pass without making you something special."

I accepted it, my head a whirl of excitement and concern.
I'd never received a birthday present in my life. How had she
managed it? "Oh, Ma, you didn't need to..." I turned the gift
over in my hands. "Are you sure we can afford it?"

"What's there to afford? I made it all myself with scraps
that won't be missed." She leaned forward, eyes alight. "Aren't
you going to open it?"

Releasing a breath, I nodded and unrolled the material.
Inside lay a pale doll in an exquisite blue gown embroidered
with tiny golden beaconflowers. Meticulously arranged burnt-
orange threads cascaded over her shoulders—hair clearly
intended to match mine.

Gratitude swelled in my chest, tightening the base of my
throat. Ma must've labored for hours on this with so much
other work to do and stiff, cramping hands.

"Ma, I...I can't thank you enough. She's beautiful."

She gave a contented sigh. "I'm so glad you like her. I know
you're too old to play with dolls, but I'll never forget how you
used to describe the dolls of the young aristocratic girls with
such longing. I just wish I'd had the opportunity to make her
for you years ago."

"I don't mind." I glanced up to find the moisture in my eyes
reflected in hers.

"Good. Now we'd best prepare you for the day." She
turned me around so she could comb my hair. "I still remember
the first moment I saw you." She paused as she undid the braid
I'd slept in. "I knew right then and there how extraordinary
you would be, especially with that head of red hair. Just
like..." Her voice caught as her hands went back to work.

I tensed, hoping she would continue. Just like what? Or
more likely, *whom*? A profusion of unanswered questions
assailed my mind, clouding my vision. Did I look like my

father? Was he there at my birth? Had he thought I was extraordinary, too?

I'd never known my father, and Ma never said a word about him. I asked on several occasions during my childhood, but she always brushed me off or changed the subject. The last time I inquired, several years before, I heard Ma weeping after she thought I was asleep. I never dared raise the topic again, though my lack of knowledge felt like an ever-widening hole in my heart.

After a few moments of silence, Ma placed a hand on my back. "Some claim it's lucky to be born under a full moon. But you know what I say?"

I strove to keep my voice light, not wanting her to suspect the direction my thoughts had taken. "What?" I knew exactly what she would say next, but I enjoyed playing along every year.

"I think it's even luckier to be born the day before, because then your eyes are open in time to see that stunning full moon —the Luminate's gift to us to light the nighttime hours."

I nodded carefully to avoid snagging my hair in the comb. Though far from convinced the Luminate ever gave us more than a passing thought, I wouldn't deny Ma the comfort of attributing nearly everything to His influence.

Ma sighed as she separated strands for a new braid. "To think you're old enough to marry now."

My laugh came out louder than I intended. "Maturity or not, I'm not ready to consider marriage."

"There's no rush, of course. But I suspect you'll have a suitor or two soon enough, pretty as you are."

My stomach churned at the thought. I hadn't the slightest idea what a girl was supposed to say to a suitor or how she should act. What if I were put in the awkward position of refusing a proposal? The entire courting process baffled me. Besides, none of the young men I encountered had ever made marriage seem the least bit enticing. None of the fellow servants I had to choose from, anyway.

My breath caught when I spied the glimmer of a candle in the window of Rafe's chambers that evening. Though I'd tried to tell myself a servant's birthday was of no consequence to a prince, I couldn't help wishing he might remember. I struggled to keep my steps measured as I made my way to our closet. Did Rafe have something planned?

I pulled open the door.

Rafe jumped to his feet and produced a small box from his pocket. Approaching where I stood just inside the door, he presented it to me with a gallant bow. "I've been waiting all day to see you. Happy birthday."

Gooseflesh crawled up my arms, and my pulse quickened. This was just the warm reception I'd hoped for, but now the reality of accepting a gift from Rafe made me want to turn and escape back down the hall. "You're sweet, but this really isn't necessary."

He took a step closer. "Of course it is. Even if it's only marked by your mother and myself, I think your reaching your Maturity is of the highest importance."

My fingertips brushed his as I took the box from his hand. The brief touch produced a rush of warmth in my cheeks. Keeping my head down, I gently lifted the lid. The sight of an emerald pendant strung on a delicate silver chain propelled a rush of air from my lungs.

"Rafe! I..." I gulped. If anything, I'd expected a pastry or ribbon. Nothing like this. Few of the courtiers around the palace possessed a jewel so exquisite, and he was giving it to *me*? "I'm not sure I can accept this."

His mouth fell open. "What's the matter? You don't like it?"

How could I explain my reservations without hurting his feelings? "It's beautiful. Stunning. But it's too much."

A trace of his smile returned. "When I saw it in the marketplace last week, it reminded me so strongly of the color of your eyes, I knew you had to have it."

That Rafe had been thinking of me in the middle of the marketplace—reflecting on my eyes, no less—sent a new surge of heat into my face. "But you must've had to barter something substantial for it."

"I'm the prince, remember?" He leaned on the wall next to him, propped up by his hand. "I'm not required to barter."

I backed against the door. "You mean you took this from the vendor without giving him anything in exchange?"

Rafe's brows knit. "That's always how it's done in the royal family. We provide food, shelter, and protection for our citizens, and in turn, they offer their services without expecting any additional reward."

Though it didn't seem right, it should've come as no surprise. The queen never offered anything for Ma's work on her gowns. "But even if it didn't cost you anything…when would I wear it? None of the other maids own anything half as fine."

"I guess I hadn't thought of that." He rubbed the back of his neck. "But still, you must keep it. Surely someday an opportunity will arise for you to wear it. In the meantime, you can hide it here and simply enjoy viewing it once in a while."

He knew me too well. In spite of my protests, I was having trouble tearing my gaze away from the rich emerald as its various facets caught the moonlight. I steeled myself to argue further.

He put out a hand to stop me. "It's yours. I'll make it an official order if I have to. I can't return it without causing the jeweler offense, and what would I do with a necklace? If it makes you feel better, I promise I'll recommend him to every noblewoman in the kingdom so that his business ought to thrive. Please, just accept it. As a token of my friendship."

I shook my head, my smile refusing to hide. "Thank you, Rafe. You will be happy to know this is the most momentous birthday I've ever had."

His deep gray eyes brightened with pleasure. "Good, that's exactly what I was hoping for. And you're welcome."

I crossed the room to sit on one of the barrels, still clutching the open box.

Rafe took a seat on an adjoining barrel. "Even if you won't be able to wear it out there anytime soon, would you like to try it on?"

"I would, but..." Embarrassment clenched my stomach. "I don't even know how to unfasten the clasp."

He chuckled, taking the box from my hands. "Who would've guessed I'd end up teaching a young lady about jewelry?" He lifted the pendant off its small satin pillow, letting it dangle as he took the clasp between each thumb and index finger. "Here, it's really quite simple."

My mind still reeled from the enormity of the gift, making it impossible to concentrate as he demonstrated the workings of the catch mechanism.

He paused and held the ends apart. "Now turn around and lift your hair."

I obeyed, holding my breath as he brought the pendant to lie at the base of my throat. His warm fingers grazed my neck as he secured the clasp, sending a tingle through my shoulders. Thank the new moon he couldn't read my expression.

Rafe cleared his throat. "There."

I lowered my braid to rest on my back once more and turned toward him. Reluctant to meet his eye, I glanced down at the gleaming jewel that produced such a stark contrast to the patched, faded bodice of my dress.

His gaze flitted to the pendant before returning to my face. "Perfect."

CHAPTER 3

The scrape of a pewter bowl against the wooden mess-hall table roused me from a daydream. I blinked and glanced up, expecting to greet Gretchen. Instead, Sam's gleaming blue eyes met mine. Ned hovered close behind.

My throat went dry.

"Might we join you?" Sam stepped over the bench and sat distressingly close in one fluid motion.

I edged my bowl away. "It doesn't look as though I have much choice in the matter, does it?"

Sam grinned into my face. "Someday, Red, you're going to give up this charade that you dislike us."

"Bound to happen one of these days." Ned took a seat on my other side, though he kept a bit more distance.

"I wouldn't count on it." I concentrated on the bland chowder sitting before me.

After making several attempts to entice me into conversation, which I stubbornly ignored, they settled for talking around me instead.

When Gretchen finally appeared, she took a seat across

from us. "Well, aren't you a lucky one? To be joined by two such fine gentlemen for dinner." She gave me a broad smile.

I rolled my eyes. "Where have you been?"

Gretchen wrinkled her nose. "The Earl of Lathrop's toddler is sick. You wouldn't believe the mess I had to clean up in the nursery."

"Ugh, say no more." Ned gripped the table and pretended to gag.

Gretchen swatted at his head. "Come off your high horse there, Ned. It's not as though the two of you don't deal with plenty of disgusting stuff caring for the animals." She wagged her spoon at them.

"Isn't that the truth?" Sam's disheveled hair fell into his face as he nodded. "Though rest assured, Red, I tidied myself up real nice before coming to dinner. I would never want to offend any pretty young maids I might come across." He gave me a nudge.

I tucked my arms even tighter to my sides.

When I'd scraped out the last of the chowder from my bowl, I rose from the bench. I turned toward Ned, hoping he would pose less opposition. "Please excuse me. Enjoy the rest of your dinner."

"Leaving so soon?" Sam clutched at my hand. "Say it isn't so."

I refused to look at him. "I'm afraid it is."

Ned slid over just far enough that I had room to glide my foot over the bench in an awkward maneuver.

"Goodnight." I directed my steps toward the door at the other end of the large hall.

"Wait, Red, you dropped something," Ned called after me.

I patted my apron pocket. My pulse pounded as I realized the doll Ma made for my birthday had slipped out. I turned around.

Sam bent to retrieve her, his smile more mischievous than ever. "Now, what have we here?"

I returned to the table in two strides, the meal I'd just eaten churning in my stomach. "Nothing. Please give it back."

"Nothing, eh?" Sam dangled the doll by one of her arms. "Looks like a doll to me." He glanced at me with a smirk. "Were you spending time in the nursery today as well, Red?"

"It's mine. Just give it to me." I gritted my teeth, my face burning as though I were leaning into a hot oven. No sixteen-year-old should carry a doll around in her pocket, but keeping Ma's gift near gave me comfort and reminded me of the pleasant memories from my birthday.

I made a grab for her, but Sam was in no way ready to relinquish his prize.

"A doll? Really, Red? I suppose a strong maternal instinct is to be desired in any young woman who hopes to marry." He pinched my cheek, and I flinched and pulled back. "But even so, this seems a little extreme, don't you think?"

"I think it's cute." Ned's tone dripped mockery.

Gretchen regarded me with sympathy. "That's enough from you two. Just give it back to her already."

"Oh, I'd be more than happy to give it back." Sam held the doll just beyond my reach. "But I'm afraid I'll need something in return... What do you think would be an appropriate payment, Ned? A kiss, perhaps?"

Ned nodded in agreement, snickering.

"Not in your wildest dreams. Keep it for all I care." I stormed out of the hall and fled straight to my closet.

I cringed when the door opened half an hour later, alerting me to Rafe's entrance. I swiped my hands across my cheeks and over my hair. Though my tears had subsided, I had a bad feeling my face remained covered in telltale red splotches.

"Good, you're here!"

I did my best to return his smile. "I am."

"What a day I've had." Rafe crumpled to the floor, pushing his hair out of his face. "The ambassador from Trellich returned last evening, and my parents thought it would be 'beneficial' for me to 'sit in on a little strategizing' today. A little? Try five hours' worth!"

Though I was still consumed by my own cares, his statement caught my attention. "Is there trouble with Trellich?"

He shrugged. "Relations with Trellich are always somewhat precarious. But Father has decided to send the Duke of Brantley with the ambassador when he makes his return journey. I've never liked Brantley much, but apparently he was very well-received in Trellich last time. Anyway, then my tutor had the nerve to be mad because the strategy session put me behind on my theology—as though any of this was my fault—and now he wants me to read three chapters tonight. Not likely."

"We could read them together if it would help."

"I guess that might be all right. You sure are a capital friend, Leah." He tapped me on the knee, then sat up and regarded me more closely. "Are you unwell? Your voice sounds a little rough, and your eyes are all red."

I turned away. "I'm fine."

He stood, bending so his face was level with mine where I sat cross-legged on one of the barrels. "No. Something's wrong, I can tell. I'm always prattling on to you about my problems. It's time you took a turn." He perched on the adjacent barrel, leaning against my shoulder. "Talk to me."

"It's silly."

"I don't care. I still want to hear about it."

Sighing, I shifted to face him. "All right, but please don't poke fun at me. I've had enough of that already today."

He frowned but raised his hand. "You have my word."

"I don't know if I mentioned it, but Ma made me a doll for my birthday. It fell out of my apron pocket at dinner, right in front of Sam and Ned—two of the boys who are always teasing me. And they wouldn't give her back." I fought against the tears prickling at my eyes again. "I know it's juvenile for me to carry around a doll, especially now that I've reached my Maturity, but she's just about the only thing I can call my own, aside from a few dresses, and Ma worked so hard on her. I guess I just like knowing she's with me."

"Makes perfect sense to me." Rafe's words betrayed no hint of laughter or scorn. "And I can guarantee you that Sam and Ned, I think you called them, have done far more juvenile things than feeling attached to a homemade present."

"Thanks, Rafe." My voice sounded like a hiccup. I covered my face with my hands as the tears I'd held back streamed down my face.

"Aw, Leah, please don't cry." My breath hitched as he leaned over to give me a hug. Would this feel as forced as Sam's mocking flirtations? Or different somehow?

Rafe's arms surrounded me, sending warmth and safety coursing through my entire being. I closed my eyes and rested my head against his chest, relishing the curious tingling where he gently stroked my hair.

Eventually he let go of me, moving his hands to my shoulders so he could look into my face. His expression was one I'd never seen before—intense, yet oddly unfocused.

I swallowed as the moment stretched out. Fire burned my cheeks, and my stomach compressed in a strange way. Uncomfortable, but not altogether unpleasant.

When I couldn't bear the silence any longer, I whispered, "You're the one who's a capital friend, you know. Should we get started on your theology?"

"Theology?" Rafe blinked, as though unfamiliar with the term.

"Your reading. For your tutor?"

He shook himself. "My reading assignment. Yes, of course. It's not going to plod through itself, is it?" He gave a weak laugh as he crossed the room to retrieve his book.

I shivered, my shoulders cold in the absence of his hands.

"But first, do you want me to find those boys and demand they return your doll?" Rafe raised his eyebrows.

I couldn't help but smile at the idea of the crown prince using his authority to get a doll back for a servant. "No, thank you. I appreciate the thought, but I can only imagine the number of difficult questions that would generate."

"Hmm, perhaps you're right." He climbed back onto his barrel. "It's aggravating, though, not to be able to help."

"You have helped."

"Good." His eyes searched mine before he held up his textbook. "On to theology, then?"

"On to theology."

He sat closer than usual, his shoulder pressed against mine, as he settled in and began to read aloud.

I surprised myself by leaning toward him.

◦

Sam approached me at breakfast the following morning.

I dropped my fork, ready to abandon my plate of eggs, but he grabbed my arm before I could get away.

"Don't go, Red. Leah. I promise not to give you grief today."

I paused at his use of my real name but wrenched my arm from his grasp. "What do you want?"

"Just to give you this." He held out Ma's doll.

I hesitated, fearing it was a trick. But when he extended his hand even closer, I snatched her. He let go without a struggle, and then looked down at his feet, shifting uneasily as I shoved the doll deep into my apron pocket.

"You seemed real upset yesterday, and Gretchen scolded us something fierce. She told me your ma made that for you. I'm sorry. I didn't know."

Since he truly looked contrite, I bit back the harsh retort that came to mind. "Thanks for returning her."

"Sure. I don't have much use for a doll anyway." A cautious smile tugged at his lips. "Say, there's a group of us planning to go to the festival next week. You should come. Gretchen will be there, and I'll be on my very best behavior. I swear it."

The Peasantry Festival was the one day each year the servants were completely freed from their duties to enjoy food vendors, musicians, and other performers that crowded the streets outside the castle.

"I usually go with my ma, but I'll think about it."

"Good." His smile broadened. "I'll let you get back to your breakfast. Thanks for not being too cross with me." He winked before heading back outside.

I sat next to Ma during our break for the midday meal. "Did you realize the Peasantry Festival is next week already? Are we going again this year?"

She shifted her food around her plate. "Some of the young folks are planning to go together, aren't they? I'm sure you'd be welcome to accompany them."

Disappointment gnawed at my stomach. "Well, yes. They invited me, but I'd still rather go with you."

"My dear, quiet girl." Ma patted my shoulder. "I appreciate your willingness to spend the day with me, but why don't you go with your friends this year? I'm not sure I'll feel up to participating in the full range of festival activities, and I'd hate for you to miss anything."

"Is something the matter?" I glanced at her plate of uneaten food.

She waved me off. "Not particularly. I'm just not as young as I once was. I don't know where my appetite's gone today." She straightened, her lips widening into a smile. "But don't you worry about me. I'll be very pleased to know you're enjoying the festival with Gretchen and the others. Just promise to get me a loaf of my favorite almond bread."

"Of course." I tried to match the brightness of her tone. "I wouldn't let you miss out on that."

She placed a lock of hair behind my ear. "You're a good girl. I hope you can allow yourself to have a little fun."

My pulse thumped worse than a carriage over a gravel road as I stood outside the closet door.

Rafe and I were childhood friends. Almost like siblings. A simple embrace couldn't change all of that. He had comforted me while I was crying, nothing more.

But no matter how I rationalized the events of the prior evening, anticipation continued to churn through my veins.

I sought Rafe's eyes the moment I entered the room, but he barely glanced up. The grim expression on his face quenched my expectancy like water dousing a flame.

When he failed to speak, I pasted on a cheerful smile. "I can't think of the last time you managed two nights in a row like this."

He traced shapes in the mound of sand he'd dragged to the closet years ago to teach me to write and spell. "I'm skipping out on an opera we were to attend with the Earl and Countess of Ferren. My parents will be furious, but I just couldn't be in the same room with them any longer."

"Oh. Then it's good you were able to get away."

I waited for Rafe to elaborate. In the past, he'd always been eager to pour out his woes—lamenting the way his parents treated various tenant farmers, balking at reports of the brutal punishments his uncles doled out to disobedient servants, or objecting to his father's choice of advisers.

But tonight he remained quiet, not even looking up at me

as the silence dragged on. Was he, too, feeling uncomfortable about last evening? Then why had he come?

I fumbled for a subject that would lighten the mood. "Everyone's looking forward to the festival. Will you be there?"

He raised his eyes, his lips twitching upward. "Yes. I've been recruited for a fencing demonstration." His expression darkened once more as he returned to the sand. "Assuming the whole thing isn't canceled."

I nearly toppled off the barrel on which I was perched. "Canceled?" The tradition of the Peasantry Festival dated back to Imperia's founding.

Rafe folded his arms across his chest. "My parents were discussing the possibility today, though I doubt they'd follow through with it. They're hesitant to do anything that might further encourage the servants to reach above their station." He held out his hands when my mouth fell open. "Their words, not mine."

"I know." My posture slumped. "But how could allowing the servants one day off a year to enjoy themselves cause any harm? It never has in the past, has it?"

"Of course not. It doesn't make any sense, but these are my parents we're talking about. They're on edge because of Viscount Renby. Well, former Viscount."

"What do you mean, former?"

Rafe's brows shot up. "You haven't heard? Sorry, no wonder you look confused. They stripped him of his title this morning." He fidgeted under my gaze as I waited for him to continue. "Because he married one of his maids."

I gripped the edge of my barrel for support. "But...how could they?" I could hardly splutter out the words. "Surely a viscount is free to marry whomever he pleases?"

Rafe's chuckle held a dark edge. "Not in Imperia. Not now, anyway. It's getting worse all the time. But I'm determined when I take the throne, my first act will be to elevate Renby to a duke."

Warmth swept through my limbs, replacing the chill produced by Rafe's news.

Gratitude overcame my hesitancy, and I crossed the short distance to sit next to him. "You're going to make a great king, Rafe. I wouldn't wish an early death on your parents, of course, but Imperia will be in excellent hands when you're the one making the decisions."

Rafe looked down at his lap, color creeping up his neck. "I don't know about that. But it means a lot to hear you say it." He cautiously reached out a hand to cover mine.

I sat, rigid, equally excited and panicked by his touch. He couldn't mean anything by it. Could he?

CHAPTER 4

$\mathcal{I}$ returned to my bedchamber in a daze, hoping Ma would already be asleep. Instead, she set aside her needlework the moment I entered, looking every bit as eager as she'd been on my birthday.

"Leah, you're finally here! I have such a surprise for you. You'll never guess."

"What is it?" Her enthusiasm was contagious.

"You're going to have a new dress for the Peasantry Festival."

"What? But how?"

"We've had a stroke of luck." She remained seated as she rummaged through the closet full of dresses she was working on for the queen and other noblewomen. "Yes, here it is."

I inhaled sharply as she held out a beautiful jade silk gown.

Ma gave me her most mischievous grin. "Lady Cartwright always likes to order her gowns months in advance so she has plenty of time for endless rounds of alterations. But in this case, her—condition—has changed such that this dress won't fit her anymore. There wasn't enough fabric for me to take it out, so she had to order an entirely new gown. She didn't want one of her rivals to benefit at her expense, and I think she has a soft spot for me since we've spent so much time together. She insisted I keep it." She held the dress out at arm's length with a sigh. "May the Luminate bless her and her little one."

"Oh, Ma, it's lovely. Truly. But you should wear it. She meant you to have it."

Ma shook her head with a laugh. "No one cares what I look like these days, least of all me. Besides, it will suit you perfectly." She held it against my chest. "Just look how the color brings out your eyes. Now, try it on for me so I can see what adjustments need to be made."

"But I don't want to create extra work for you." My protest sounded half-hearted, even to my ears.

"This won't feel like work, I promise." She cupped my chin. "What a pleasure it will be to finally see my daughter in one of the fine gowns I'm forever toiling over."

A dark thought marred my elation as Ma slipped the dress over my head. "But do you think it's appropriate?"

"What do you mean?" Ma leaned around from where she'd begun fastening buttons at my back.

I ran a hand over the smooth, vibrant fabric. "I'm not sure the king and queen would approve."

Ma released her grip to walk around and face me, leaving the dress to sag over my shoulders. "Why should the king and queen have anything to say about a girl wearing a dress that's been freely given to her?" She narrowed her eyes. "What's troubling you?"

Could I reveal what was on my mind? Rafe assumed I'd heard about the ousted viscount, so he must not have told me anything meant to be kept private.

"I heard a rumor today. About the Viscount Renby."

"Ah." Ma took my hands and led me to sit on the bed. "Leah, I know I've always told you to keep your distance when it comes to the royal family."

Guilt bubbled in my stomach, making me squirm with the

reminder that I'd heedlessly flouted her advice for years.

"But I only meant it for your protection. I hope I've never made you feel inferior. Because you're not. You have every reason to take pride in yourself." She raised my chin to make me look at her. "I don't care what the king and queen say, and it wouldn't matter to me if you were the maid assigned to empty chamber pots. In my eyes, and more importantly, in the Luminate's, we are all equals. Do you understand?"

"Yes, Ma." I nodded and stood so she could finish pinning the dress.

I appreciated her reassurances, but I couldn't help noting that, even if she were right, the Luminate's notions of equality didn't seem to matter here in Imperia.

By the day of the festival, Ma had tailored the dress so the bodice hugged my chest and waist, and the ribbon trimming the bottom edge of the skirt grazed my polished black shoes. After I'd twirled enough times to satisfy her, then gathered the small stack of embroidered handkerchiefs and gloves to use for bartering, I took off to meet Gretchen.

I paused in the hall to clasp Rafe's emerald pendant around my neck, shivering at the recollection of his fingers brushing my skin. Such thoughts were foolish, but I couldn't help taking this opportunity to wear the necklace, since it suited the new dress so perfectly. I hoped a vague explanation that someone had lent it to me would satisfy any inquiries.

Gretchen's mouth dropped open when I caught up with her at the end of the hall. "Just look at you. You could easily be mistaken for a countess! And here I'm stuck in the same dress I've worn for the past three years." She fingered the edge of one of my tapered sleeves. "Well, if that doesn't catch Sam's attention, I don't know what…"

Her voice trailed off when Sam stepped into view, followed

by Ned. The wave of heat searing my face intensified under their stares. Perhaps the gown hadn't been a stroke of luck after all. Could I still back out of attending the festival?

Recalling Ma's counsel, I took a deep breath and squared my shoulders. She'd worked hard on this dress; the least I could do was try to appreciate it.

Gretchen took the arm Ned extended to her as we set out. Sam offered his to me, but I hurried past as though I hadn't noticed. He lowered it without a word.

The streets just beyond the grounds of Dorendyn Castle were already bustling. The laughter and energy flitting through the air made me giddy. Vibrant flowers hung from the side of the palace, so numerous it appeared as though the very walls were made of them. The crowd, dressed in their finest, turned the road into a living, breathing rainbow. Decadent aromas of bread and spices enticed us to delve among the food carts, and merry songs floated through the air from wandering minstrels like a chorus of invisible birds.

We roamed as a unit for some time, getting our bearings. We paused at a draper's stand so Gretchen could choose fabric for a new shawl. Then we followed the inviting sounds of dulcimer and flute to a group of lively musicians.

I noticed Rafe on a raised platform constructed for the fencing demonstrations. His foil dangled from his right hand as he scanned the crowd. His eyes widened when he caught my gaze, sending a flush crawling up my cheeks. He broke into a familiar grin and raised his fingers to his neck.

I lifted the pendant that lay just above the square neckline of my gown and nodded, smiling back.

Sam tapped my shoulder. "Well, what do you think? Shall we join them?"

I gasped and released the pendant. "Join who?"

"Gretchen and Ned." He pointed toward the group of dancing couples. "Would you like to dance?"

My gaze darted back to him. "Dance? I hadn't really

planned on—"

"Aw, come on, Leah, please? I promise I won't step on your toes or anything. And look, they need another couple to fill their set."

I studied the dancers. Gretchen caught my eye and waved me over. I didn't relish the thought of dancing with Sam, but his eager expression softened my resistance. My next opportunity to dance would likely be next year's festival.

"All right. I guess one dance couldn't hurt."

Sam whooped and grabbed my hand to pull me into the open space near the musicians. As we took our places, I glanced back at Rafe. He was still watching me, but now his shoulders sagged. When I tried to smile at him again, he turned away. Before long, the steps, claps, and jumps of the dance claimed my full attention.

I partnered with Ned for the next song, then Sam convinced me to dance with him once more before we made a collective decision to seek out the food carts. Sam lifted his arm again as we set out, but I shook my head and kept my distance. A twinge of guilt pricked my stomach when he charged forward, his hands clenched into fists. Surely he hadn't expected this one pleasant day to erase years of teasing?

I sighed, quickening my pace to keep up with Gretchen and Ned.

Sam had resumed a neutral expression by the time we were enveloped by the heady scents of seared meat and roasting vegetables. We enjoyed mugs of cider and hearty pastries filled with lamb and gravy before I got in line to barter a small handkerchief for the promised loaf of almond bread for Ma.

By the end of the afternoon, exhaustion nipped at my limbs, but the day had been more enjoyable than I'd ever imagined so much time in the company of Sam and Ned could be. I directed my steps toward my bedchamber, trying to dismiss the vision of Rafe's downcast expression that kept forcing itself upon my mind's eye.

CHAPTER 5

"*W*ell, if it isn't Red. Good evening to you."

Sam gave me a mock bow when our paths crossed in the hall, provoking a chortle from Ned. In the two weeks following the festival, their interactions with me had already devolved back into teasing and mock flattery.

"Good evening, yourselves." I lengthened my strides, making the leather soles of my flats slap against the marble floor.

"You are looking quite lovely today." Sam's voice chafed my ears as he kept pace beside me. "Your hair is like the orange of the sun's rays…"

"As it makes its slow descent behind the mountain," Ned finished in a dreamy tone.

"I would've never guessed the two of you were cultured enough to spout sonnets."

"A man could be capable of almost anything with such inspiration before him." Sam tried to take my hand as he knelt before me.

"Oh, lay off it." I sidestepped him, careful to stay beyond his reach.

"You cut me to the quick." Sam sniffed and rose to his feet. "Still, you must do us the honor of letting us escort you to dinner." He looped his arm through mine.

"Indeed, you must." Ned took my other arm.

"As though I'd want to be seen walking the halls with the likes of you two." I made a feeble effort to free my arms from their grasps.

"Aw, come now, Red. We insist." Sam tugged my arm closer to his side. "We'll try to behave ourselves, truly we —"

"Unhand her at once!" The shout came from behind us.

We froze mid-step.

I groaned inwardly, recognizing Rafe's voice. While grateful for the interruption to my forced stroll with Sam and Ned, I couldn't picture the upcoming confrontation ending well.

The boys dropped my arms like branding irons, and we all faced Rafe. I dipped into a low curtsy, keeping my head down. Sam and Ned spluttered for a moment before following my example with delayed bows.

Rafe stalked up to us, the two gentlemen he'd been walking with trailing behind. "You should be ashamed of yourselves, accosting this innocent maiden in such a manner." His fierce glower softened as he turned to me. "Are you all right, Le—miss?"

"We were just teasing her, having a little fun." Ned broke in.

"Silence," Rafe barked, and Ned resumed his bowed stature. "I want to hear from the young lady."

I released a breath and looked up at him. "He speaks the truth, Your Highness. I am quite well. They meant no harm."

"Hmm." He searched my face, and the tension in his posture eased. "Well, in that case, I will let you go without punishment, as long as you leave at once and vow to importune this maiden no further."

"Yes, Your Highness," Sam mumbled on top of Ned's "Of course, Your Highness."

I held back a giggle as they both scurried off in the direction of the mess hall.

"You may go as well." Rafe now addressed his peers. "I shall escort this young lady to her destination."

The taller of the gentlemen raised his eyebrows at the other before they resumed their stroll down the corridor. My stomach sank. This was bound to be the subject of much gossip before the night was out.

Rafe took my arm and steered me in the opposite direction, keeping silent until his friends' footsteps retreated. "Are you really all right, Leah?"

I tried to pull away. He was whispering so close to my ear, I could feel his breath on my neck.

"What was going on back there? Who were those young men?"

"I'm fine, Rafe, truly. Those were two of the stable hands. I've known them all my life, and they've been teasing me almost as long. They get on my nerves, but I can assure you they're harmless."

His jaw remained set. "Even if they meant no harm, they need to learn the proper respect due to a lady."

I laughed, then checked myself and lowered my voice. "A lady? I appreciate the thought, but you need to remember I'm merely a servant. As such, I don't command quite the same level of gentility required for a noblewoman."

"Well, perhaps you should."

A lady's maid stared at us as we passed, sending searing heat into my cheeks. "While we're on the subject of my lowly status…are you sure this is a good idea?"

"What do you mean?" His brows knit.

"Walking through the corridors like this." I waved my free hand at our linked arms.

Rafe puffed out his chest. "I'm the prince, aren't I? How could I do any less than escort the maiden I rescued to safety?"

"I'm not sure that quite constituted a rescue." I stole a glance at him. "Is it customary for you to attend to damsels in distress in such a manner, then?" I bristled at the idea of Rafe walking through the halls arm in arm with other young women, but I shook it off.

"Well, no. But I still don't see how this could be objectionable."

"I'm concerned what people might say..."

"Oh, Leah, will you cease your endless worrying? I'm trying to be your knight in shining armor, and you're ruining it."

A smile tugged at my lips as I conceded defeat.

We rounded a corner, and Rafe's expression grew thoughtful. "Wait, you said those delinquents back there were stable hands, right? They weren't Sam and Ned, were they?"

"Yes." I was surprised he remembered.

"Were those the same boys you danced with at the Peasantry Festival?" Rafe studied my face with a strange frown.

I nodded.

"Oh." His frown deepened. "So you enjoy their company, then. I'm sorry I intruded."

"*Enjoy* is a generous overstatement. They were unusually tolerable at the festival. Ordinarily, I don't find their society very pleasant."

"Hmm," was Rafe's only response, but the set of his mouth became less grim. "I very much wanted to dance with you," he added after we'd walked a few steps in silence.

I hoped he couldn't feel my arm quiver. "I certainly would've rather danced with you than those two oafs."

"I'm glad to hear it." He covered my hand, rubbing his fingers over my knuckles. The pleasant sensation sent goosebumps trailing all the way up to my shoulder. "That green dress was lovely on you."

I tried to swallow past the growing lump in my throat. I couldn't recall Rafe ever giving me such a direct compliment. "Thank you. Your gift matched it perfectly."

"Yes, I'm glad you had an opportunity to wear it after all." He stopped and turned to me, a warm, intense look in his eyes. "You were easily the most beautiful maiden at the festival."

For a moment I heard only the pounding of my pulse in my temples until distant laughter shattered the illusion that we were alone.

I tugged at Rafe's arm to keep walking. He matched his pace to mine as I glanced around, trying to clear my head. "Where are you taking me, anyway?"

"To the dining hall, of course. I assumed that's where you'd be heading this time of day. You haven't eaten already, have you?"

"No, but I don't eat in the dining hall."

"You don't? But I've seen you there before."

Heavens above, Rafe could be oblivious. "The times you've seen me in the dining hall, I was serving the food, not eating it."

"Really?" He let out a sigh. "I guess I should've known that. Sorry. Then where do you eat?"

"The servants have a separate mess hall."

"Oh. Well then, I'll take you there. Just point me in the right direction."

"I appreciate the thought, but I'd rather you didn't. We've already churned up plenty of gossip for one day. Your showing up with me would be enough to turn every head in the palace."

Rafe held my arm with determination, his hand clasped over mine. "Then I'll at least escort you to the door."

With great effort, I talked him into releasing me when the door of the mess hall came into view. Though he agreed, he seemed reluctant to let go of my hand.

"I hate not knowing when I'm going to see you again."

"I know." How much could I afford to elaborate? Though I

wanted to cherish this moment, something urged me to run before someone saw us. "Hopefully soon enough."

"Soon enough for you, maybe." He lifted my fingers briefly to his lips before letting them go. "Goodnight, Leah."

"Goodnight, Rafe," I whispered for his ears alone. I could still feel the exact spot where his mouth had touched my hand. "And thank you."

The corners of his mouth turned up slightly as he bowed and strode back down the hall.

I wasn't hungry enough to contend with the curious faces and endless inquiries awaiting me at dinner. Sam and Ned were probably busy divulging their tale to anyone who would listen. And I didn't want the memory of my walk through the halls, with my hand encased in Rafe's, marred by the chaos of the mess hall.

Instead, I slipped through the kitchen. I grabbed several biscuits and tucked them into the pockets of my apron. One of the cooks spotted me but merely winked. Giving her a grateful wave, I took off down the corridor.

I would have to face the gossiping mob at some point, but it could wait until the morrow.

Ma regarded me with unusual interest when I returned to our chamber that evening. My empty stomach crumpled like a dried-up leaf. I turned from her to retrieve my nightdress.

"I didn't see you at dinner tonight."

I shrugged, failing to meet her eye. "I wasn't particularly hungry. Sarah allowed me to steal a snack from the kitchen."

"I see."

I tried to perform my bedtime preparations with as normal an air as possible, sensing her gaze on my back.

Ma cleared her throat. "I understand Prince Raphael took

Ned and Sam to task this afternoon. Were they...did they harm you?"

"Oh, no." I faced her, shaking my head. "I never appreciate their teasing, but it was nothing out of the ordinary."

The straw in our mattress rustled as she leaned back on her hands. "You certainly do have an unusual number of personal encounters with the prince."

I clutched the flimsy material of my nightdress. What did she mean by that?

My grip eased as I recalled the first time Rafe had stumbled into our closet. He'd torn his pants climbing rocks, and I helped him avoid a scolding from his governess by taking them to Ma to mend while he hid in the closet wearing my apron.

I gave a small laugh. "Yes, lucky me."

She continued to study me with knit brows.

My mind raced, grasping for an explanation that would satisfy her. "He was very grateful that time you patched up his trousers. I think he was eager to do me a kindness in return. Perhaps he remembered me because of my hair."

Ma released her breath through pursed lips. "Yes, that would make sense. But, Leah?" She reached out to stop me as I walked past. "Do be cautious. You're growing into a very pretty young woman, and the prince is seventeen now. It would do you no favors to attract any extra attention from him."

"Heavens, Ma. It's nothing like that."

"I'm glad to hear it."

As I crawled into bed, the expression in Rafe's eyes as he called me beautiful crossed my mind, but I pushed it aside. Rafe was the crown prince, and I, a chambermaid. Even if he could think of me in that way...

I buried my head under my pillow. Rafe and I were friends, nothing more.

~

Gretchen pounced on me at breakfast the following morning. "Is it true? *Prince Raphael* came to your rescue last evening? And you never said a word about it—I had to hear it from Monica." She swatted my shoulder as she sat next to me on the bench, facing me with wide eyes.

"It can hardly be called a rescue. Sam and Ned were just teasing me as usual."

"Still, how romantic."

"Romantic?" I nearly choked on my porridge. "Awkward would be a more apt description."

Her posture drooped. "Why? What did you say to him?"

My shoulder lifted in a half-shrug. "I had to defend those imbeciles to keep them out of trouble. I told him they were harmless."

"Oh no, Leah, you didn't!" Gretchen threw her hands up. "What a missed opportunity. You should've acted scared of those scoundrels, made it look worse than it was. Not enough to get them thrown in the dungeon or anything, but you should've made the most of something like that. You could've told him he'd come just in time, that you didn't know what you would've done without him, and then swooned into his arms." She gazed past me, her hands clutching her heart.

I grunted. "Careful, or you may swoon right onto the floor. What would the prince think of you if your dress got covered in smut? You of all people should know I'm hardly the swooning type."

"Anyone could be the swooning type when it comes to Prince Raphael. That black hair you just want to run your fingers through, those brooding gray eyes…"

I shifted my weight on the hard, wooden bench. "Well, let's hope next time it's *you* Sam and Ned are harassing when Prince Raphael happens to walk by."

"I should be so lucky. But that would never happen anyway. They don't tease me like they do you."

"I suppose not. I get singled out for my hair."

"You do know it's more than that, right?" Gretchen narrowed her eyes. "They just use your hair as an excuse to start up a conversation. Sam's had his eye on you for some time now."

My spoon landed in my empty bowl with a *chink*. "You must be joking. All he ever does is call me Red and give me a hard time."

"How else is he supposed to get your attention? You're so quiet, and you're always disappearing for hours at a time."

My only response was a raised eyebrow.

"You know, you really should at least consider him, especially now that you've blown it with the prince. From what I hear, Sam has a decent shot at becoming the head stable hand one day."

I shook my head. Me—marry *Sam*? Aside from his crooked teeth, his boyish looks were attractive enough. And though I'd never admit it aloud, she was right. A stable hand was a very reasonable match for a chambermaid. Still, I couldn't begin to wrap my mind around the idea.

"Head stable boy or not, I'm not ready to think about marriage yet. I've just barely turned sixteen."

Gretchen rolled her eyes. "I know you're very innocent, Leah, but you needn't be so naïve. It's not at all unusual for girls to get married at our age. You would be wise to start thinking about it before all the good matches are snatched up. I'm hoping Ned arranges things with my pa long before my next birthday."

"Ned?" My mouth fell open. "You can't be serious."

Gretchen placed a hand on her hip. "Of course I'm serious. You can't tell me you haven't noticed."

I bit my lip. What was I supposed to have noticed? "But... have the two of you spoken of marriage?"

"Heavens, no. We've never had the privacy for a conversation as momentous as all that. Believe me, you'd be the first to know. But he doesn't pay much mind to any other girls at this point, aside from you, and I know he wouldn't dare steal you away from Sam."

"He can't steal me when I in no way belong to Sam."

"Yes, yes, fine. But how fun would it be if I ended up with Ned and you with Sam? Even you have to admit we had a jolly lark at the festival. Sam simply couldn't keep his eyes off you." She nudged my ribs.

"The festival was lovely." I studied my calloused hands folded in my lap.

"See?" Gretchen bent to look in my face. "Unless, of course, you have your heart set on someone else."

"Certainly not." Rafe's face appeared in my mind, but I blinked, trying to clear my head. I needed to change the subject. "Where does Clara have you assigned this week?"

I released a sigh as Gretchen took the bait, listing her complaints about yet another week cleaning the nursery. I had to get a grip after my hazardous thoughts last night and now this morning. Rafe and I could never mean anything to one another outside the world of our broom closet, no matter how many times he held my hand or gazed into my eyes. I'd been clear on that all along, and I couldn't afford to start thinking differently now.

I jumped, sending my head crashing against the wall when Rafe made his next appearance in our closet a few evenings later.

He seemed to have trouble meeting my gaze.

After staring at his book for a few moments, shifting all the while, he closed it with a snap. "I'm so sorry, Leah, about the other night. It was stupid to interfere like that, then insist on escorting you through the palace. I don't know what I was thinking."

I smiled, hoping to lighten his contrite expression. "I know you had the best of intentions, and the gossip seems to have died down. No real harm done."

"But you knew this was going to happen, didn't you? I should've listened to you. I always end up regretting it when I don't."

"It's gratifying to hear you say that, though I doubt it will have any effect on your future behavior." Several months ago I would've thought nothing of jabbing him in the side to tease him out of a bad humor. But tonight, with Gretchen's dreamy recital of Rafe's attractive features still fresh in my mind, the thought of touching him brought warmth to my cheeks.

The corners of his mouth quirked up, but the attempted smile didn't reach the rest of his face. "You're probably right. As usual. But I still don't understand why it's caused such a fuss. Even my parents heard about it."

I stiffened. "Your parents? What did they say?"

"While commending my chivalrous instincts, they..." He coughed. "Never mind, it was a senseless conversation."

"Rafe—" I couldn't let him back down on this one. "If the king and queen have taken notice of me, presumably for the first time, it's important I know what they said."

"Fine. But remember, you asked for it." He traced the design on the cover of his textbook. "They reminded me, in no uncertain terms, of their high expectations for my marriage, and cautioned me against being taken in by 'merely a pretty face.'" His eyes were glued to his lap more intently than ever. "Shows what they know."

My face burned as though it'd been lit on fire. My conversation with Ma had been embarrassing enough, but now the king and queen? I stole a glance at Rafe, whose face looked as red as mine felt.

Hoping to clear the air, I forced a laugh. "Well, as long as you seek out a more high-ranking damsel in distress next time, I'm sure they'll be placated easily enough."

Rafe kept his head down, offering no response.

Clearly we needed to move on to a safer topic. "I understand some visitors from Trellich are on their way? Ma's had fittings with dozens of noblewomen. Apparently they're all hoping to get their latest gowns perfected before the Trellans arrive. I suppose there will be many banquets and parties."

He raised his eyes, though the set of his jaw remained grim. "You suppose correctly. It's going to be dreadful. Everyone making small talk and celebrating as though we can pretend the extra companies of guards patrolling the border are just out for a scenic walk."

"It's a good sign they're coming at all, though, isn't it?"

"We'll see. I have a bad feeling about it." He slipped back into silence.

My chest constricted at his continued melancholy. "Rafe… you're not still worried about the gossip, are you? It'll die down soon enough, especially with the Trellans coming. I truly appreciate that you came to my rescue. Even if I didn't need it."

He chuckled and rose to sit on the barrel next to mine. "Sorry I'm such a grump this evening. There are just so many things my parents and I don't see eye to eye on. And I can't shake the sense they're up to something." He leaned over until his arm brushed my shoulder. "Nothing new in any of that, though, is there? Perhaps we should just read tonight since I'm such miserable company."

"Sounds good to me. Though you're never miserable company."

His eyes searched mine for a moment before he grinned. "If only I could hide out here for the duration of the Trellans' visit. You'd bring me food and water, wouldn't you?"

"Of course. I'm certain no one would ever even notice you were gone."

He tapped his book on my head. "Merely a pretty face, my foot."

CHAPTER 6

I pushed through the kitchen door into the dining hall, balancing a tray of steaming bowls of bouillabaisse. The party from Trellich had arrived several days before, sending the palace into a frenzy as servants readied rooms, hauled trunks, and prepared elaborate meals. Tonight, the entire palace staff had been recruited to serve at a banquet honoring our guests.

My steps faltered at my first view of the hall. Thousands of candles lit the walls, rendering the room hardly recognizable. Lavish floral arrangements spilled over their vases, nearly covering each long, rectangular table. They must've left the gardens practically barren.

I glanced to the head table. Rafe wasn't seated at his usual post on the queen's right. Instead, he was placed well to the left of the king and queen. On his right was a dignified, sharp-looking older man whom I presumed to be the King of Trellich. How odd — Rafe's parents ordinarily kept their unenthusiastic son as far from foreign royalty as possible.

To his left sat the most beautiful young lady I'd ever seen. Her hair was almost as dark as Rafe's, swept up in a stylish updo studded with jewels. Her large, amber eyes and porcelain skin glowed in the candlelight as she gave Rafe a shy, flawless smile.

I frowned, then shook my head and looked away. The beautiful Trellan princess was welcome to smile at Rafe all she liked. I had a job to do.

But my gaze returned to Rafe each time I emerged from the kitchen with a new platter. While the Trellan king did most of the talking, the princess remained involved in the conversation throughout. She shifted to survey the room, and I hoped she might open a dialogue with her other neighbor. Instead, she laughed at something Rafe said and placed a hand on his arm.

My foot caught on a chair leg. I straightened, irritation nipping at my stomach. *I'm here to serve a meal, not spy on Rafe.*

Weariness weighed down my feet and wrists after serving all seven courses, but at last we were down to clearing the delicate china dessert plates and refilling wine glasses.

King Frederick rose, silencing the crowd. I reached for the empty goblet of the odious Earl of Spencer, maintaining a safe distance from his leering face. The king began a formal welcome to the royal family of Trellich.

I brought the glass close to the mouth of the wine bottle to minimize the sound as I poured.

"…and we are especially pleased to announce the engagement of our son, Prince Raphael, to Princess Penelope of Trellich, and look forward to the solidification of our countries' alliance."

My hand jerked, sloshing wine onto the floor.

"Don't they make a charming couple?" The king beckoned them to stand, then looked to Queen Beatrice, who gave him a solemn nod of approval.

I fumbled to set down the wine bottle and goblet, silently cursing the proliferation of flowers encroaching upon every open space.

Rafe was engaged—to the stunning Trellan princess.

It made perfect sense. Imperia had been trying to make peace with Trellich for ages—how better than through marriage? My insides coiled, and black spots marred my vision. Had Rafe known the last time we were together? Why hadn't he told me?

I sought Rafe and found my answer. Princess Penelope smiled timidly at the cheering assembly, but Rafe stood frozen, bewildered.

He hadn't known.

It was just like the king and queen, planning Rafe's entire future without bothering to ask his opinion. And what objection could he raise now, after it was announced in front of hundreds of people?

The earl patted me on the hip, shaking me from my grim reflections. Avoiding his gaze, I set his glass before him and retreated to the shadows in the back of the hall.

Soon Gretchen was at my side. "What a disappointment. The Princess Penelopes of the world get everything, don't they? Just look at her. She must've deployed some form of dark magic to get her hair to stay in place like that, and her teeth have to be fake." She squinted at me. "Leah? You look so pale—are you all right? Surely this news can't have distressed you. I know you don't care two straws about the prince. And let's face it, who among us wearing serving aprons had a chance with him anyway, eh?"

I tried to smile. "No, you're right. The news doesn't affect me in the least. A closer alliance with Trellich can only benefit us all. I think I'm just taxed. We haven't served a banquet this involved in years."

"Don't I know it." Gretchen shifted her weight. "They should've let us alternate courses or something, but that would never occur to our dear queen." She peered at the bottle in my grasp. "That's nearly empty, you know, and no one's paying us any mind. Drink it," she urged in a whisper. "It's clear you need something to fortify yourself for a cleanup of this magnitude."

"That won't be necessary, but I may as well dispose of it."

Once in the kitchen, I leaned over the counter, inhaling deeply. Steeling myself for the long evening ahead.

$\sim$

I lay awake for hours, listening to Ma's slow, steady breaths from the other side of the bed.

Rafe is engaged.

No matter how many times I thought the words, they never seemed real.

Grief swelled in my chest like water boiling over in a kettle until sobs racked my entire body. I clamped a hand over my mouth to avoid waking Ma.

What was wrong with me? I knew such a change would happen eventually, and I should be happy for Rafe. He'd marry a beautiful princess, someone of his proper station. Once he got past his initial shock, no doubt he'd be thrilled with the match.

So why was I crying and harboring such fierce resentment toward Princess Penelope?

I was in love with him.

The certainty struck me like a physical blow, and I winced. I'd basked in his affection, relished the exhilarating hints that our friendship might be taking on a deeper meaning. But how had I let it go this far?

Without even realizing it, I'd fallen in love with sweet, stubborn, scatterbrained Rafe.

If not for my sleeping mother, I would've been consumed by bitter laughter. I'd put up meager defenses, thinking I could avoid the idiocy of hoping for a future with Rafe by holding tight to my rationality.

It seemed in guarding my mind, I had neglected to guard my heart.

I spent the next week trying to forget about Rafe, a task made virtually impossible by the incessant gossip surrounding his betrothal to Princess Penelope. My closet no longer represented a sanctuary, only a bittersweet reminder of all the moments we'd shared. At times I even thought I could catch a whiff of his scent.

I was dead-set on tormenting myself, and no amount of logic could persuade me otherwise.

Even books provided little solace. Rafe would probably never loan me a book again. For all I knew, I would never see him in private again—a thought too painful to dwell on.

Still, I cherished my last book from him. I sat pressed against the window, straining to see the pages by the light of the quarter moon.

The door of the closet burst open, and Rafe appeared.

I jumped up, sending the book clattering to the floor.

"Rafe, you're here. I didn't think..." My first instinct was to throw my arms around him, but my feet remained immobile. The depth of my feelings unsettled me, and his engagement created an almost palpable blockade between us.

He reached behind him and closed the door, his eyes never leaving my face. "I lit the candle in my window. Did you see it?"

"No. I must've already been here." The incessant thumping in my chest set my nerves on edge.

"Oh." He rubbed the back of his neck, shifting his gaze to the floor.

My breath hitched as he bent to retrieve my fallen book.

He straightened and held it out to me, a glint of humor

piercing the uncertainty in his eyes. "I believe this belongs to you, miss."

A breathy giggle escaped my lips. "Thank you, kind sir." I took hold of the book, but he didn't release it. I could practically feel his touch spanning the pages to reach me.

All at once, he let go and paced away. Lacing a hand through his hair, he leaned his forehead against the wall.

I sank back onto a barrel, closing my eyes to gather my scattered thoughts. If only I could know what was going through his mind. Was his behavior unusual, or was I interpreting his actions differently? I folded my hands in my lap. What would a *friend* say at a moment like this? The obvious answer struck me just as he inhaled sharply and turned to face me.

"I should be saying congratulations."

"What?" His brows furrowed.

"For your betrothal."

"Oh, that."

"You must feel very fortunate. Princess Penelope is lovely, and I'm sure she must be quite accomplished."

Rafe coughed. "I hadn't noticed."

"Hadn't noticed? Every member of the palace staff has noticed—"

"I hate that they've taken up every moment with their ridiculous balls and excursions." His voice deepened to a growl. "I can't even remember the last time I was here."

"Yes, it's been a while, but I suppose we should get used to that." Something in his expression disarmed me, cutting through my attempts to stay poised and distant. "I've missed you." I clutched the end of my long braid and began to study it, heat rising to my cheeks.

My throat constricted with Rafe's every footfall as he came to stand before me.

"Have you?" He placed a finger under my chin and raised my head. His eyes looked fierce as they bored into mine, until his face softened with a concerned frown. "You seem pale. Are you unwell?"

I tried to give a dismissive wave, hoping he didn't notice the goosebumps on my arm. "My skin has always been pale."

He shook his head. "This is different. Let me see your hands." He took my hands in each of his and turned them over.

I flinched as the familiar tingling wound up through my shoulders.

"Blistered all over, just as I feared. They've clearly been working you too hard. I'll speak with Clara first thing in the morning."

"Please don't. Nothing has changed in my workload." I fumbled for an explanation that would satisfy him. The truth wasn't an option. "My spirits have been rather low lately, but it's nothing to concern yourself with."

Keeping his hold on my hands, he bent so our faces were level. "They've been teasing you again, haven't they?" His gentleness threatened to melt away every barrier I'd ever tried to raise against him. "I'm so sorry I haven't been able to help, that I wasn't here to comfort you." He looked down, rubbing his thumbs across my knuckles. "I've failed you, time and again..."

The longing to console him engulfed me. Swallowing hard, I disengaged a hand to touch his cheek with trembling fingers. "You have never failed me, Rafe. I don't think you ever could."

He lifted his head, so close his breath warmed my face. Time simultaneously accelerated and slowed as he closed his eyes and leaned forward. Every precious moment we'd spent together seemed to coalesce in the instant he placed his lips on mine. He moved one hand to the back of my head, the other resting at my waist. I clutched his arms, my stomach quivering as his muscles tensed under my fingers.

All too soon, his lips released me from their spell. He settled beside me, carefully untangling his hand from my hair to stroke my face. "I first suspected I might be in love with you the night you were crying. I couldn't bear to see you hurt, and then when I held you for the first time…I nearly kissed you right then and there."

Warmth coursed through me at the memory.

He traced his thumb along my cheek. "I knew for certain at the festival, when I saw you dancing with Sam. The thought of you in his arms, the possibility he was courting you—it was enough to drive me mad. It took everything I had not to jump off that stage and run him through with my sword."

I shook my head, lowering my gaze.

"What is it?"

When I glanced up, his brows were knit with concern. "I just…it doesn't seem possible that you could be so in love with me."

He gave a soft laugh and tucked a strand of hair behind my ear. "Surely you can't be so blind, Leah. Of course I am. Every moment I have to spend out there I'm wishing desperately I could be here with you in this ridiculous closet. You're the only one who treats me like a real person, who doesn't care that I happen to be a prince. You listen, you make me laugh, you challenge me. How could I not be in love with you?"

My head spun as though I'd been transported to another realm. Rafe was at my side, declaring a love more ardent than I could've hoped for. His words filled my mind and heart, driving away every lingering doubt and insecurity.

"I know what you mean." I didn't dare break the moment with anything above a whisper.

He straightened, his eyes lighting up. "That's it! I can't believe I didn't think of it before." He grabbed my hands again. "We'll run away together!"

I blinked up at him. "What?"

"Isn't it obvious? All either of us wants is to be together, away from everyone else. So let's go. What's stopping us? Let's get married—start a life where we can be together outside the confines of a broom closet."

I could only stare at him in bewilderment. "Run away together? I don't think…"

"Why not? It's perfect, unless…" Rafe frowned as he studied my face. "I'm such an idiot. All this"—he indicated our close proximity—"you've just been trying to spare my pride. You're not in love with me." A pained look twisted his face as he dropped my hands. Dipping his chin, he turned and strode away.

I stepped forward and gripped his shoulder. "Rafe, that's not it at all. I'll admit, I made a concerted effort not to fall in love with you. But it seems you won me over in spite of myself."

He spun back to me, and I tentatively brushed a lock of hair off his forehead.

"When your betrothal was announced, I was so miserable I could hardly function."

I caught a glimpse of his grin before he pulled me against him, covering my mouth with kiss after kiss. I clung to him, allowing my senses to be overwhelmed by his closeness, his touch, the certainty that he loved me.

His betrothal… What was I doing? Reality snapped me back to my senses as if I'd been cuffed by a rug beater.

I backed away. "This isn't right. You're engaged."

His smile didn't waver. "Not for long, now that we've come up with a solution. I hope to leave within the week. I'll begin packing and mapping a route tomorrow. It won't be easy to see you again in the meantime, but I'll try to leave messages here when—"

"Rafe, no. Stop." I turned from him in an attempt to clear my head.

He followed, sending shivers down my spine as he rubbed his hands along the length of my arms.

"What is it, my love? Is a week too soon? Two, then. Will that suffice?" He leaned forward to whisper in my ear. "You won't make me wait much longer than that, will you?"

I took a deep breath. "We can't run away together."

Rafe dropped his hands, and I took the opportunity to turn and look into his face.

"You're the crown prince of Imperia. The only heir to the throne. You can't just run away from that."

He set his jaw, a vein pulsing in his neck. "I don't care. I refuse to live without you. You're more important than —"

"I'm not more important. We're talking about our entire country. Who would inherit the throne in your absence?"

"Uncle Bernard, my father's next oldest brother." A hint of uncertainty clouded his eyes. "Though Alexander and Harold would be unlikely to let it go without a fight. As it is, those three have been feuding for years."

My head spun with the implications. "So your disappearance could result in a civil war?"

Rafe crossed his arms. "That would no longer be our concern."

"Not our concern? Come now, Rafe, you don't mean that. It would impact our families, our friends. Their suffering would be our fault. People could die because of us." I gazed out the window. There had to be a better solution. "What about your parents?"

"What about them?"

"Have you spoken with them? Maybe if they knew how desperately you wanted to be free from this engagement, they'd relent."

"It's no good. I've already tried." He buried his head in his hands. "I ranted, begged, threatened...believe me, no stone was left unturned. But they feel it's high time I step into my responsibilities as the prince, and that my marriage to Penelope is the only way to solidify our alliance with Trellich. What I want doesn't matter to them in the slightest." He strode up to me again, gripping my shoulders. "That's why we have to run away together. Please, Leah. It's the only way."

The temptation to agree tugged until my knees nearly

buckled. Why couldn't we run away together? We'd be so happy, and surely his uncles could sort out the inheritance among themselves.

But doubt crept through my mind like a poison. Could I abandon Ma like that? And even in the absence of bloodshed, did I want to be responsible for putting Imperia's leadership into the hands of one of the king's brothers, knowing the countless reports of their cruelty?

My vision blurred with tears. "I can't. I'm so sorry."

He let go of my shoulders as his posture sagged.

"Rafe, listen to me. This country needs you. You can improve so many lives when you take the throne. You'll finally have the power to right so many injustices. I can't deprive Imperia of that, no matter how much I want to."

He sighed. "You'd have us go our separate ways, then?"

"I'm not sure we have a choice. The fact that you're willing to give up everything for me...it means so much." The tears welling in my eyes spilled down my cheeks. "No one could ever be as dear to me as you are now, and that will never change. But you must marry the princess, and I must find a way to let you go."

He opened his mouth to protest further.

"I think it would be best if I leave." But I couldn't wrench my gaze from him. Would we have the opportunity to be alone like this ever again?

He wiped the tears from my face with his thumb. "Then goodnight, my darling Leah."

He leaned forward as though to kiss me again. As much as I wanted him to, I forced myself to move to the door, remembering I would be kissing someone else's betrothed.

"Goodnight, Rafe." There was so much more I wanted to say, but the look in his eyes was unbearable. If I hesitated a moment longer, I would be in his arms again.

I closed the door and fled down the deserted halls.

CHAPTER 7

*H*elplessness threatened to smother me as I went about my work the following day. Maids rushed through the palace, tending to the needs of our extra guests, but they seemed distant, part of a world that no longer included me. Remorse surged through my veins in an unceasing cadence.

My dearest friend—my love—was miserable, and I couldn't help him.

As soon as my necessary tasks were complete, I staggered back to our closet, desperate to be alone. I couldn't survive many more days like this, pretending all was well when my mind couldn't focus, my chest constricting with doubt and regret.

I crossed the small room, nearly tripping on the new books Rafe had stacked in a neat pile. Tears stung my eyes, and I fell to my knees. I'd hurt Rafe, refused to go along with his plan for us to be together. But even when I pushed him away, he remained as constant a friend as ever.

If only I could run to him and plan our immediate escape. But surely we'd regret it. Sacrificing the best interests of our family, friends, and country couldn't help but taint our relationship. And how could I hold Rafe back from all he could accomplish as Imperia's future king?

I rubbed a hand across my face, my breath escaping through clenched teeth. Rafe's best chance of happiness would be to accept his fate and make the best of his engagement to the princess. Jealousy strangled my heart, but a whisper in the back of my mind told me I was right.

Princess Penelope would have the chance I was being denied to be Rafe's partner in life, and if she made a genuine effort, surely he wasn't hard-hearted enough to shut her out forever.

Princess Penelope. I sat up. What if she didn't know how to catch Rafe's attention? I couldn't aid him, but maybe I could be of use to her. If I could help her better attract Rafe, perhaps she could win his love, and he would be happy. And I...

I didn't want to think about that part.

I pushed a sheet down the rails of a washboard. Up, down, up, down. The incessant vibrations made me jittery. Wiping an arm across my brow, I sat back on my heels.

Clara deposited a pile of bedclothes at the adjacent washtub.

I lowered my gaze and met my wide-eyed reflection in the frothy water. This would be my best opportunity to speak with her, before I could talk myself out of my plan.

I gripped the edge of the tub. "Clara?"

"Mm?" She brushed the stray hairs from her face.

I inhaled, the scent of the rosewater soothing my anxiety. "I've been thinking...do you remember when you told me you didn't think I'd be a chambermaid my entire life?"

"I suppose I do. What of it?"

I fiddled with the ribbon trim of the sheets I'd been scrubbing. "I thought perhaps this would be a good time for a change."

She gave a pillowcase a sharp twist. "Is that so? Well, what did you have in mind, then?" A teasing glint lit her eyes. "I don't look ready for a replacement quite yet, do I?"

"No, I wouldn't dream of suggesting such a thing." Warmth flooded my cheeks. "I thought, perhaps, that I could...Princess Penelope must need a great many lady's maids."

She plunged the pillowcase into her tub, sending a cascade of droplets onto her apron. "Princess Penelope?" She lowered her voice to a harsh whisper. "You're telling me you want to be put on the staff of that little Trellan chit? Why?" She straightened and squinted into my face.

"I've never known anyone who's lived in a foreign country, and I find it fascinating. And I would love an opportunity to study her dresses. The materials they use in Trellich are so delicate."

Confusion still creased her brows.

"I am my mother's daughter, after all." I forced a laugh.

Clara sighed. "So it would seem. Well, her full staff hasn't been assembled yet, so there would be space for you." She scanned me from head to toe. "Your behavior has always been proper, and your face is pretty enough. I can only assume your needlework's up to snuff if Therese has been teaching you." She shrugged. "I guess I don't see why not. You'll need something more suitable to wear, though."

"Oh, of course." I looked at my faded cotton dress. The hem had been patched more times than I could count.

"Nothing wrong with it in my eyes, mind you, but in Trellich, it seems the maidservants dress nearly as elegantly as their mistresses. I could spare a length of material if you and your mother can sew it into something appropriate."

I bobbed my head. "Yes, I'd be happy to work on it, and I'm sure Ma will help where necessary."

"All right, then. If you're sure about this—"

"I am, Clara. Thank you. I won't let you down."

She chuckled. "You'd best not."

∿

Gretchen practically upended my bowl of oatmeal the following morning. "Going off to be a lady's maid for the princess? And you weren't even going to tell me?"

I took a moment to catch my breath. "Of course I was going to tell you. I just wasn't sure if it was official yet."

Her jaw tightened. "Not *official* yet? That's why you didn't tell me? I would've told you the instant such a thought even crossed my mind, and I certainly would've consulted you before breathing a word of it to Clara." She shook her head. "You used to confide in me. I feel like I don't even know you anymore."

"Gretchen, I'm sorry. It's just…I wanted a change. You can understand that, can't you?"

"Of course I can. That's part of the reason I'm so upset you didn't tell me!" The table vibrated as she thumped down her bowl and spoon. "What if I wanted a change with you? You do realize the lady's maids all spend the day together, right? They usually even eat their meals together. We'd hardly see each other!"

My head swirled. I needed to do this for Rafe, but Gretchen had a point. I hadn't taken her into consideration at all when I threw myself into my plan. "I guess I hadn't thought of that. I'm so sorry. It was a hasty decision, and I seized the chance to speak with Clara when we worked together yesterday. But you're right, it was thoughtless of me."

"Well, I'm glad you can at least acknowledge it." Gretchen folded her arms across her chest. "Now we just need to hope Clara's willing to add yet another maid to Princess Penelope's staff."

"What do you mean?"

"You don't think I'm going to let you leave me behind, do you?" She lowered onto the bench beside me.

"But, Gretchen…you just said the lady's maids often keep to themselves."

"Your point?"

I leaned close and whispered, "Ned. I thought you were hoping — the two of you —"

"We'll work it out. I can still find my way to the stables when I have a break. Who knows? Perhaps Princess Penelope has a horse or two that need extra looking after." She waggled her eyebrows. "He won't forget me as easily as that. He may even miss me."

I laughed and gave her shoulders a quick squeeze. "I know I would."

My stomach churned as I made my way to our chamber at the end of the day. If Gretchen had already heard about my new endeavor, perhaps Ma had as well. Even if she hadn't, I needed to speak with her tonight, before she was the last to know.

My conscience pricked me for not telling her right away, but the necessity of explaining myself sent rivulets of dread through my veins. If Ma was more perceptive than Clara and Gretchen, I could only imagine the difficult questions that might arise.

The weight of my secrets pressed upon me as I opened the door.

"Leah, how are you this evening?" Ma set aside the gloves she'd been embroidering.

I leaned down and hugged her, catching the faintest scent of ginger. Though her smile was warm, she looked pale and tired.

"I am well." I took a deep breath. The longer I waited, the

more firmly my announcement lodged in my throat. "I have some good news, actually."

"Indeed? I'd love to hear it." She patted the spot next to her on the bed.

I perched beside her, making an effort to still my fidgety hands. "I've been assigned a new position—as a lady's maid for Princess Penelope."

Her eyes widened before crinkling with her smile. "That is good news. What an honor! Clara must think very highly of you to allow you to represent our country to the new princess. I'm so proud of you, Leah." She squeezed my knee. "Just think, this means you may be on the staff of our queen one day!"

I lurched forward and gripped the edge of the bed. Why hadn't that occurred to me before? If I worked for the princess now, it would only be natural that my service would continue after her wedding and beyond. Watching Rafe become someone else's husband, the father of her children, would've been painful enough from a distance. Now I'd doomed myself to a front-row seat.

Feeling Ma's eyes on me, I roused myself. "Thank you. Yes, I suppose it is quite an honor."

A line formed above her nose. "You are happy about this, aren't you? If not, we'll speak to Clara. I'm sure she'd see reason—"

Tempting as it was to consider turning back, I smoothed the blanket and formed my lips into a smile. "Thanks, Ma, but I'm happy about it. I promise. This is what I want. I'm just nervous about making such a change."

"Of course you are." Ma rubbed my arm. "But I have no doubt you'll do extremely well. I'm sure the Luminate has set you on this path for a reason. Trust Him to provide everything you need."

I basked in her warmth, wishing fervently she would prove to be right.

"All this food for one person, and then she doesn't even eat a third of it." Gretchen glared at the plate of lingonberry tarts she was conducting back to the kitchen. "What a waste."

After days of wheedling, Gretchen had finally convinced Clara to allow her a trial as a lady's maid for Princess Penelope. She, too, had been granted a length of fine material, and we'd spent our evenings sewing alongside Ma until our dresses met Clara's approval.

"I suppose it'd be considered bad form to eat her leftovers."

"I would imagine so." I indicated the tray in my hand. "The eggs are cold by now, anyway."

We deposited the dishes in the kitchen, and I took off back down the hall while Gretchen lingered, chatting with our fellow lady's maids.

Based on our first week of service to the princess, the work didn't suit me well. I preferred to work hard and efficiently, at which point I could spend my leisure time as I liked. As a lady's maid, there was often no work to be done at all, but such idle time was not our own, since we were required to be ready whenever the princess might need us.

My lack of occupation left me bored and restless, but I strove to bear in mind my goal. The sacrifice would be well worth it if I could make some meaningful progress toward helping Princess Penelope win Rafe's heart.

I hovered in Princess Penelope's doorframe. She stood at her wardrobe, sifting through gowns. She would be attending an exhibition of grounded archery, a form of target shooting unique to Imperia, scheduled as an amusement for our Trellan guests that afternoon.

Her hand rested on a frilly pink brocade.

I cleared my throat. "If I may be so bold, my lady, I have heard it said that green is Prince Raphael's favorite color."

She twisted to face me, a frown pinching her delicate

features. "The prince? Why should I—" She bit her lip. "Of course, the prince. Yes, I understand now. Perhaps..." She rifled through several more dresses before turning back to me with a gown of emerald silk. "Do you think he would prefer this one, then?"

"Yes, I think that will be lovely."

I laid out the dress and began rummaging through drawers for appropriate undergarments.

"What a stunning gown!" Harriet, one of the maids who'd accompanied the princess from Trellich, swept into the room. "The poor gentlemen'll hardly be able to concentrate on their sport."

"They won't be able to take their eyes off ye." Victoria, the other Trellan maid, appeared at Harriet's side. "Shall we draw yer bath, m'lady?"

"Yes, that would be fine."

Following the princess's bath, we began the elaborate ritual of fitting her into a gown, sprinkling her with accessories, and styling her hair.

I pinned a curl in place and reached for another hairpin. Beside me, Gretchen released a strand of hair from the curling iron.

Princess Penelope met our gazes in her vanity mirror. "You'll all be accompanying me to the exhibition later, so make sure to be ready after lunch."

The pin I held dropped to the floor with a faint *clink*. We had to go with her? It would be my first encounter with Rafe since...

I chewed my cheek. "But surely you won't need all of us. I'd be happy to stay behind to finish the hem on your yellow gown."

Princess Penelope turned to me, her lips curving upward. "No, no, I expect you all to be in attendance this afternoon. I wouldn't want to deprive anyone of the opportunity to enjoy the festivities."

I was stuck, then. With any luck, Rafe would be too caught up in the games to wonder at my presence or would assume all the servants had been given the afternoon off to enjoy the fresh air.

A messenger rapped on the doorframe. Victoria hurried over to retrieve his tray, upon which lay an envelope. The princess rose and snatched up the letter as soon as Victoria reached her. Turning from us, she paced away and tore it open. She scanned the contents, crumpled it, and tossed it into the fire.

Her cheeks flushed as she spun back to face us.

Victoria returned the tray to the messenger. "A note from yer betrothed, m'lady? Ye're wise to be so discreet."

The princess gave a self-conscious giggle. "Yes. Words of courtship are best seen only by the intended recipient."

Rafe was sending Princess Penelope love notes? My initial surge of jealousy was soon overtaken by skepticism. Perhaps it was expected among the upper classes, but I still couldn't believe Rafe would be penning words of affection to the princess when he'd recently expressed such indifference toward her. And though I only caught a brief glance of the envelope's address as Victoria passed, it looked far too elegant and scripted compared to Rafe's usual blocky handwriting.

We were perching a jewel-studded tiara atop the princess's curls when another messenger appeared at the door. This time Harriet went to fetch the missive, which appeared to be a hasty scribble from Rafe accompanying a corsage for the princess to wear to the exhibition.

If the initial note was from Rafe, wouldn't he have sent the corsage with it?

I shook my head. Any letters passed between Rafe and Princess Penelope were their business and had nothing to do with me. Apparently, there was a great deal about courtship I didn't understand.

CHAPTER 8

$\mathcal{W}$e shuffled behind the princess through the arena, passing noblewomen in vibrant silks with wide, plumed hats, stately gentlemen too elderly to compete, and maids and footmen bustling to attend them.

Apprehension bristled my nerves. Even with a scarf covering my hair, Rafe was bound to notice me.

We ascended the dais where King Frederick and Queen Beatrice already sat on elegant thrones. After dipping into deep curtsies, we settled just behind the small throne intended for the princess.

A lump swelled in my throat when the competitors stepped onto the field, led by Rafe. Images from our last encounter inundated my mind, and I averted my eyes, fearing the intensity of my gaze might draw his attention.

He stopped in front of Princess Penelope. Almost close enough to touch, yet the entire country seemed to stand between us.

Bowing, he placed a kiss on the back of the princess's hand, his expression stony. He raised his head, and his eyes met mine for a fraction of a second. I trembled with the effort of keeping my body still, my face neutral. His brows lowered, but he quickly glanced back to the princess before turning toward the field to begin the exhibition.

My knees buckled, and my thoughts dispersed in every direction.

Fortunately, Princess Penelope had little need of us as she chatted with the queen and clapped politely for each competitor.

A perceptible rise in the crowd's volume caught my attention. The Duke of Brantley stepped forward for his first trial. He strode up to the platform and gave the queen, and then Princess Penelope, a gallant bow and kiss on the hand before returning to the field.

He placed an arrow with a round, weighted tip across his bow.

"I've been waitin' to see the duke." Victoria flicked open her fan. "Isn't he just the most handsome gentleman ye've ever seen?"

"The prince looks like a gawky boy in comparison," Harriet agreed in a loud whisper.

My fingers curved into fists at my side. "But shouldn't our loyalty lie with the prince? He is our mistress's betrothed, after all."

"And Prince Raphael's first round was very impressive." Anne had been the first Imperian maid assigned to Princess Penelope. "He scored the maximum number of points, didn't he?"

"He did." I flashed her a grateful smile. Grounded archery was one of the few childhood studies Rafe had truly enjoyed.

"Oh, Leah, don't be such a ninny!" Gretchen turned to our Trellan companions. "The Duke of Brantley is very handsome. I imagine you saw him quite a bit while the engagement was being arranged."

Harriet nodded. "It's thanks to him the engagement happened at all. I don't think the king, or the princess, for that matter, liked the idea one bit at first. But the duke spent so much time with 'em and lobbied for it so persuasively, he won 'em over."

Princess Penelope didn't want to marry Rafe either? It was hard to imagine anyone not wanting to marry Rafe, but then she hardly knew him. My shoulders drooped. My task would be even more difficult than I'd expected.

Victoria's voice broke into my reverie. "I'm just glad he wasn't wooing her for himself as we feared. As long as he remains a bachelor, my hope lives on." She nudged Gretchen. "Do ye know which of the young ladies here in Imperia are vying for his affection?"

"Nearly all of them." Gretchen giggled. "Do you see the young woman over there, in the burgundy dress? She's the Earl of Harper's eldest daughter…"

I watched the duke direct his arrows into the decorative wooden canisters scattered throughout the field. His appearance certainly wasn't lacking, though an air of superiority rendered his smiles false.

"I'm not that impressed by the duke, either."

Startled, I looked up to find Anne beside me. "Thanks for taking my side."

"You're welcome." She shifted her feet. "You're Therese's daughter, aren't you?"

I nodded.

"I so admire her work. Her embroidery is stunning. I've never seen anything like it."

I pivoted away from the field to give her my full attention. "I'm sure Ma would be very pleased to hear that."

Her shy smile brightened. "I hope to become a seamstress one day, especially if I could be trained under your ma. That's why I took this position. I don't particularly enjoy this aspect"—her gaze swept across the dais—"but I hope working on the princess's gowns will improve my needlework."

"I'm sure it will. You're already far more patient with your sewing than the rest of us. I think Ma would agree that's the most important skill a seamstress could possess." I leaned closer. "Truth be told, I'm not enjoying this aspect either."

She gave me a conspiratorial grin. "I can tell we're going to get along just fine."

~

Princess Penelope retired early after dinner, releasing us from our duties. Too restless to head to my bedchamber, I instead roamed the gardens flanking the eastern wall of the palace, where I had a clear view of the North Wing.

Gretchen jogged to catch up with me. "I'm sorry about earlier. It was unkind to call you a ninny."

"I understand. I'm sure I sounded like one."

"I just…I wish you would make more of an effort with the other girls. I know they may not be the most intellectual lot, but you must admit they're friendly. Unless something's happened I wasn't aware of—"

"No. You're right. They've been very welcoming."

"What then? You've been so distant of late and always eager to sneak away."

The wind rippled the delicate petals of a moonbud. "I guess I've found the adjustment to our new positions more difficult than I anticipated."

Gretchen curled and straightened her fingers. "You're working twice as hard as the rest of us, you know. Except maybe Anne. But you could certainly stand to lighten up a bit. I'd hoped being lady's maids together would bring us closer and help you relax a little."

I attempted a genuine-sounding laugh. "I got a new job, not a new personality."

She giggled. "That's better. But is everything all right with you? I never know what you're thinking these days."

In that moment, I yearned to tell Gretchen everything.

What a relief it would be to have a confidante, to get her advice on what had passed between Rafe and me and how to approach the princess.

But it was too late now, the risk too great. Instead, I plastered on a reassuring smile. "I'll be fine. Even though I volunteered for it, I don't handle change well. And I worry about Ma."

Gretchen squeezed my shoulder. "Yes, she's been rather pale lately, hasn't she? Has she consulted Mistress Donna?"

"No, she—" I spied what I both feared and hoped might appear—the flicker of a candle in Rafe's parlor window. "I have to go."

She took a step back. "You have to go? Right now?"

"Yes, I'm sorry." I flinched at the skeptical glint in her eyes. "Speaking of Ma reminded me that I promised I'd help with her sewing this evening."

"Oh, well then, why don't I go with you? I'd be happy to help, and we'd have more time to chat."

The hairs on the back of my neck rose. How far would she press my lie? "Thank you, but perhaps another time. As I said, Ma hasn't been feeling well, and I don't know if she'd be up for a visitor tonight."

"Of course." Gretchen searched my face. "Give her my regards, and I guess I'll see you in the morning."

"I will. Goodnight."

My insides twisted painfully as I walked back toward the palace, but whether from guilt over my conversation with Gretchen or anxiety for my upcoming meeting with Rafe, I wasn't sure.

An odd mix of emotions simmered as I wound through the halls leading to our closet. Half of me wanted to fly into Rafe's arms, the other half gnawed with doubt. Anticipating the temptation of being alone with him made my stomach constrict as though gripped in an iron fist.

I replayed the moment our eyes met at the exhibition. Was he displeased to see me with the princess?

Putting aside my fears, I strode on. I had to take this opportunity to find out how he was faring after weeks of silence.

By the time I reached the south corridor, trepidation surged through my veins. I pushed open the door with unsteady hands.

"There you are!" Rafe jumped up as though he'd been waiting for hours.

"I came as quickly as I could." I leaned against the closed door. My legs grew weak just being in his presence.

He walked over and stood before me, jaw clenched. "What do you think you're doing?"

"I'm not sure what you mean." Heat crept up my neck as I met his gaze.

"You know exactly what I mean. A lady's maid for the princess? Please tell me I'm mistaken."

I stepped around him and crossed to the window. "You're not mistaken. My duties were reassigned."

"Who makes such decisions?"

"The head housekeeper. Clara."

"So this is *her* fault?" Some of the anger left his voice.

"Not entirely. I initiated the discussion." I gripped the windowsill. "I wanted a change."

"But why Penelope? No doubt a duchess or someone else would've been happy to accept your services."

"Princess Penelope has been very kind to me." I bit my lip, knowing I was evading his question. "It doesn't need to impact you, does it?"

His fist struck the wall. "Not impact me? I'll have to pretend not to see you. Anything less could put you in harm's way."

"But you don't need to interact with me. I'll just blend into the background."

"That's the problem." He reached out a finger and stroked my cheek. "You could never blend into the background. How will Penelope react when she notices my gaze never meets hers directly but instead fixes on one of the maids? I doubt it will take her long to determine which one."

I leaned into his touch, my resolve faltering. "I'm sure it won't be as bad as you think."

"It will be that bad." Rafe bent forward, inching closer to my face. "When you're in the room, how could I possibly focus on anyone else?"

The pull of his eyes entreated me to close the distance between us, but I clutched my skirt and stepped back. "Please try, Rafe. I'm sorry. I didn't think this through, but I had no intention of making things difficult for you. I only wanted to help." Tears pricked the corners of my eyes. I wanted to ease Rafe's pain and was only making it worse.

"Help?" His lips twitched. "The green gown today. That was your doing, wasn't it?"

"I may have made a suggestion…"

His expression failed to soften.

"I thought I could use my knowledge to aid the princess. To help her make an inroad with you." My shoulders sagged. "I just want you to be happy."

"You *know* what would make me happy."

I couldn't look away from his ardent gaze. The delirium of the dream of running away with him washed over me again, threatening to overcome every argument against it. I dug my nails into my hands. "Yes, but you need to be happy with the princess."

"Ugh, Leah! How can you be so sweet and so aggravating at the same time?" He exhaled, then approached me cautiously, placing his hands on either side of my face. "Thank you for the thought, but I'd much rather you speak with the head housekeeper and get yourself reassigned. Please."

"I can't. I'm sorry. At least not yet. Don't you think that

would provoke more suspicion? It took some convincing for Clara to allow me to take this post. I shudder to think what she'd say if I backed out so soon."

His eyes warmed as he rubbed his thumbs along my jaw. "All right. I'll just have to do my best, then. But if this causes you the slightest hint of trouble, I'm going to sweep you up and take you far away from here, understood?"

I nodded, my pulse leaping at the thought.

He mirrored my nod, then turned away.

"Rafe?"

He was at my side in an instant. "Yes?"

"Did you—?" My cheeks warmed as I struggled to put my query into words. "This will sound like an odd question, and I know it's none of my business, but did you send Princess Penelope two notes this morning?"

A line formed between his brows. "Two notes? No. I dashed off a quick line with that ridiculous flower I had to send her, but that was it. Why?"

I didn't know whether to feel relieved or concerned. "She received a note shortly before your flower arrived and implied it was also from you."

He shrugged. "Perhaps from her father, or a letter from home. Believe me, I don't waste time penning missives to Penelope. If I were to write love letters, you know exactly to whom they'd be addressed." He leaned forward to kiss my lips.

I turned, redirecting him to my cheek.

"I should go." My voice wavered.

Rafe slipped his arms around my waist, resting his forehead against mine. "If you must. But be careful, my love."

My arms wound around his neck. "You too. And give Princess Penelope a chance." I tipped back to look into his eyes. "For my sake, if not yours. I can't stand to see you so miserable."

He raised an eyebrow. "I'll only consider it if you can turn her into a perfect replica of yourself. This hair"—he tugged at a stray curl—"these lips"—he brushed a finger across my mouth—"eyes just this shade." His voice caught as he gripped my head, his thumbs at my temples.

Every fiber in my body yearned to melt into him, to pretend nothing else mattered but the two of us together.

A painful twist in my stomach brought my senses rushing back, and I disengaged his hands.

"Goodnight, Rafe." I studied his face, wondering whether we'd ever meet like this again. "Take care of yourself. Please, try to be happy."

"I'd much rather be miserable if it means you might change your mind." He ran his fingers through my hair, then let them drop with a sigh. "Goodnight." He raised my hand to his lips, allowing them to linger far longer than necessary.

In one last, desperate act of willpower, I opened the door before he could entrance me further.

Heedless of my direction, I wandered the halls. Doubts crowded my mind as soon as the haze from Rafe's affection cleared. Had I been wrong to request a position as Princess Penelope's lady's maid? Could I ever make enough progress with her to overcome the additional strife I'd caused Rafe?

My face tingled at the recollection of his touch.

With Rafe's effect on me increasing every time our eyes met, did I even have the strength to try?

CHAPTER 9

I splashed tea into a dainty, floral-patterned cup for Princess Penelope the following morning, exhausted and shaky from a sleepless night.

"Is there anything else I can get you, Your Highness?"

The princess stifled a yawn. "No, this will do for now. Thank you."

I blinked, trying to dismiss the images of Rafe that kept creeping into my mind's eye, and returned the ceramic teapot to the tray harder than I intended. The loud *clink* made me jump.

"Are you well, Leah?" The princess bent forward to study me.

Heat burned my cheeks as I met her gaze, praying she couldn't read my thoughts. "Yes, thank you. I apologize for my clumsiness." I shifted the tray farther back on her nightstand. "If I may trouble you, my lady, where is the gown that needs its beading replaced? Anne and I planned to work on it this morning."

She pulled the sheets off her legs and rose from the bed,

motioning over her shoulder. "It's hanging at the far end of the closet."

"Of course. Thank you." I retrieved the dress and draped the frothy, peach-colored material over my arm.

The princess rummaged through her writing desk and pulled out a sheet of parchment.

"Would you like me to stay in order to post your letter?"

Her head jolted up, and a quill clattered to the floor. "No. I will ring for one of you if I need assistance."

I shrank back. Perhaps I had erred in making the suggestion. "Very good." I reached for the door handle but paused again. "My lady?"

Her "Hmm?" was scarcely audible as she bent to retrieve the quill.

"How did the prince like your dress at the exhibition yesterday?"

She straightened, and her face relaxed into a smile. "He liked it very well. In fact, I believe that's the first time he's ever given me a compliment. Your suggestion was a good one."

"I'm glad to hear it." A flicker of hope rose in my chest as I curtsied and left the room.

My clumsy efforts might yet achieve some small amount of good.

A messenger appeared as we cleared dishes from Princess Penelope's drawing room, where her father had joined her for luncheon. The princess took the note from the tray and tucked it behind a vase on the mantle, giving her distracted father a sidelong glance.

The Trellan king departed with an affectionate kiss on his daughter's cheek. She followed him to the door and waved at his retreating figure before hurrying back to retrieve the letter.

After scanning its contents with pursed lips, she crouched before the hearth and carefully placed it amidst the flames.

I averted my gaze as she straightened and smoothed her skirt. Sidling to the far end of the table, I retrieved the dessert platter and stole a glance at the smoldering paper.

The same scripted writing as the missive from the day before.

Who were these letters from, and why was the princess so eager to be rid of them? If only I could venture close enough to decipher the text.

Princess Penelope soon dismissed us for the entire afternoon.

Gretchen's eyes sought mine as we shuffled out of the parlor. Her smile radiated only a fraction of its usual exuberance. "You can probably guess where I'm heading. I assume you have no interest in accompanying me?"

I certainly could guess—Gretchen dreamed up excuses to stop by the stables whenever we were granted a spare moment.

None of her prior attempts to convince me to join had succeeded, but her hurt look yesterday when I abandoned her in the gardens haunted me. "Actually, a walk outside sounds lovely."

Her face brightened in an instant. "I'm so glad you're coming. It's been ages since you've seen Ned and Sam. Sam will be thrilled."

I suppressed my groan as she squeezed my wrist.

While I wasn't looking forward to the smells of hay and manure, the welcoming sun warmed my back, and the fresh air calmed my turbulent thoughts.

Ned, who led a black gelding through some sort of exercises, grinned when he spotted us. Sam appeared only moments later as though they shared some form of telepathic communication.

Gretchen waved to him, then gave my elbow a tweak

before she strolled over to talk with Ned. Sam propped his pitchfork against a wall and headed directly toward me.

My stomach clenched tighter with his every step. Why didn't I devise some other way to make peace with Gretchen?

"Well, well, if it isn't Red. We thought you'd forgotten all about us—gotten too high and mighty now that you associate with royalty."

I shrugged and avoided his gaze. "I'm still a servant. Nothing to boast about."

"But admit it, you've missed me at least a little."

I nearly choked on my laugh. "Missed your incessant teasing? Hardly."

"Aw, now, Leah, that's not fair." He frowned and rubbed the back of his neck. "You know I like to have a bit of fun with you, that's all. I wouldn't have you trade that beautiful hair for the world."

I gulped. Was Gretchen right about his feelings for me? Sam's smile turned shy.

It would be best to join the others.

Sam leaned close as I walked, keeping up with my gait. "Are you sure you want to disturb them? Gretchen's been visiting a lot lately, and I don't think the visits have been unwelcome."

I stopped and looked at him, and he waggled his eyebrows.

"You're probably right." Keeping my head down, I redirected my steps.

"Why don't you let me show you around, maybe introduce you to the horses?"

I winced at the eagerness in Sam's voice.

"Oh, all right." I edged away from his offered arm as he led the way to the nearest stable.

Gretchen, all smiles, finally rejoined me to head back to the palace half an hour later. "Did you enjoy your visit with Sam?"

"Not particularly. But perhaps his manners have improved ever-so-slightly. I gather your visit with Ned went well?" I didn't think I'd ever understand her giddiness about Ned, but I wanted to try.

"Oh, yes." She giggled. "They always do, you know. I just hope he decides to propose soon. I suppose you don't understand since you and your ma aren't stuck in the dormitories, but I'm really looking forward to sharing a room with only one other person."

"You're planning to get married so soon?"

"Why not?" Gretchen tossed her braid behind her shoulder. "I know all my prospects, and Ned is my choice. I'm excited to start our life together."

A pinch of jealousy curbed my desire to protest further. Gretchen's future was so clear, and she could accept it so cheerfully.

Glancing back to ensure we were no longer in view of the stables, I gave her a hug. "I'm happy for you."

She regarded me with surprise for a moment, then squeezed me tight. "Thank you, Leah. That means a lot. It sounds like poor Sam will need to be a little more patient, though, eh?"

"If he has his heart set on me, he's going to need infinite patience. He'd best resign himself to bachelorhood right now and be done with it."

"I wouldn't say that. Just give it another year or two, and you may be surprised. I have a feeling love is going to sneak up on you one of these days, Leah Wellstone, and when it does, you're really going to be in for it."

If she only knew the half of it.

I returned with Gretchen to the sitting room reserved for our use when not attending the princess. Anne sat at the table, threading her needle through a crystal bead to affix it to the peach gown I'd retrieved that morning.

I hurried to her side. "I didn't know you were planning to keep working, Anne. I'm sorry I left."

She shook her head. "No need to apologize. Enjoy your free afternoon. I don't mind beadwork, and I need more practice."

"At least let me help." I took a seat across from her.

"Any word from Penelope?" Gretchen asked.

"Nothing." Anne shrugged. "I think she's out somewhere."

"Hmm. Well, in that case, I'm off to pester Sarah for more of those divine sticky buns from breakfast." Gretchen waved as she headed out the door.

Anne and I worked in silence for some minutes.

An idea struck me. "Anne, have you ever been to the sewing room?"

She glanced up with wide eyes. "No, why do you ask?"

"I haven't stopped by in ages, and it's early enough that Ma should still be there. Shall we pay her a visit?"

"Are you sure they won't mind?"

"Not at all. I used to spend a lot of time there when I was younger." Guilt tugged at my conscience. I couldn't even recall the last time I'd stepped foot in the sewing room.

"Then I'd love to." Anne prodded the string of beads she'd just attached.

I helped her tidy up the sewing table before we set off.

The sewing room was one of my favorite places as a child. Its enormous, south-facing windows made it one of the brightest rooms in the palace. The hum of the seamstresses' chatter trickled into the corridor as we approached.

We reached the door, and I peered in. The heavy curtains positioned at each corner of the room bunched together to reveal open dressing rooms—no noblewomen were present for fittings.

I motioned Anne inside as several of the seamstresses glanced up from their stitching.

"Why, Leah! How good to see you. Just look how you've grown."

"It's been so long. Therese told us you've reached your Maturity. It's hard to believe how those years have marched by."

"A lady's maid for Princess Penelope, we heard. What an honor!"

"Thank you," I interjected. "It's wonderful to see you all. It has been too long. This is Anne, another of Princess Penelope's lady's maids. She's always the princess's first choice when there's needlework to be done."

Anne ducked her head, pink tinting her cheeks. "It's nice to meet you all. Leah exaggerates. I have much yet to learn."

"Feel free to stop by anytime you like," offered Lucy, the senior seamstress.

I frowned, scanning the table. "Where's Ma? I don't see any work set up in her usual spot. Unless you've all changed places on me."

"No, no, we're such creatures of habit, it would take nothing short of a royal order to swap us around." Lucy gave a throaty chuckle. "Therese is paying one of her regular visits to Mistress Donna."

I stepped back as though she'd dealt me a physical blow. One of her *regular* visits? To Mistress Donna, the healer?

"Is Ma unwell?" I bit back the other hundred questions hurtling through my mind.

"Nothing worse than usual, near as I could tell. Just those joints troubling her again."

The iron grip on my heart loosened a notch. I knew of Ma's joint pain, but I had no idea she consulted Mistress Donna at all, let alone regularly.

Lucy leaned over to gaze out the window. "She ought to be back soon, I should think." She glanced around the table and received a few nods. "You're welcome to wait here. Not much is known about this princess. We're curious to hear your take on her." She motioned to two empty chairs.

"Thank you. As much as I'd like to catch up with all of you, I should find Ma." I turned to Anne, trying to signal an apology.

She gave me a determined nod.

"Of course." Lucy's understanding smile wrinkled the corners of her eyes. "It was lovely to see you girls. Stop by again soon."

"We will, thank you."

I hastened to the infirmary. "I'm sorry for the short visit, Anne. I know that's not what you were hoping for."

"Nonsense." Anne kept pace beside me. "Of course you want to check on your ma. Are her joints really ailing her so badly?"

"I don't know. They've been troubling her for some time, but I had no idea…"

Anne squeezed my arm, and we fell into silence for the remainder of our trek.

At the infirmary, Anne tapped on the door.

One of Mistress Donna's apprentices peeked out. "May I help you?"

"We heard Therese Wellstone is here."

Thank the new moon Anne was willing to take the lead. My breath came in short huffs, making me dizzy.

"Yes. Just over here." Smells of vinegar and herbs assaulted me as we stepped inside. The white-clad apprentice led us past two closed doors and indicated the third.

This time I knocked. "Ma?"

"Leah? Is that you? Come in."

We entered to find Ma wrapped in towels, holding a teacup.

I exhaled. "Ma… We went to the sewing room, but Lucy said you've been coming to see Mistress Donna."

Ma's lips curved upward. "I'm fine, Leah. Really. Take a

seat and catch your breath. I'm sorry I didn't tell you, but I didn't want to cause you any alarm. I only visit Donna when the pain interferes with my work. She has me bathe with epsomite and ginger."

"And drink willow bark tea." Mistress Donna ambled in behind us. "I also make her a salve."

I dropped into a wooden chair, grasping the arms. The treatments didn't sound so bad, and Ma didn't seem to be in any immediate danger. Still, the fact I knew nothing about this rankled me.

Ma looked to Anne. "Who is your friend?"

"Oh, yes, sorry. This is Anne."

Anne nodded to her. "It's a pleasure to meet you, Mrs. Wellstone. I'm very sorry to hear you've been in such discomfort."

Ma pulled a towel tighter around her shoulders. "Thank you. It's nice to meet you, too."

"Anne is one of my fellow lady's maids. We were dismissed for the afternoon, and Anne was curious to see the sewing room."

"Ah. Well, I'm just finishing up the last of my tea. Why don't you two step out while I get dressed, then we can all walk there together?"

"Don't you dare." Mistress Donna planted her hands on her hips. "No more work today, and that's an order. You need rest."

Ma's shoulders sagged.

Seeing Ma like this, inhaling all the scents I associated with illness...

The need to escape the infirmary propelled me out of the chair. "Either way, we should let you get dressed. We'll wait for you in the hall."

I gulped a lungful of air the moment we returned to the main corridor.

Anne faced me. "I should go. I'm sure you and your ma

could use some privacy. Thank you so much for taking me to the sewing room. I appreciated seeing it, even though our visit was brief."

"Yes, that might be best. And you're welcome. Hopefully we'll have a better opportunity another time. I'll return to our sitting room shortly."

"Take your time." Anne pressed my hand before setting off down the hall.

Several minutes later, Ma appeared at the door. Was she always this pale?

"Anne had to leave so soon?"

"She wanted to finish some beadwork."

"I see." Ma pressed her lips together. "She seems like a nice girl."

"Yes, she's been very kind."

I held out my arm, and Ma leaned on it as we walked toward our bedchamber.

After the silence stretched for some minutes, Ma raised her head. "I'm sorry, Leah. I should've told you. There's just so much I want to protect you from..." She rubbed my arm. "I tend to forget you're not a little girl anymore."

"Is it really so bad?" I swallowed. Did I want to know the answer?

"I'm in no mortal danger. That we know of, anyway. But my hands aren't working the way they used to, and my back aches dreadfully when I sit at the sewing table for too long. It's a difficult thing, not to be able to sew and embroider as I once did. I feel so useless —" Tears thickened her voice.

"Ma, don't say that." I gripped her hand. "You've been doing the work of three seamstresses for years. You'll just need to cut back, that's all." Hopefully my statement expressed more confidence than I felt.

"You're right, of course, though I'll hardly know what to do with myself."

"I'll help on free evenings, whenever you need me. And I

can apply the salve if Mistress Donna wants to send some along next time."

She patted my hand. "Thank you. You've always been a great comfort to me, Leah."

We arrived at our bedchamber, and I got her settled on our straw mattress. Looking back at her delicate frame as I closed the door, a renewed sense of helplessness washed over me.

First Rafe, and now Ma. Why couldn't I do more for the people I loved?

CHAPTER 10

$\mathcal{T}$he princess's silver bell tinkled against the mahogany wall of our sitting room.

I jumped up, motioning to the other maids who played five-stones near the fire. "Don't cut short your game. I'll go."

I hurried into Princess Penelope's bedchamber. "Good evening, my lady." I unfolded a lacy nightdress from the dresser and draped it across the end of her bed.

"Ah, Leah. Good evening." She placed her tiara in a velvet-lined box on her vanity.

"Shall I undo your laces?"

She nodded and crossed the room to stand near the bed.

I released the knot just above her waist and tugged the ribbon free from the lowest eyelets. A book on her bedside table caught my attention. "Do you enjoy reading, my lady?"

"What?" Her jerk made me lose my grasp. She glanced back, her expression apologetic. "Forgive me, I must've been lost in my thoughts. What did you say?"

"I apologize for startling you, Your Highness. I was merely inquiring whether you enjoy books."

"Ah, yes. That is, I'm fond of romances."

"Yes, I believe those are favored among the ladies of Imperia as well." I inserted what I hoped felt like a natural pause. "I've heard that Prince Raphael prefers books about the sea."

"Is that so?" Princess Penelope turned to study me. "You seem to know a great deal about his tastes."

I froze. Over the past month, I'd introduced tidbits of information about the prince on occasion, such as his favorite dessert, his fondness for his hunting dog, Perry, and his dislike of charades. Had I taken it too far?

"No more than anyone else, Your Highness." I shrugged, trying to summon a giggle. "We have only one prince in our country, after all. His likes and dislikes have long been the subject of much speculation, especially among the young ladies."

"Yes, I suppose that should come as no surprise. But I still don't understand why you insist on acquainting me with such gossip."

I wiped my clammy hands against my skirt. "Well, it's common knowledge the prince wasn't pleased with the manner in which King Frederick and Queen Beatrice brought the engagement about. And a happy union between Prince Raphael and yourself, and the resulting peace for Trellich and Imperia, would surely benefit us all. But please forgive me if I've been too forward."

Instead of anger, sadness and a hint of fear flashed in her eyes as she continued to examine me. "I appreciate your honesty. But you're also very cunning. I can see I'll have to keep an eye on you."

◦～◦

I filed into the chapel behind the princess the following Sunday.

Lucy sat with Ma in the back pew. *Thank heavens others are looking out for her.* Ma's condition hadn't altered, but I'd increased my vigilance since discovering her visits to the infirmary. I wouldn't allow any further decline in her health to escape my attention.

Rafe and I exchanged a glance as he passed us to take his seat across the aisle. Despite his concerns, he'd avoided drawing attention to me whenever we couldn't help being in each other's presence at banquets, balls, and the princess's other social engagements.

But the ardor in his eyes never wavered.

As the sturdy, clean-shaven priest stood at the pulpit reciting a prayer, Princess Penelope craned her neck to look behind us. The jewels in her hair reflected the sunlight streaming in from the stained-glass windows. She repeated her scan of the chapel minutes later.

Upon the third iteration, Anne leaned forward. "Can we get you something, my lady?"

The princess jumped, her cheeks glowing pink. "Oh, no, thank you. I'm fine."

I followed her gaze across the aisle to Rafe. He studied her, his brows knit. She gave him a reassuring smile, which he returned.

Averting my eyes, I balled my hands into fists in my lap. My stomach sank as though filled with lead. These affectionate moments were exactly what needed to take place for Rafe to have any chance of happiness, but I couldn't bear to watch them unfold.

I delivered Princess Penelope's tea the following morning. She gasped, snatching a letter and thrusting it into a drawer.

"Leah! I wasn't expecting anyone...that is to say—" Her eyes were red and puffy as though she'd been crying for some time.

"Are you unwell, my lady? Shall I summon the healer?"

She swiped a hand across her cheeks. "I am distressed, but it is nothing to concern yourself with." She straightened, resuming a fraction of her usual royal bearing. "You may pour me a cup of tea, but I'll need no further breakfast. Please inform the others I am indisposed and would prefer not to be disturbed."

"Of course, Your Highness." I set down the tray and served the tea.

"I'm sure I shall be quite recovered by midday. I'll ring for you then. In the meantime, please fetch a messenger for me."

"Very good, my lady. Right away." I curtsied and slipped from the room.

My mind raced as I hurried down the hall to find a messenger. Why couldn't I deliver her letter? And why was she crying?

After the messenger departed, I conveyed the welcome news that we could take the morning off. Gretchen invited me to walk to the stables, but I declined. Something odd was going on with the princess, and I didn't want to miss an opportunity to find out more.

A messenger strode in several hours later, making me miss a stitch and stab my finger. I pressed the wound to my apron, my eyes fixed on the note balanced on his tray.

I lurched from my chair before he could knock on Princess Penelope's door. "Wait, please. Her Majesty is indisposed this morning and requested not to be disturbed. Allow me to convey your letter."

He bowed. "Thank you, miss."

I took the note, guilt permeating my insides like ink spreading in a tub of water. I stood before the princess's bedchamber, dangling it at my side until the messenger's footsteps sounded far down the hall.

Retreating to a corner, I examined the envelope. *Her Royal*

Highness, Princess Penelope was scrawled across the back in the same script I recognized from my first weeks as a lady's maid.

To my knowledge, she hadn't received a message from this source in almost a month. There was no direction aside from her name, so it must've come from someone within the palace city. But the wax sealing the envelope bore no insignia to indicate who sent it.

The only way to find out more would be to read the letter itself.

Struggling to steady my trembling hands, I tapped on the princess's bedchamber door. I paused a moment, then opened the door a crack.

Princess Penelope's brows lowered when she spied me, but she beckoned me inside.

"I'm so sorry to disturb you, my lady, but this just arrived. I thought you might not want to wait until midday to see it."

"Oh, yes. Thank you." She darted over, snatched the letter, and collapsed onto her settee. After ripping open the envelope, she unfolded the enclosed parchment.

Holding my breath, I bent until the words came into focus.

Meet me outside the North Gate after dinner. —NA

I straightened and retreated several paces as Princess Penelope rose to her feet.

She flung the note into the fire and turned back toward me. Her jaw dropped. "Oh! Leah, you're still here. Well, thank you for delivering the message. No response is needed, so you may go. Though following luncheon, I will need help getting dressed. I find I'm quite recovered, so I think I'll venture out this afternoon."

I sensed nervous energy behind her chatter. "Very good, my lady."

"Off with you, then." She smiled and made a shooing motion.

I curtsied and ducked out of the room, impatient to be

alone with my thoughts. My pulse teemed as I stumbled toward our sewing table.

The solution to the princess's clandestine correspondence was within my grasp. I just had to be brave enough to take it.

~

I feigned surprise when the princess dismissed us after an early dinner. The other maids sat down to eat in our sitting room, but I made hasty apologies of indigestion and took my leave for the evening.

The halls seemed longer than usual as I hastened toward the front entrance of the palace. What if I encountered Princess Penelope?

I nodded to the guards as I exited, not trusting my voice.

As soon as I encountered a narrow trail, I stole into the gardens on the north side of the palace, eager to be off the main thoroughfare.

The curling black iron of the North Gate came into view over the pruned hedges. My stomach heaved. Thank the new moon I hadn't eaten anything.

After scanning the open area beyond the flower beds, I took off at a run before I could convince myself to turn back. I slowed prior to reaching the guards. Hopefully they hadn't heard my pounding footsteps.

They opened the gate, but one stepped in front of me before I could proceed into the cover of the trees beyond.

"I wouldn't stay out too late in this forest if I were you, miss."

"Thank you. I won't be long. I…" What excuse could I give for being out this late? "I only hoped to find some willow bark for my ma's ailing back."

He nodded and clicked the gate shut.

I set off toward the forest edge, inhaling deeply in an

attempt to keep my pace even. From what I could tell, I'd preceded the princess and whomever she planned to meet.

Having no experience scaling trees, I took cover in some heavy undergrowth. Minutes dragged by as I waited. The musky scent of damp leaves filled my nostrils, and every tingle on my skin seemed to derive from a yellowback spider or Flynnite beetle.

At last the gate creaked open, followed by rustling footsteps in the nearby foliage. Princess Penelope's slippered feet wandered about until she took a seat on a tree stump within ten feet of my hiding place.

I scarcely dared to breathe as she waited in silence for her mysterious correspondent, fitfully running her hands over her skirt.

Heavy footfalls sounded far to my right. The princess's accomplice must've left through a different gate to approach under the cover of the trees. My pulse hammered in my ears as tan, leather boots neared Princess Penelope.

The Duke of Brantley strode into view.

I stifled a gasp, my thoughts racing in a hundred directions. What was the duke's name? Surely I'd heard it before. In a flash, it came to me. Nicholas Alberle — NA.

The princess rose to meet him. Their voices were barely audible over the chirping crickets and squirrels skittering through the leaves.

Lines of concern etched across the duke's face as he pressed the princess's fingers in his. "What is it, my love? Do you realize how dangerous it is for us to meet like this?"

"Yes, but I needed to see you." Princess Penelope nudged a fern with her slipper. "I just don't know if...I'm having so many doubts."

"Doubts?" The duke clutched his chest. "About us?"

Confusion and pain spun into a cyclone in my head. Even if the princess's feelings toward Rafe didn't run very deep yet, how could she be unfaithful to him?

"No, of course not." She placed a hand on his arm and glanced around. "What troubles me is...the plan. Can't we just get married and return to Trellich? Wouldn't that be enough for you?"

The duke pulled away from her grasp. "You know we can't do that. Think of all the people who are counting on us to succeed—the Earl of Ferren, the Barons of Camberlet and Estern, the Viscount Rothwald—the list goes on and on. Not to mention their families. Our *plan* is what will save this country from destruction."

The princess sighed. "I know you've been saying that all along, but now that I'm here...Frederick and Beatrice are difficult, I grant you, but I certainly don't see any signs that Imperia is on the verge of destruction. And while Prince Raphael is a reluctant suitor, there's a great deal of kindness in him. I think he has the makings of a good king once he grows into it. He's done nothing to deserve the fate you have in mind for him."

I ground my nails deep into my palms.

"Ah, so that's it!" the duke spat out in a whisper. "You're developing feelings for the boy. Well, it's only natural, I suppose, being forced into his company day in and day out. I must bear my jealousy as best I can."

"No, that's not it at all." Princess Penelope's voice shook as though she were on the verge of tears. "I've never wavered in my love for you. But I can't stand being the instrument of harm for these people who have welcomed me."

"Sacrifices are an unfortunate necessity in achieving the greater good. It pains me as well." He clutched her shoulders. "But think to the future, how we can improve the condition of the Imperian people. Besides, you yourself won't be the instrument. All that is required of you is to marry the prince as planned. The remaining steps to eliminate the royal family have been arranged without any need for our involvement. In fact, I've just returned from meeting with our comrade in the north. He is more than prepared to fulfill his end of the bargain."

"So that's where you've been? You could've let me know — I've been worried sick!" The princess visibly trembled.

"I've told you, I can't let you know my every move. The notes, the meetings, they're all dangerous. If our plans are discovered, we'll never have our chance to be together."

Princess Penelope's expression softened as he tucked a curl behind her ear.

"But the point I was trying to make is that our hands will remain clean. You won't have to touch your *precious* prince."

The princess lurched back. "That's not fair. I told you he's nothing to me. And what of you? How do you think it makes me feel to hear you talked about among the ladies, the maids, even? All speculating whom you may be courting, whom you've been flirting with?"

"Now, now, Penelope, don't trouble yourself with idle gossip. My heart is ever yours, my love. But how would it look if I were to ignore the other ladies completely, when my devotion to you must be kept in the utmost secrecy?"

"But that's what I'm saying. Why must it be secret? Can we not marry and be done with it?"

I shrank farther under my bush as the princess turned, placing her hands on her hips.

"You know we can't." The duke walked around to face her again. "But take heart, my dear. It will be difficult while we wait, but once our ally completes his assignment, we'll be free to wed at last and spend the rest of our lives together."

Princess Penelope pouted but didn't argue further. The duke leaned forward and pressed his lips to hers. I closed my eyes, fighting a wave of nausea.

I crouched there, numb, long after they bid each other farewell and their footsteps receded in different directions.

They planned to assassinate Rafe and his family so the duke could take the throne. Apparently with support from a significant portion of the peerage, several of whom were among the king's closest advisers. Their co-conspirator in the north could be nothing but a low-life of the worst degree.

My chest tightened as though someone were squeezing the last of the air from my lungs.

How could they? At least the princess was having second thoughts, but her treachery still seared like a dagger in my ribs. I was trying to help her win the affection of the man I loved while she secretly plotted his demise. Any fondness he ended up feeling for her would only make her deception all the more painful.

As the last light faded from the sky, I forced myself into action.

CHAPTER 11

$\mathcal{I}$ marched through the palace halls, determined not to lose any more time. At the far end of the North Wing, I turned toward the east and knocked at the door, hoping I had correctly interpreted the location of Rafe's chambers. One of the prince's valets opened the door.

"Red! It's been too long."

I tried not to wince. "It has, hasn't it, Stephen? Good to see you again."

He leaned against the doorframe. "You know, you're getting prettier all the time."

Stephen was reputed to be a notorious rake. Repulsion rippled through me, yet…perhaps I should use such information to my advantage.

"You're too kind." I attempted to flutter my eyelashes. "Is the prince within?"

"No, though I'd guess he'll return soon. Is there anything I can help you with?" He raised his eyebrows suggestively.

I squared my shoulders to mask my disappointment. My secondary plan would have to suffice. "Actually, there is. Do you think you could do me a little favor?"

"I certainly hope so."

Taking a deep breath, I launched into the story I'd rehearsed on my way inside. "Well, you see, I'm a lady's maid for Princess Penelope now. She's missing one of her blue gloves, and she has her heart set on wearing them tomorrow. She insists the prince stole it as a romantic token and sent me to retrieve it." Distaste bubbled in my chest as I whispered close to his ear. "Though between you and me, I'm convinced she simply misplaced the silly thing."

He winked. "Search all you like. I'd hate for your lovely mistress to be deprived of her glove." He stepped out of the doorway, waving me in with a gallant bow.

I lightly touched his arm. "I'm so grateful, Stephen. Thank you."

"Anytime, Red."

I did my best to return his smile, then hurried into Rafe's chambers.

Once through the doorway, my steps slowed. These were the rooms where Rafe ate, slept, read—the only place he had privacy outside of our broom closet. The desire to soak in his presence overpowered me, but I propelled myself forward. I had to pretend to search in case Stephen followed me.

I made my way around the sitting room, lifting paper-weights and opening drawers. Stephen's voice sounded in the hall. I jumped, listening carefully.

My shoulders relaxed. He was speaking to someone else. With any luck, his distraction would last a while longer.

On the far side of Rafe's parlor, a candle sat in the window recess. How odd to finally see it up close after years of antici-pating its flicker from afar. Now, for a packet of matches. Unable to find any in the nearby vicinity, I snatched up the candle, brought it out to the sitting room, and tipped it against one of the lit candles until its wick ignited.

Stephen poked his head in. "Having any luck?"

I stifled my gasp. "Not yet. I thought it would help to light a candle since it's so dark in the back rooms. I hope you don't mind."

"You're welcome to anything you like."

I returned to the parlor and pretended to search again. When enough time had passed, I placed the candle back on the windowsill, hoping desperately Rafe would have a chance to see it before its flame was disturbed.

Catching Stephen's eye on my way out, I shook my head. "If her glove is here, the prince hid it well. I can't search all evening."

He shrugged. "At least you tried. You're welcome to resume the search anytime you like. I would never be less than delighted to see you."

I pasted on a smile. "I appreciate the offer. Goodnight." Dipping into a brief curtsy, I set out down the hall.

"Goodnight, Red," he called after me.

I headed to our closet, burying my trembling hands in the folds of my skirt. If only Rafe would see my gesture and understand.

Restlessness made it impossible to focus on my book. I paced the closet, occasionally gazing out the window, though I didn't know what I expected to see.

The wait stretched on, but I couldn't abandon my post.

Rafe burst through the door at a run. "Leah! I came as quickly as I could. Is everything all right? I saw the candle — that was you, wasn't it?"

His sudden nearness and concern roused every ounce of affection I'd fought to repress.

"Yes, I put the candle there. But I'm fine." I took hold of his arm.

The crease in his forehead relaxed, and his eyes lit. "You've changed your mind, then? I'll begin making plans this very night—"

I let my hand drop. He hadn't been here a full minute, and I was already causing him pain. "No, Rafe. I'm still resolved not to elope. I'm sorry."

The air deflated from his chest. "Well, what then? And how did you manage to get that candle lit?"

"Stephen allowed me into your rooms." Heat crept up my neck. "I didn't think any young lady would find it difficult to persuade *him*..."

"What do you mean by that?" His jaw muscles flexed.

"Just that I gave him a few extra smiles to ensure he'd let me pass. It was nothing. I needed to see you, and it seemed to be the safest way—"

He embedded a hand in his hair. "You're satisfied to break my heart again and again, only to go off and flirt with my valet."

I lowered onto a barrel, overcome by a wave of exhaustion.

Rafe's gaze rested on me, and he cut himself short. He sat down, placing an arm around my waist. "I'm sorry. You made an effort to see me, and all I can do is give you a hard time. But I'm not sure you fully comprehend the agony I've been suffering being parted from you."

"Believe me, I do. It's hard for me as well. Almost unbearable at times."

He leaned his head against mine, his soft hair caressing my temple. I allowed myself a moment to enjoy his warmth before moving to stand before him. I couldn't afford to be distracted.

"Rafe, I heard something tonight... There's something about your engagement you must know."

"What do you mean?"

Pacing and rubbing my forehead, I unraveled my tale piece by piece—the gossip of the Trellan lady's maids regarding the duke, the notes in the mysterious script Princess Penelope delivered straight into the fire, her increasing agitation the past few weeks, all leading up to their clandestine meeting.

Rafe looked alternately puzzled, distressed, and angry as I spoke, producing no interruption save an occasional huff or grunt.

At last, I lapsed into silence.

He dragged a hand across his face. "I just can't believe Penelope got caught up in all of this. She never struck me as the conniving type. And I had thought...it seemed as though we were on friendly terms."

The pain in his eyes pinched my heart like a vise. "I think the Duke of Brantley is behind it all. As I said, Princess Penelope just wanted to get married and return to her family. She didn't seem nearly as enthusiastic about the idea of disposing of you and your parents."

"Well, that's something." Rafe gave a forced chuckle. "The duke I can certainly envision as the mastermind of such an undertaking. He's about as two-faced as they come." Cupping his hand around the back of his neck, he stood. "But this is beside the point. What you've described is clearly incriminating, but what's to be done about it? Much as I like the idea of exposing Brantley, it would hardly do our relations with Trellich any favors."

He turned back to face me.

"His entire plan rides on my impending marriage to Penelope, right? So if it didn't take place, he would be out of luck, but the ties to Trellich might be salvaged. Especially if I could get Penelope to call off the wedding. Hopefully all it would take is a hint that we know their plans to send her running back home."

I nodded as he spoke. "She's been so jittery lately, I think she'd be more than happy to go. But shouldn't your parents be warned of the duke's plans in case he seeks another way to take the throne?"

"Yes." Rafe heaved a sigh. "I hate to involve them, but I'm

afraid we have no choice. Even taking Brantley out of the equation, they'd never allow my engagement to Penelope to break off quietly without this knowledge. If she tried to jilt me and run off to Trellich, they'd likely follow and beg her to come back, or at the very least harass me endlessly about what I did to drive her away. No, they must know, and the sooner, the better. I will arrange a private audience for us as soon as possible."

"Us?" Black spots swarmed my vision. A private audience with the king and queen was certain to reduce me to a blubbering mess. "Surely now that you know it all, you can inform them in the way you see fit, without my interference."

Rafe hooked a strand of hair behind my ear. "You have nothing to fear, Leah. I'll be right there with you. I understand your hesitation, but if I tell them myself, they'll think I fabricated the entire story. I've made it no secret that I'm not keen on this engagement. Besides, since you're the one who read the letter and overheard the conversation, you'll be able to describe them with more accuracy and be better able to answer their questions."

I bit my lip. "I suppose. But if they wouldn't believe you, why would they believe me?"

Rafe shrugged. "Why wouldn't they? You have no reason to try to break off my engagement." A grin crossed his face. "Well, at least as far as they know."

He leaned toward me, looking as though he'd like to remind me why I, too, should want to break off his engagement.

I stepped back, forcing words through the sudden dryness in my mouth. "All right, I'll accompany you if I must. But how will I know when the audience is scheduled?"

Rafe pointed to our long-neglected sand pile. "I'll write it there as soon as I have a chance."

I nodded, feeling the color drain from my face.

He took my hand and rubbed his thumb in circles along my

palm. "All will be well, I promise. Remember, I'll be there by your side the whole time. And just think how grateful they'll be —you could be saving all our lives." His voice softened as he moved closer. "Perhaps grateful enough to extend their blessing upon our marriage." He reached out to stroke my hair.

My heart lifted at the thought. "Do you really think it's possible?"

"I'm clinging to that hope with all my might." His gaze moved to my mouth, and he bent forward.

I took a sharp breath and put my fingers to his lips. "Rafe, don't. You're still engaged."

Sighing, he pressed his forehead against mine. "An engagement that will be broken—hopefully within a matter of days— to a woman who loves another. So much so that she's going to let him kill me. Does that really need to stand between us?"

It would've been so easy to be swayed by his logic, but I removed his hand from my hair and took a painful step back. "Yes, it does. But hopefully soon…"

His eyes anchored to mine, but he kept his distance. "You're right. As always. But it pains me not knowing when I'll see you again."

Tears welled in my eyes. "I know. I've missed you terribly. But the audience will be scheduled within the week, right? And maybe things will improve after that."

Rafe gave me a dark look. "They'd better."

I laughed in spite of myself. At times like this, he so resembled the impetuous ten-year-old I'd met so many years ago. "Ma would tell us to have faith that it will all turn out well." I only hoped I could follow her advice. "For now, I must say goodnight."

I rose to my tiptoes and gave him a peck on the cheek.

Though my kiss caused his lips to twitch upward, his "Goodnight" came out as a grumble.

～

I could hardly bear to look at Princess Penelope the following morning as I stood behind her, fixing her hair. My hands shook with rage as I removed the curling iron from the hearth and wrapped a dark strand around it. How could she betray Rafe like this, all while acting the role of his fiancée? Her every smile, every false remark, filled me with disgust.

As much as I dreaded my audience with the king and queen, I was eager for the princess's charade to be at an end.

I checked the closet the first moment I could get away.

Rafe had been there.

My pulse thundering through my veins, I darted to the sand pile. I bent closer and deciphered, *Monday, after luncheon.*

My knees buckled as lightheadedness blurred my sight. I sat against the wall, watching the light from the window dim to murky blue. In two days I would stand before the king and queen to proclaim the duke and princess's guilt. Would they be angered by such unwelcome tidings? Or grateful? Could they ever be grateful enough to allow their son to marry a servant?

My nerves tingled at the prospect.

I avoided the princess's gaze the next few days, fearing the anxiety and resentment in my eyes would arouse her suspicion.

Monday arrived at long last. I rose silently, trying not to disturb Ma. Standing at our wardrobe, I ran my fingers across the green dress but opted instead for a pale-blue satin with a darker sash. Distracting reminiscences of the Peasantry Festival wouldn't do me or Rafe any favors in our upcoming audience.

My hands quaked throughout the morning, making the simplest tasks a challenge. When I asked the princess to excuse me after luncheon, she sent me away without further questions. My pallor must've made my claim of illness believable.

I passed through the halls, increasingly certain I'd be ill in truth.

The enormous, carved wooden doors to the throne room came into view, sending a chill rippling down my back.

Rafe rushed up beside me. "Are you ready?" He squeezed my hand before dropping it again.

The guard nearest us regarded the interaction with curiosity but said nothing.

The doors moaned as guards heaved them open. Rafe motioned for me to walk with him, which I did, trapped in a daze. The queen eyed us with her brows drawn, while the king appeared bored, almost to the point of dozing off. Each wore a golden crown inlaid with rubies, the king's buried in his mass of gray hair, the queen's perched atop her dainty updo. The backs of their gilded thrones towered high above.

We stopped at the foot of the dais, and I swept into the lowest curtsy I could manage without toppling over.

"Mother, Father," Rafe nodded to each in turn. "This is Miss Leah Wellstone, who wishes to convey information of the utmost importance to you regarding a plot against the throne."

The queen folded her hands in her lap. "How were you informed of Miss Wellstone's urgent conveyance, Raphael?"

He squared his shoulders. "I provided assistance to Miss Wellstone some time ago when she was being accosted by several young men. On the basis of that interaction, I believe, she felt comfortable confiding in me."

"Ah, yes. So this is the chambermaid." The queen's lips formed a hard line. "Well, then, Miss Wellstone, do enlighten us."

I rubbed my sweaty palms against my dress as inconspicuously as I could. "Certainly, Your Majesties. I was assigned a position as one of Princess Penelope's lady's maids several months back. During that time, I noticed she received a number of notes that seemed suspicious—"

"Suspicious how?" the queen broke in.

I tried to summon comfort from Rafe's close proximity. "Every time she received a note, she threw it directly into the fire as soon as she read it."

The queen released her breath in a sigh. "But you don't know the contents of any of these *suspicious* notes?"

I nearly choked on my tongue as the realization hit me. I couldn't tell them what I had seen in the note because I wasn't supposed to be able to read. "No, Your Majesty."

"I see."

A glance at Rafe's narrowed eyes confirmed my fear that the interview wasn't going well. But I couldn't back down now. "I also overheard a conversation between Princess Penelope and the Duke of Brantley," I continued, trying to sound bolder. "They were speaking of their love for one another."

The king sat up, his sleepy haze vanishing.

"It seemed they developed an attachment when the duke accompanied the ambassador to Trellich. The duke expressed his intent to marry the princess one day, but first he wanted her to go through with her marriage to Prince Raphael. He said he had arranged for your assassinations, including the prince, so that once the duke and princess were married, he would become king."

Relief bubbled in my chest. Hopefully the worst was over.

"Shocking!" The king leaned forward to study me.

The queen placed her manicured hands on the arms of her throne and rose. "Do you realize what you're saying? About your mistress, no less?"

I gaped at her. "I…yes, Your Majesty. But my loyalty to our country is greater than what I owe to my mistress. I could hardly let such treachery against yourself and King Frederick proceed in secrecy."

"Treachery?" The queen's voice dripped with disdain. "The treachery is yours, in fabricating such a shameful slander!" She pointed a long, bejeweled finger at me as I stood rooted in place. "Against Princess Penelope, the future queen of Imperia, and the Duke of Brantley, one of my husband's most trusted friends and advisers."

The king nodded with an affirmative grunt.

I could only stare, my limbs trembling.

Rafe stepped forward, his fist clenched at his side. "Leah—Miss Wellstone—has fabricated nothing. We have no reason to doubt her. What could possibly motivate her to invent such a story?" He ascended the first step of the dais. "Now, I thought the best course of action would be for me to confront the princess privately about this matter. I'll convince her to break off the engagement and return home, which will hopefully preserve our ties to Trellich as much as possible—"

The queen rounded on him. "You will do no such thing. Confront the princess? On what grounds? Of course you believe this pretty little maid. You'd seize on anything that would free you from this marriage out of spite, because we didn't think you fit to choose a wife for yourself. But how could you know whether she speaks the truth?" The queen looked back to me. "Where is your proof underlying these hefty accusations?"

I shrank under her cold gaze. "I have none, Your Majesty. As I said, the notes have all been burned to ashes. I can give you nothing but earnest assurances of my sincerity."

The queen gave a mirthless laugh. "Earnest assurances of sincerity? From a servant? I've heard enough. This girl has committed treason for bringing slanderous, false accusations against Princess Penelope and the Duke of Brantley."

Treason? My head spun with the implications, clouding my vision. Somehow I remained upright.

"What?" Rafe stomped up the last two steps to the dais. "You can't do this, Mother. Leah is telling the truth. We are in danger, and she seeks to help. You would punish her for trying to save our lives?"

"I don't care if you saved this girl from a dragon's keep, it does not do for the Crown Prince of Imperia to be on such familiar terms with a maidservant." The queen practically spit the last word at him, as though she spoke of a rodent or insect. "I will punish her for not knowing her place, for spinning vicious lies about her superiors, and for daring to repeat them to her rulers without a morsel of proof to back them up. As punishment for her treason, Leah Wellstone is henceforth banished from the kingdom of Imperia."

"*No!*" Rafe's shout echoed through the marble hall. "This is my fault as much as hers. It was I who encouraged her to share her story with the two of you, since I assumed you would appreciate the warning. If you are to banish Leah, you must banish me as well."

With a scornful laugh, the queen motioned to the guards posted at the doors. "Tempting as it may be, I'm afraid we have need of you here. Titus and Franz will ensure you make it back to your chambers without delay. I was planning to be merciful and give your little friend twenty-four hours to say her good-byes and arrange her affairs. I'd hate for any bad behavior on your part to change my mind."

Rafe hung his head. As the guards lined up on either side of him, he glanced down to where I still stood, paralyzed. "Leah, I'm so sorry. I should've seen this coming. I should never have dragged you into this. I will find a way to help you, I swear it..."

I put on the bravest face I could muster. "This isn't your fault. We had to try. Please don't worry about me, Rafe. All will be well."

"*Rafe?*"

I cowered at the piercing register of the queen's voice.

She made a shooing motion to the guards. "Take him out."

Rafe's eyes bored into mine until the guards led him around a corner, at which point the queen turned to face me. "You are hereby relinquished of your duties as Princess Penelope's lady's maid. A guard shall be stationed with you at all times. Aaron?" She beckoned to a young guard, and he hurried to my side. "Be at the front gate of the palace by midday tomorrow, at which point you will be escorted to the border of your choice.

Failure to abide by these instructions will result in your immediate execution. Do we have an understanding?"

I swallowed hard. "Yes, Your Majesty."

"Then get out of my sight."

The large door still stood open from Rafe's departure. The
moment the queen turned from me, I bolted through it.

CHAPTER 12

*B*anished.

I walked in a daze, seeing nothing but the scene replaying in my head. *Leah Wellstone is henceforth banished from the kingdom of Imperia.* Had the words truly been spoken, or was I living a nightmare from which I couldn't wake?

Rafe—my steadfast champion, the crown prince, their *son* —dragged away by guards. I never would've believed it if it hadn't taken place before my very eyes.

Sorrow punctured my heart like a spear. I would probably never see him again.

My feet shuffled forward until I arrived at our bedchamber. Poor Ma. No mother should have to suffer the pain of her daughter's banishment. Would her declining health bear such a blow?

I glanced at Aaron. He nodded to me, then positioned himself to the left of the doorframe. At least I'd have some privacy. A tremor passed through my arm as I pushed the door open, but no one was within. I stared about, lost in my own room. How did one prepare for exile?

While my mind continued to reel, my body took action. I

retrieved a ragged but sturdy satchel and gathered my few possessions, then removed my dresses from the closet and folded them neatly. My hands faltered when I reached the green gown I'd worn to the festival. What a happy time that had been, before I knew anything of heartache or a Trellan princess. I stroked the material before placing it within the bag.

My apron sagged with an odd weight as I lifted it from its hook. My doll. Setting the apron aside, I dug her out and smoothed back her hair. Soon my face would look every bit as blank as hers—anonymous, familiar to no one.

I stared at the beloved, now haunting, doll until Ma burst into the room. Tears coursed down my cheeks as she ran to me.

"Leah! I saw the guard—what happened?" She collected me into her arms, murmuring in a soothing voice. "Whatever it is, we'll set it to rights."

Swiping my nose with the handkerchief Ma offered me, I sank onto the bed.

"What is it, darling?" She sat beside me, concern brimming in her eyes.

The right words wouldn't come. "I must leave. Tomorrow. I've been—banished." Another whimper escaped my throat. "I'm so sorry, Ma."

Her mouth fell open. "Banished? Surely that can't be. What could you have possibly done to deserve such a punishment?"

I turned toward her. My secrets no longer mattered, now that I was forced to leave behind everything I held dear. Grasping her hands, I told her everything in hushed tones, leaving out only the details of Rafe's declaration of love and plan to elope.

Ma listened, regarding me with wide eyes. When I finished describing my audience with the king and queen, I leaned against her shoulder. "I'm so, so sorry, Ma. Can you ever forgive me?"

"There's nothing to forgive." She rubbed wide circles on my back. "You've done nothing wrong. You were right to inform the king and queen. It's not your fault they didn't believe you." Though her voice shook, her words emanated serenity and strength.

"But you warned me to keep my distance from the prince, and I didn't listen. And worse, I've been dishonest with you — for years." I covered my face with my hands.

"None of that matters now, Leah. It sounds as though Prince Raphael has been a devoted friend, and I understand why you wanted to learn to read. I'm only sorry you didn't feel you could be truthful with me about it." She cupped my face, compelling me to look at her. "You are forgiven, my dear child. The punishment you've been dealt is far worse than any of your misdeeds."

Her posture tensed as she lowered her hands. "Now, it sounds as though we don't have much time. I'll need to pack a few things."

I jerked upright. "What? Why?"

"I'm coming with you, of course."

It had never occurred to me that such an idea would cross Ma's mind. I rose, shaking my head. "You can't come with me."

"How could I let you go off to a foreign country alone? You're my only child. Without you, I have nothing left here."

"Oh, Ma, I so appreciate..." My supply of tears was endless. I swallowed hard. "But I can't let you come. Your home, your work, your friends are all here. And your health is so fragile, you mustn't take such a risk. I can't allow you to travel such a distance."

"No, Leah, I am determined. I can still walk just fine, and —"

"Please, hear me out." I gripped her shoulders. "I see you at the end of every day. Your weariness, your pain doesn't escape my notice. Without Mistress Donna's remedies, I doubt you'd ever get a good night's rest. I refuse to take you into the unknown, where we may not be able to reach a healer, where we may not even have a bed to sleep in. If something happened to you because of me, I'd never forgive myself."

Ma's posture drooped. "Perhaps..." She released a heavy sigh. "Perhaps you're right. I'm hardly fit for a journey of this magnitude, and I don't want to be a hindrance. But I can't bear the thought of your being alone." She pressed a fist to her lips and clamped her eyes shut. "Have you thought about where you'll go?"

"I need to go to Trellich." A plan emerged in my mind as I spoke. "If there's anything I can do to protect Rafe, I have to try."

Ma nodded. "I do understand, though I hope you won't be in any further danger. You may even feel somewhat at home in Trellich. Red hair is much more common there." She paused, threading her fingers together. "That's where yours came from. Your father was Trellan."

"Truly?" Questions pelted my mind. Marriages with foreigners were rare in the aristocracy, unheard of among servants. I resumed my seat on the bed. "But how did you meet? What happened to him?"

"I should've told you long ago, I know. But I wasn't sure how you would respond to such news. And it's so difficult for me to think about, let alone speak of...I'm sorry." She glanced to the door and lowered her voice. "Reginald came as part of the Trellan ambassador's entourage, mostly to take charge of the horses. But they also used him as an errand boy, which is how we met. The ambassador's wife found a slit in her finest gown just before the welcome banquet, and he was sent to fetch me to stitch it up.

"I'd never thought to marry, but I lost my heart to your father almost in an instant. He had the kindest smile and gentlest manner, and his green eyes sparkled just like yours." She returned her focus to me, cradling my chin in her hand. "Well, we managed to make our paths cross many times and soon were deeply in love. We were married in secret, uncertain whether permission could be obtained by either royal family. But then the negotiations went downhill, and the ambassador left more quickly than anticipated. Your father was required to go with him, but he promised he would return as soon as he could."

My stomach clenched. I could imagine what might be coming next.

"Not long after, Trellich was struck by a terrible illness—the Gravedigger's Bounty, they called it—and the borders closed for some time. When I found I was with child, I confessed my secret marriage to Rosanna. Do you remember her? You were only about seven when Clara took over as head housekeeper. Anyway, she allowed me to stay but urged me to take Reggie's last name and to tell everyone my husband had enlisted in the militia and been sent abroad. I did as she asked and waited for the borders to re-open, but he never came." Her eyes glistened with unshed tears.

"Oh, Ma, how terrible. To wait so long and never know what happened." I hugged her. "I'm certain he would've returned if possible."

"Thank you." She tightened her arms around me. "I never thought my only child would be lost to me as well."

"I'm so, so sorry." I clung to her, my lifeline of love and support. "But I know you will be strong, Ma. You must. And perhaps I might even return one day, if I can uncover proof of the duke and princess's plans."

"I'll be praying for you. Remember that you are in the right, and the Luminate will be by your side on your journey, every step of the way."

I pulled back. "The *Luminate* will be with me? You still believe that?" Anger rose in my throat, bitter as wormwood. "Why hasn't He stopped the duke and princess? Where was He when the queen pronounced my banishment?" I slumped onto my pillow. "How could He let this happen?"

"Leah, please. Don't." Ma ran a hand along my arm. "You're scared and upset, and I don't know why He's set you on this path. But He must have a reason. Trust Him. He may yet bring some good out of all this pain." She curled up next to me, drawing me close. "Please place yourself in His protection, since you can no longer be in mine."

∼

I swatted at a fly with irritation as I waited outside the stables the following morning, a new, sterner guard hovering several feet away. I'd cut short my time with Ma so I could see Gretchen. Where was she?

A vibrant pink bonnet bobbed at the top of the hill. *At last.* I stepped out from my hiding place in the shadows of the trees, and my guard, Silas, mirrored my movements. I subdued the urge to roll my eyes. Waving, I caught Gretchen's attention and motioned her over.

She broke into a run, gasping as she reached me. "Leah! I heard you were banished. But surely that's not—"

"Not here." My whisper came out as a hiss. "We need to get farther away." I inclined my head toward the guard.

Gretchen followed my gaze and nodded. She grasped my hand and held it close to her side as we edged closer to the stables. Silas glared but kept his distance.

She faced me as soon as we stopped, concern and disbelief warring in her eyes. "Is it true, then? But how? Why?"

"Yes, but it's all a misunderstanding. I was trying to help…" I massaged my temples. "I won't tell you the details and risk dragging you into this mess, but I uncovered a plot against the royal family. When I tried to warn the king and queen, they didn't believe me and accused me of treason."

"They didn't! You poor thing. And you just know if it'd been the daughter of a duke or even a baron, they would've believed her straightaway. It's infuriating." The hard set of her jaw softened as she squeezed my arm. "Where will you go?"

"Trellich, escorted by guards. We set out at midday."

"So soon." She peered up at the angle of the sun. "But why Trellich? Wouldn't one of the Flynns be more welcoming to an Imperian?"

"I may be able to find evidence there. To prove my innocence, and to save..." Perhaps I ought not go into detail on that count. "But Gretchen, will you do something for me? The plot I mentioned—it involves Princess Penelope. They want to use her marriage to Prince Raphael to take the throne."

"The princess? I shouldn't be surprised. Too pristine and so flighty. I knew I never liked her."

I almost wanted to smile. "I need you to watch her for any suspicious behavior. You're in the best position to do so now. Ma knows the whole story, so discuss it with her if you notice anything unusual. And if the two of you determine it's important enough, find a way to inform Prince Raphael."

Gretchen's eyes widened. "Prince Raphael? But I don't think I could—"

"Tell him you're a friend of mine."

"A friend of *yours*?" The corner of her lip twitched. "So the two of you...how could you not tell me?"

Leave it to Gretchen to jump to such a conclusion. "Nothing to get excited about. He's just the first person I told about Princess Penelope, and he believed me."

Her eyes narrowed as though she didn't quite accept my explanation.

I quickly moved on. "But it's critical that if you consult the prince on this matter, the king and queen mustn't find out. I don't want you banished alongside me." My foot traced a line in the damp earth. "And would you...? Will you look after Ma for me?"

"Oh, Leah. Of course I will." She hugged me. "I won't let you down."

"I know." Dear Gretchen. I could search the continent and never find another such faithful, comical friend. "Now, I'll give you a head start before I return to the castle. I don't want you to be seen with me." I glanced at Silas, who continued to watch us, his arms folded across his broad chest.

She straightened. "I'd be proud to be seen with you no matter what. But it would be best to say our goodbyes now, so no one catches me blubbering like an idiot."

I gave her another squeeze. "You're a dear friend and a wonderful person, Gretchen. I shall miss you terribly."

"I'll have no one to listen to me, no one to scold me when I gossip, and no one to give me sage advice. What will I do without you?"

I pressed my lips together. "I hope Ned takes good care of you."

"You know I won't let him get away with any less." She giggled but sobered quickly. "Oh dear, poor Sam will be so disappointed. What should I tell him?"

"Tell him—tell anyone who asks—that I displeased the queen and was sent away. No one needs to know anything further."

She nodded. "I'll do my best, but I doubt they'll be willing to let it go at that. I'm not the only one who's going to miss you, you know." A fierce look crossed her eyes. "Mark my words, we'll find a way to bring you back someday."

"I hope so." I pressed her hands. "But I must let you go. So we'll just say goodbye, for now."

A tear trickled down her cheek. "Goodbye. For now." She blotted her face with the corner of her apron before marching in the direction of the stables.

After she disappeared down the hill, I took several wavering breaths. A glance at the sun spurred me into action. The noon hour was quickly approaching. Silas kept pace with me as I walked back through the gardens. But I couldn't let him follow me to my next stop. Finding an open trail, I broke into a run and swerved through winding paths until his boots no longer pounded behind me.

Still jogging, I sneaked into the palace through a side entryway. My heart threatened to burst from my ribcage as I took the maze of corridors leading to the broom closet for what might be the last time, so familiar I could've traversed them with my eyes shut. I opened the door, and disappointment quashed my last ray of hope. No sign of Rafe. The king and queen must've done everything in their power keep him away from me.

I knelt at the sand pile, words of love and regret coursing through my mind like a garment raked across a washboard. There was so much I wanted to say, but I settled for my words from the day before.

All will be well.

I rose and went to the window, reaching into the far corner of the sill to retrieve the emerald pendant. After losing myself in its subtle glow for a moment, I pressed it to my lips and slipped it into the depths of my apron pocket.

It wasn't enough, somehow. My gaze returned to the sand pile. Bending before it, my quivering fingers traced, *I love you.*

Tears slipped down my cheeks as I ran from the room and through the halls, pausing at my bedchamber to retrieve the satchel I'd packed the prior afternoon. I continued my flight down the wide staircase of the main entrance, heedless to the stares of everyone I passed. Silas met me on the lawn, his glare darker than ever. Without a word, he gripped my elbow and dragged me forward.

He released me beside the iron bars of the front gate with a huff. I stumbled to a stop, then slumped to the ground, my arm throbbing.

I'd barely curled my knees to my chest when the vibrations of approaching hoofbeats roused me. Two armed guards on proud horses made their way toward us, followed by a smaller bay tied with a lead. *All this, just to get a chambermaid out of the country.* Shuddering, I rose to my feet.

The guards dismounted, and the taller addressed Silas. "Is this Leah Wellstone?"

"It is, and you're welcome to her. Best keep your wits about you—she tried to get away."

"I see." He eyed me with a frown. "Well, we'll take her from here."

Silas shook his hand, then marched away. *Good riddance.*

"Miss Wellstone?" My new sentry stepped closer, the set of his jaw grim.

I nodded.

"We are to accompany you out of Imperia. Have you chosen your destination?"

"Yes, sir. Trellich."

The other guard coughed, causing the first to turn. They exchanged a significant look before the taller again regarded me. "Very well." He motioned to the smallest horse. "Marron shall convey you during the course of our journey."

My eyes widened. The third horse was for me? "But, sir, I...I've never ridden a horse."

He blew a breath through his teeth. "You'll manage."

The other guard advanced, drawing Marron toward me. "Don't worry, you'll find her calm and good natured." The squint in his eyes softened. "Why don't you two take a moment to get to know each other while I have a word with Harrison?" He handed me the lead. "I'm Jedd, by the way."

I accepted the thick leather strap, wringing it in my hands as Jedd led Harrison away. Marron barely noticed the exchange as she sniffed at the dirt path beneath her feet.

When Jedd paused before his comrade some feet away, his urgent whisper grazed my ears. "*This* is the girl they've banished? She doesn't look like she'd hurt a beetle. Why would they assign two of their top-ranking guards to escort her? And to..."

"It is not our job to question orders." Harrison folded his arms. "If you hope to retain your position, you'd best obey them."

Jedd lowered his chin with a grunt of assent.

As they turned back toward me, I darted my gaze to Marron and reached out to stroke the horse's coarse hair. She raised her head and sniffed my hand, giving a soft whicker before she returned her attention to the ground.

"Are these your things?" Jedd nodded to my bag.

"Yes, sir."

His lips twitched as he picked it up, weighing it in his hands.

He grasped Marron's saddle. "Should be easy enough for her to carry, especially since her rider will hardly add to her load." He winked at me as he tightened a strap around the bag, then whispered, "We have plenty of food packed for the journey, so you needn't worry about that."

"Thank you." I glanced to where Harrison tapped his foot, frowning at us.

Jedd followed the direction of my gaze. "It seems my commander is eager to depart. Shall I give you a leg up?"

I eyed the stirrups, panic constricting my throat.

He bent, cupping his hands. "Here. Step on, and then swing your other leg up and over."

"But, I...I'm wearing a skirt."

"So you are." He straightened and exhaled in a laugh. "But I'm afraid I don't know what else to do with you. Sidesaddle is best attempted only by an experienced horsewoman. It won't be that bad, I promise."

He leaned down again, and I followed his instructions, heat searing my cheeks as my skirt rode up to my knees.

Jedd grinned. "There, see? You're off to a promising start. Are you all set?"

Swallowing, I took the reins and nodded. Jedd patted Marron's shoulder before returning to his dun, effortlessly hopping up and walking it alongside Harrison on his dappled grey.

The gates opened, and they proceeded through. I gripped the saddlehorn as Marron lurched forward. Swiveling back, I soaked in the view of Dorendyn Castle one last time. Was Ma or Rafe watching to bid me farewell? Every window reflected insipid blue in the bright sunlight.

I would never see them again.

My life, everyone I loved, lay behind me, the distance between us already widening. Only vast emptiness lay ahead.

CHAPTER 13

A dream-like state enveloped me as the minutes lengthened to hours, then days. Marron was as docile as promised, and though my seat was unstable, I remained on the saddle at all times. But by the time we stopped to camp each night, my backside was too sore to sit, and my legs so cramped they could hardly straighten. My teeth protested meal after meal of stale bread, and the gamey aftertaste of dried meat lingered on my tongue. The occasional bird or small animal brought down by one of the guard's arrows came as a welcome reprieve from our limited diet.

The guards set up a separate makeshift tent for me each night by draping a canvas over low-hanging branches. But even with relative privacy, sleep eluded me. I'd never spent a night outside before, and the hard ground prodded my back through my thin bedroll. Every rustle and snap assailed me with tremors of fear. Though neither guard seemed to suspect me of attempting escape, they took turns keeping watch, perhaps to ensure any roaming nocturnal creatures steered clear of our campsite.

Harrison made fewer and fewer efforts to conceal his impatience with my clumsiness on horseback, but Jedd chatted about the counties we crossed and pointed out notable land-marks—a large, glassy lake, a steep cliff sheltering a peculiar cave, a snow-capped mountain far in the distance.

How odd to be traveling through the wilderness instead of on roads, which presumably would've made for easier riding. But I knew better than to question my escorts. Besides, I was an exile now, separated from my loved ones with little hope of return. It hardly mattered where I was deposited.

The terrain grew wilder and rockier as we progressed north. I gaped at the hills, then mountain ranges, that appeared on the horizon, the lush landscape stunning but void of habita-tion. The grass seemed greener here, and hillsides brimming with trees glowed yellow, orange, and red.

But the natural beauty did little to allay the weight pressing ever tighter about my heart. I missed Rafe as never before. Previous separations had been far longer, but until now, I never appreciated the comfort of knowing he was safe within the palace grounds and if anything happened to him, I would hear of it.

Now the bond between us frayed as though it were a tangible object, soon to be stretched to the point of snapping. What then? I didn't know how long I'd survive with holes in my heart that would never heal. Or if I even wanted to.

I lost track of how far we traveled, but patrolling guards alerted me to our close proximity to the Trellan border. My ears burned as Harrison informed them of my status as an exile, entreating them to keep watch lest I attempted to return to Imperia.

We crossed into Trellich around midday, though I saw nothing to indicate the precise boundary between the coun-tries. The guards allowed me to share one last meal with them before they prepared to depart.

Jedd unfastened my pack from Marron's saddle. He

balanced it thoughtfully, then placed it in my hands. "Wait here a moment."

Harrison approached, and I gave Marron a final pat before he led her away to tether her to his own horse.

Glancing at his retreating figure, Jedd hurried back to my side. He thrust a small packet into my hands, then draped a blanket over my shoulder. "You'll need these if you're to have any hope of surviving out here."

The packet weighed down my palm, and I peeked inside. Dried meat and hard biscuits. If I hadn't appreciated them before, I would now.

The corners of his mouth quirked up, as though he could read the question in my eyes. "Don't worry about us. We always pack extra." He backed up a few paces as Harrison drew near.

"Everything ready, Jedd?"

"Yes, sir."

"Good." Harrison eyed the blanket and parcel of food but refrained from comment. "Then let's mount up. If we hurry, we may be able to reach Millington before dark." He returned his attention to me. "I trust you understand the terms of your exile and will not seek to violate them."

"Yes, sir." I gulped. "But, could you tell me—where does the Trellan royal family live?"

He narrowed his eyes. "Glonsel Palace."

"Where is that?"

Jedd pointed ahead. "Straight north from here. But you—"

Harrison cleared his throat. "That's enough. I wish you well, Miss Wellstone."

He strode away, his loud footfalls covering my murmured "Thank you."

Jedd grasped my free hand. "Good luck, Miss Wellstone. If only there was more I could do." A sigh hissed through his teeth. "I'd give you the tent if I could, but I fear someone would notice."

I did my best to smile into his earnest face. "You've done plenty. More than the king and queen would've liked, I'm sure, and I'm very grateful. Thank you. May the Luminate bless you." I almost laughed at the statement, but it couldn't hurt. The Luminate hadn't seen fit to bless me lately, but Jedd was certainly deserving of His favor.

He squeezed my hand, then jogged over to his stallion and swung up into the saddle. Turning to give me a wave, he followed Harrison back into Imperia—a direction forbidden to me forevermore.

Their figures vanished over a far hill, and my last connection to home disappeared with them. My last connection to Rafe.

But even if I never saw him again, I had to at least try to keep him safe.

I turned to survey the landscape in the direction Jedd had pointed. Straight north.

All that stretched before me appeared uninhabited. A grassy meadow with a thick forest beyond led to foothills dwarfed by the mountain rising behind them like a fierce protector.

I had no idea a place could be so beautiful—or so remote. Already the hoofbeats of the soldiers' horses echoed into the void, leaving only the faint calls of birds and rustling of chipmunks.

A new sense of hope filled me as I set off into the meadow, breathing deeply of the clean air, scented only by grasses and flowers rather than human sweat and gaudy perfumes.

The forest lurked ahead, all shadows and entangled limbs. But I couldn't stop with hours of daylight left. I roamed the edge of the tree line, scanning the thick underbrush for a path. Nothing.

Hadn't someone, or even some*thing*, made their way through this wood at some time or another?

Gritting my teeth, I ventured in, hoping to cut a direct

course through. Soon brambles caught hold of my skirt and tugged me backward. A quick yank freed me from their clutches but tore my hem in the process. I fought my way farther into the thicket. The branch of a gnarled pine caught my arm, leaving a deep scratch. I winced and retrieved my handkerchief to press against the wound.

At length, the seemingly endless twilight of the heavy tree cover gave way to darkness. After stumbling over a dozen stray branches, I had to stop for the night. I folded myself into the relative shelter of the massive roots of a fallen tree, curling up tightly before tucking the edges of the blanket all around me. At least the trees blocked some of the chill wind passing overhead.

Weariness consumed my limbs, but apprehension plagued my rest. My mind swam with images of Ma sleeping alone, of Rafe worrying for me and in danger himself, and the question I had tried to avoid ever since my disastrous audience with the king and queen—what would become of me? I drifted into a fitful sleep, awakened often, each sound in the surrounding trees magnified by my acute awareness of my solitude.

Far from rested, I welcomed the morning light trickling through the thick foliage. I stood and stretched, pausing only to relieve myself and gather my packet of food and waterskin before setting off once more. *Please, let me escape this wood before nightfall.*

I traveled in haste, stopping to rest only when black spots swam before my eyes, threatening to steal my consciousness. Though my boots were sturdy and my body used to hard work, my calves burned like the core of an oven, and I couldn't seem to suck in enough air. I nibbled only morsels of sustenance from my meager food supply and paused several times to collect berries from prickly shrubs. My fingers stung more with each gathering.

Ignoring my groaning stomach and aching feet, I pressed

ahead, propelled by the fear of spending another night in the forest.

As the sun dipped toward the horizon, the trees before me became less crowded. I lurched forward, desperate to reach the light beyond. A cry of relief escaped my lips when I at last emerged into a clearing at the base of a grassy hillside.

But my exhilaration was short lived. I'd taken for granted there would be signs of civilization on the opposite side of the dense forest, but this land looked every bit as unoccupied as what I'd already traveled through.

I sank to my knees. Was this what Jedd tried to warn me of before Harrison cut him off? Perhaps I should've followed the border to the east or west instead of diving straight toward the heart of this desolate country. Unless they intended it to end this way, purposely taking me to a spot where I would be days away from any possibility of aid. Was my banishment simply a kinder front for a death sentence?

I wrapped my arms around myself, shivering uncontrollably. How could they do this to me? The injustice reverberated in my head like the howl of a ravenous dunwolf. I'd done nothing to deserve such a fate. I closed my eyes, picturing Ma. If only I could replicate her wisdom, her calming presence.

Certainty weaved through my mind like twine in the hands of a basket maker. She would tell me to pray. The notion of praying to the Luminate, who allowed me to undergo so much suffering, produced little comfort. If He was deserving of the trust Ma placed in Him, how could this be His plan for me?

I lay down on my side, too weary in body and spirit to continue.

My sleep was more peaceful that night. Hunger and cold nipped at my limbs when I woke, but joyful birdsong and the stunning pinks and purples of the sunrise cheered me. After eating a strip of dried meat and a small hunk of bread, I stood to assess my surroundings.

As I walked along the base of the hill, a small footpath

leading to its crest caught my attention. I followed it, taking heart in this evidence that someone, at sometime or another, had been here before me.

I kept on the trail for the remainder of the day but met with no other signs of habitation. The irony encased me like a downpour of chilling rain. All my life I'd longed for more opportunities for solitude, but now after only a few days of it, an almost physical ache for human companionship overpowered me. If only I'd appreciated Ma, Gretchen, and the other servants more.

Despite strict rationing, my food supplies ran out the following day. The footpath continued down the far side of the hill, then led me up the mountain itself. Beholding the vast cliffs above, it didn't seem possible I'd have the strength to follow the path to its conclusion. But there was no other choice. My only hope of finding evidence to protect Rafe lay north.

A glittering mountain stream ran beside the path for a lengthy stretch. I picked some cattail swaying along the shore and twisted them into the shape of a small noose. That night, I tied it between two trees. If only a rabbit or squirrel would wander in, I might at last get a satisfying meal.

But the next morning, the trap hung limp. Disappointment clawed at my chest as I knelt beside the water to wash my face and fill my waterskin. No sign of any fish. Heaving a sigh, I rose and foraged among the brush. A small handful of purple berries sank to the bottom of my empty stomach like granules of sand trying to fill a cavern.

The days blurred, my steps staggering over the rising trail. The stream had swerved down another facet of the mountain, and every morning my trap came up empty. My spirits sank further each time a new bend in the path failed to produce any sign of civilization.

After a time, my hope gave out completely. I leaned against a tree, then slumped to its base. I could manage no more than to lift my waterskin to my mouth, and even that soon ran dry. I sent up a desperate prayer that the Luminate would look after Ma and find another way to ensure Rafe's safety, since I had let him down.

As peace embraced me at last, my eyelids fluttered closed. *If You're there, Luminate, take me home. My time has come.*

CHAPTER 14

I was wrong. It wasn't my time.

A muffled cry sounded in the distance, stirring my groggy mind.

Footsteps pattered to my side. "Heavens, child, there you are!"

My eyelids were as stiff as a starched frock, but I managed to force them open. A waif of a woman crouched over me. The white band edging her face revealed a thin crescent of mousy hair at her forehead, and a black veil fluttered behind her. A nun?

Her blue eyes searched mine, filled with concern. "At least you're able to waken. Let's get you some water." She untied a waterskin from her belt. Lifting my head, she tipped the spout to my mouth. Cool water drizzled over my cracked lips. She helped me sit up so I could drink more. Though my dry tongue blocked my throat like a wadded cloth, nothing ever tasted so sweet.

"There, now. That ought to do you some good." She dabbed my lips with a handkerchief, then returned the waterskin to her side. "Do you think you can walk? I'm not sure I can carry you all the way to the manor, even with the help of the other sisters."

I must've moved my head enough to imply a nod.

She positioned her hands under my arms. "Easy does it, now. You've been lying here for some time. Poor thing. I'm ever so sorry I didn't find you sooner. The visions aren't always clear, you see, so I've been searching this hillside all afternoon. I even called out a number of times, but no doubt you were asleep. I was beginning to think I'd misinterpreted…well, here you are now, anyway."

She pulled me to my feet. A headache throbbed at the base of my skull, but I could stand with her support. We took a few tentative steps as I leaned on her as heavily as I dared. My legs held me upright, so we began our painstaking ascent. Her chatter ceased after a few yards, and she began to pant.

What vision could've prompted her to search for me? My starved, exhausted mind was no match for such an inquiry. I focused on putting one foot in front of the other as we trudged through the dirt.

At last, a bend in the path opened to a plateau. On the far side, nestled in a copse of trees, stood a wide brick house with two rows of windows, topped by a steep face of black shingles.

Relief coursed through my veins, making my steps stagger. Perhaps the Luminate hadn't entirely forsaken me after all.

My rescuer heaved a sigh. "Let's pause a moment—there's a good girl. I'll see if anyone's around to help." She took several deep breaths before calling, "Mabel? Sister Helen? Sister Rochelle?"

It seemed an odd place for nuns to congregate, but I wasn't going to question my good fortune.

"I suppose they can't hear us this far out. I'll try again as we get closer."

Her third round of cries brought a short, sturdy woman hurrying to the front of the house. She gawked at us before taking off at a run. Huffing, she slowed as she drew near.

"What in heaven's name have ye here, Sister Marianne?"

"Luminate bless you, Mabel. I'm not sure I know. But He's sent her to us, and we must see that she's cared for." The woman holding me — Sister Marianne, apparently — tightened her grip on my arm.

Mabel bobbed her head and placed herself at my other side. In a daze, I was led inside the house, up a flight of stairs, and into a small, bright room.

"Will ye be wantin' a bath, or something to eat, afore ye lie down?" Mabel's muted voice seemed to come from the other side of the wall.

I was already sinking onto the bed stretched out before me, dismissing a fleeting twinge of guilt for the damage I was about to inflict on the pristine sheets.

"Maybe just some water," Sister Marianne whispered. "And some broth, if you have any. I think the bath can wait."

Mabel's plump form disappeared down the hall as Sister Marianne shifted my arms and legs around until she could tuck me under the covers.

My weary eyes closed before she exited the room.

My dreamless sleep was broken only by visits from a concerned Sister Marianne and multiple attempts by Mabel to wheedle me into taking some food and water.

Two days later, I accepted her offer to sit up and drink broth from a mug while she changed my bedsheets.

"What a scare ye've given us, little miss. We weren't sure ye was goin' to make it that first evenin'. But now that ye can eat something, ye ought to be set to rights soon enough." She turned to me with her hands on her hips and a grave expression.

I hastily swallowed and set down my mug.

"We'll need to get the sisters in here, ye know, to figure out what's to be done with ye."

My face must've registered fear, for the taut lines in her face softened.

"Not to worry now, child. They'll deal kindly with ye. Don't ye be doubtin' that." She squinted as she appraised me. "And perhaps we'll leave it 'til the morrow, shall we?"

I opened my mouth to speak, but she waved a hand.

"No, no, whatever ye have to say can wait. Save yer energy to drink that broth." She smoothed the blanket on top of the fresh sheets. "Not that I ain't right curious, though. What a story ye must have to tell!"

She assisted me back into bed before gathering the soiled sheets piled in a corner. "Perhaps we'll give ye a bath on the morrow, too—nothin' lifts the spirits quite like that fine-smellin' soap o' Sister Rochelle's."

"Thank you." My voice had no more substance than the whisper of reeds.

"Ye're right welcome, little miss." The corner of her lip turned up, creating a dimple. "I'm just happy to see how far ye've come."

I awoke the next morning still feeble, but far more like myself. The promised bath stirred a waft of anticipation, though the prospect of meeting with the sisters generated less optimism.

Hopefully they wouldn't toss me out with the soiled bath-water when I confessed my banishment.

Sunshine poured through the yellowing lace curtains, illuminating my surroundings. Scuff marks dulled the ornate floral carvings on the dresser and matching vanity and chair positioned against the far wall. The room's sole adornment was a painting of a lone cross perched atop a hillside.

Mabel arrived with a bowl of porridge and a steaming mug

smelling of apples, cinnamon, and autumn evenings in the palace kitchens. My stomach gurgled appreciatively.

Honey and oats mingled on my tongue as I sampled the porridge in small bites. Mabel hauled a metal tub into my room, and then bustled in and out with buckets of water, a bar of soap, and a towel.

I set the bowl and mug aside to examine the soap. Hints of lavender teased my nose. Princess Penelope used such luxurious products for her baths, but never servants.

Mabel gripped the edge of the tub and turned to me. "Shall we give it a go, then?"

I smiled and nodded. She rushed to my side as I set my feet on the floor. Dizziness crowded my mind, and my knees buckled. A sigh seeped through my gritted teeth. It would likely be some weeks before I'd return to full strength.

Leaning on Mabel's arm, I made it to the tub. Together we peeled off my filthy dress and underclothes, my embarrassment vanishing under her motherly care. Invigoration stirred in my bones as I sank into the water and let the layers of sweat and dirt float away. Mabel scrubbed me like a tarnished piece of silver, and by the time she finished, my numb skin tingled from scalp to toes.

She helped me into underclothes too large for my wasted frame and a plain black dress with a stark-white apron. She regarded me with a shrug. "It's all we have, I'm afraid, but it'll do well enough. Ye're a great deal more presentable than when we started, ain't ye?"

I tested my voice. "Yes, thank you."

"Ye're a polite little thing, I can say that for ye. And yer vowels're long, not like a Trellan. Traveled a long way, did ye?" She rummaged in the top drawer of the vanity and produced a comb. "Now, let's see about that hair."

I leaned my head back as she set to work coaxing out knots. "What is this place?"

Mabel's hands paused. "Well, ye might call it a convent, I

suppose. Not in the traditional sense, mind ye, but it's a group o' nuns right enough. The manor was inherited by Sister Rochelle, and she's been kind enough to provide room'n board for the others. I keep house for the sisters and do the cookin'.""

I nodded, trying to decipher her dialect well enough to absorb the information. "Will I be speaking with Sister Rochelle, then? Is she the—Mother Superior—I think she would be called?"

"To think ye were barely conscious just days ago, and listen to ye now! The sisters don't have a Mother Superior—they're so small in number, ye see—but I expect ye'll be talkin' with Sister Johanna, and maybe Sister Clarice."

She gave my hair an extra yank at the mention of Clarice.

Sister Marianne peeked around the doorframe. "Well, look at you. So well recovered." She entered with a warm smile. "My, see how your hair shines! I didn't even realize you were a redhead. You must be a native of Trellich, then?"

I shook my head, careful not to tug on the comb Mabel continued to wield. "No, I'm from Imperia. But my father was Trellan."

"Yes, I can hear it in your voice now. Your father a Trellan. That is interesting. You don't hear of many marriages across that border." She shook her head, causing the fabric of her veil to creep over her shoulder. "Just listen to me babbling on. This is hardly the time for such chitchat. How are you feeling? You certainly look as though you've returned to good health."

"Just about." I took a steadying breath. "I shouldn't trespass on your hospitality much longer. I need to find a way to Glonsel Palace."

Sister Marianne crossed the room and sat on the edge of my bed. "It is no trespass, my child. Glonsel Palace, you said? That may prove difficult. But no doubt Sister Johanna will come up with something. Have you the strength to speak with her?"

Mabel pressed a hand to my back. "Beggin' yer pardon,

Sister Marianne, but can it wait 'til this afternoon? I was hopin' the poor thing could take a rest afore luncheon."

"Of course." Sister Marianne patted my arm. "I'm sure these exertions have been taxing after such an illness. Will this afternoon be sufficient for you, Miss — ?"

"Leah. Leah Wellstone." I cringed. I'd been here for days, and they didn't even know my name. "And yes, that would be fine. Thank you."

"Very well, I'll let her know." She turned as she reached the door. "It's a pleasure to see you looking so well, Leah. I'm so glad the Luminate sent me to you in time."

"As am I."

She nodded and left, pulling the door closed behind her.

Sister Marianne reappeared that afternoon accompanied by a taller, middle-aged woman attired in a black dress and white apron, matching the clothes I'd received. Her kind eyes seemed to peer into my soul, making me squirm.

Sister Marianne cleared her throat. "Sister Johanna, this is Miss Leah Wellstone."

I shifted forward to edge my feet to the floor.

Sister Johanna held up her hand. "Please, stay seated. It's a pleasure to finally meet you, Leah. Or do you prefer Miss Wellstone?"

The familiar lilt in her voice suggested she, too, hailed from Imperia. She must've been in dire circumstances to end up on a remote mountainside in Trellich.

"Leah is fine."

She pulled a chair over and sat across from me. "You're very welcome here, Leah. I understand you've traveled all the way from Imperia."

"Yes."

"That was once my home as well. You will find many of the

sisters here at the manor are Imperian. But what could've taken you so far from home? And all alone?"

I opened my mouth, formulating my answer. "I..."

Hasty footsteps echoed in the hall. Another woman clad in black and white shadowed the doorframe, younger than Sister Johanna but with frown lines etched across her face.

"Ah, Clarice, I'm so glad you could join us." Sister Johanna rose at the newcomer's entrance.

Sister Clarice. I fingered my hair, recalling Mabel's tug at the name.

"Meet our guest, Miss Leah Wellstone. Leah was about to explain what brought her from Imperia to our fair country of Trellich."

"What does it matter?" Sister Clarice's voice had a pinched quality. "We merely need to determine what's to be done with her. She doesn't belong *here*, in any case."

Sister Marianne threaded her fingers, darting glances between them.

"There's no need for such hostility, Clarice." Sister Johanna squared her shoulders. "We must do our best to discern the Luminate's purpose in sending this young woman into our midst. The best way to proceed may be highly dependent upon the circumstances that brought her here. Surely it would cause no harm to listen to the girl's story."

Sister Clarice grumbled something like assent.

Sister Johanna turned her attention back to me. "Now, child, please go on with what you were about to say."

I gulped. My disclosure was unlikely to find a sympathetic listener in Sister Clarice, but I couldn't bring myself to lie to women who had taken religious vows. "I left Imperia because I had to. I was—banished."

"Banished? Shame on you, Sister Marianne, for bringing an outlaw into this house of devout women." Sister Clarice pointed to the door. "Send her out immediately."

My posture drooped. Was this the reception I should expect from now on?

Sister Johanna rubbed her forehead. "We honor the Luminate by seeing the good in everyone, dear Clarice. We do not yet know if Leah has done anything deserving such rebuke. She hardly looks as though she intends to cause us harm, in which case we can permit her an opportunity for further explanation. After all, we know as well as anyone how easy it is to get on the wrong side of King Frederick and Queen Beatrice."

Her statement piqued my interest, but she didn't elaborate.

The corners of her lips twitched upward. "But, if you feel your safety is in jeopardy, you're welcome to return to your chamber while Sister Marianne and I conduct our interview."

Sister Clarice folded her arms across her chest, voicing no further objection.

"You have nothing to fear from me, I assure you." My voice crept forth like a timid mouse from a crevice. "My banishment was the result of a misunderstanding. I uncovered a plot against the royal family, which implicated several members of the nobility. The king and queen didn't believe my account and accused me of treason."

"I wish I could say I'm surprised." Sister Johanna blew out a breath through pursed lips. "You've been through quite an ordeal. How can we best assist you?"

"I need to travel to Glonsel Palace."

Her brows rose. "To find work?"

"No. Well, yes, but only temporarily. I hope to find evidence of the plot I uncovered."

"I see." Sister Johanna straightened the edges of her apron. "So you will require a place to stay afterward."

The straw mattress crinkled as I fidgeted. I hadn't thought that far ahead in my plan. "Yes, I suppose so." I longed to return to Imperia, but I could hardly depend on such an outcome.

"Have you any connections here in Trellich? Anyone who could take you in?"

"None that I know of." My doll's featureless face appeared in my mind's eye. *Alone. Recognized by no one.*

"Of course you wouldn't, dear, so far from home." Sister Marianne gave Sister Clarice a sidelong glance as she edged past her and perched on the bed beside me.

Sister Johanna pressed her palms together. "Back in Imperia, you must've been in close proximity to the royal family, having such encounters with them."

I blinked, dragging my thoughts back to the present conversation. "I was a servant at Dorendyn Castle. A chambermaid until recently, when I became a lady's maid."

"Did you do any work in the kitchens?"

"No, aside from serving at banquets. But I'm willing to learn. I can sew, and—" I bit my lip, pausing to consider. "And I can read and write." The revelation could cause little harm this far from the Imperian palace.

All three sisters gaped at me.

"Now that is interesting." Sister Johanna studied me anew, as though searching for a clue she'd missed. "How did—?"

Sister Clarice interrupted her. "There, you've heard it yourself. She has plenty of marketable skills and should have no trouble finding a position."

"I sure wouldn't mind some help 'round here." Mabel stood in the doorway, polishing a candlestick. "These legs ain't as young as they used to be."

"You stay out of this." Sister Clarice shook a finger at her.

I pressed my lips together to mask any hint of a smile.

"She raises a fair point," Sister Johanna countered. "There's plenty of work to be done around the manor. Perhaps it's time we enlist some help for our dear Mabel. Some of the sisters may even appreciate assistance with their correspondences."

Sister Clarice rounded on her. "Are you truly suggesting we permit an exile to become a member of our household?"

"If we don't take in an innocent exile, who will?" Sister Johanna's voice remained steady against Sister Clarice's glower. "Much of my prayer has focused around Leah for the past few days, and I've come away with the impression that her journey with us isn't meant to end here."

"I feel the same way." Sister Marianne leaned forward, making the edge of the bed quake.

Sister Johanna's attention returned to me. "Would you like to stay with us, Leah? Or would you prefer we find you a position elsewhere?"

I glanced among them, noting Mabel's encouraging nod. "I'd be happy to stay, if I could be of some use. If not, I'd be grateful for any honest work that can be obtained."

"This is absurd," Sister Clarice growled.

Sister Johanna silenced her with a glance. "We shall discuss the matter with the others, at which point you will be as free as anyone to voice your opinion." She laid a hand on my arm. "Now, why don't you get more rest, Leah? Thank you for putting up with our commotion and for your honesty. I'll be sure to let you know when we've made our decision. But rest assured, we will not let you go without food or shelter again."

"Thank you." The churning in my stomach slowed. Sister Johanna didn't strike me as the type of person who'd go back on her word.

Mabel, Sister Marianne, and Sister Clarice filed out the door. Sister Johanna turned to follow.

"But what about Glonsel Palace?"

Sister Johanna faced me again, grasping the doorframe. "Yes, I'll need to give that matter some thought. None of us ever travel such distances, but I'm confident we'll devise a solution. We shall revisit the matter in a few days, when you've had more of a chance to recover."

"All right, thank you. For everything."

"You're very welcome, Leah."

She shut the door behind her.

With nothing to do but rest, I lay down. The white and silver stripes on the wall blurred, overlaying one another. What would they decide?

Helplessness flooded in from every direction, turning the bright, airy room into a smothering cupboard. My fate was always in the hands of someone else.

CHAPTER 15

I jumped when someone rapped on the door.
Clutching my sheets, I sat up.

Mabel charged in, a grin spread across her face. "Ye're
to stay!"

I could stay? Tears dampened my eyes. I'd have a home
once more. Not the home I longed for, but a place of comfort
and safety nonetheless.

"Sister Clarice put up a stink, o' course, but the others were
in full agreement. I'm just thrilled. My heart ached near to
burstin' at the thought of turnin' you back out to the wilderness." A shudder shook her wide frame. "And your help will
sure be appreciated, though we'll start ye out real slow and
easy. If ye've got the energy, tomorrow I'll take ye 'round the
place and show ye what I do."

"That sounds wonderful. Thank you, Mabel."

"'Tis I who should be doin' the thanking. Now, get some
more rest. That's an order." She narrowed her eyes, but smile
lines crinkled the corners of her lips.

A tentative prayer permeated my thoughts as I settled back

under the covers. *Thank you, Luminate, for providing for me when I least expected it.*

~

Sister Johanna stopped by the following morning. "Ah, good, you're awake. It's nice to see more color in your face."

I rose from my chair.

"I know Mabel wasted no time informing you of our decision yesterday. I must confess: it was the outcome I'd hoped for."

"She did." I adjusted my skirt. "I'm so grateful you and the other sisters are willing to give me a chance."

"Of course. Now, the reason I'm here is I've come up with a way to get you to Glonsel Palace." She clasped her hands together. "The Luminate always provides."

"Thank you. I—" Sweat laced my palms. Another venture into the unknown. But a surprising calm eased my heart. This small effort toward helping Rafe seemed to bring him closer within my reach.

"You should know it probably isn't the mode of transport you'd prefer. We don't keep any horses or carriages on hand. You'll travel with Horace."

Horace? I didn't even know if she spoke of a man or an animal. "This *Horace* will be able to get me to Glonsel Palace?"

"Yes." Her eyes twinkled. "Sister Helen and Sister Rochelle bake hosts for priests all over Trellich to use for communion when they celebrate Mass. It's our sole source of income, except for the years Mabel's garden produces an especially bountiful harvest. Horace stops by every third new moon to pick up boxes of hosts to deliver where they're needed, including the palace."

"Oh…" I racked my brain for an image of the moon the prior evening.

"The moon is in its first quarter," Sister Johanna supplied. "But we don't expect him until the next lunar cycle."

My shoulders drooped. Seven weeks. Longer than I'd hoped, but anything was better than traveling on foot.

"You'll likely stay at inns during your travels. Trellans use a monetary system, mostly coins. Do you have anything you can sell?"

I thought of the emerald pendant hidden in my dresser drawer. *No.* I'd never part with that. "Ma and I used to embroider handkerchiefs and gloves to barter with. But I didn't have time to prepare anything when I was banished."

"That ought to suffice. I'll see what I can do to round up some items for you to get started." Her brows lowered. "I must ask—do you expect this to be a dangerous mission?"

I chewed my lip. Searching private chambers in the palace would certainly have risks. The less I considered it, the better. "Perhaps. But I don't feel I have much to lose."

"I understand." She smoothed the fabric of my sleeve. "Though be careful not to discount the value of your own life, Leah, even if it must be lived apart from your family and friends."

Weeks passed, and I settled into life at the manor. I took over many of Mabel's cleaning and sewing tasks, and helped her tend the garden and prepare meals in the dim, cramped kitchen. In spare moments, I embroidered handkerchiefs and practiced my penmanship with a quill, ink, and scrap paper provided by Sister Johanna. The library soon became my favorite room, with its dusty bookshelves lining the walls and assortment of overstuffed armchairs. Though the only literary works were theological in nature, I appreciated the freedom to read without fear of discovery.

Sister Clarice kept her distance, but the other sisters

welcomed me into their midst. Sister Valeria, another fellow Imperian, insisted I call her Sister Val and grinned every time we crossed paths, and I shared an instant affinity with Sister Rochelle, whose graying hair was threaded with hints of red.

The sisters led a quiet, structured existence. They gathered for morning and evening prayers in a large sitting room they'd altered to resemble a miniature chapel. The remainder of each day was spent in prayer in their private chambers, though occasionally I spotted one of the sisters out for a solitary walk on the mountainside. Mabel and I conversed in hushed tones, and I tiptoed up and down the steep staircases and narrow corridors, which sent the tiniest sound echoing to the farthest corners of the house.

Life at the manor ought to have suited me well, yet restlessness tormented me. The stillness provided ample time to fret over what might be happening at Dorendyn Castle. Had Ma's condition worsened, and was anyone helping care for her? Images of Rafe, miserable from my exile and Princess Penelope's betrayal, haunted me by day, and his pleading voice trickled through my dreams in the quiet of the night. Was he finding any snatches of happiness, or had he fallen into despair?

The scenes leading up to my banishment cycled through my mind again and again. If only I'd kept the last note for Princess Penelope instead of delivering it, perhaps the king and queen would've believed my story. I could've prevented my banishment, provided for Rafe's safety...but it was too late. Now all my hopes centered on Glonsel Palace.

The moon filled itself out and waned in preparation to begin its cycle anew. Sister Helen and Sister Rochelle requested my assistance making hosts to ensure they'd be ready for Horace's arrival. The work kept my hands powdered with flour and my back soaked with sweat from the sweltering oven. But the smell of freshly baked bread and the sisters' kindness and good humor made the tasks pleasant.

As the waning crescent approached, I gathered my few belongings into my bag once more. Memories of the last time I performed the task chafed the corners of my mind like a scab torn too soon from a wound.

The day of the new moon arrived at last. My shaky hands clanged pots and pans and tipped over jars of preserves until Mabel sent me to work in the garden. I donned a borrowed bonnet and applied myself to extracting weeds, pausing every few seconds to listen for clicking hoof-beats or groaning wheels on the path leading up to the manor.

Wiping an arm across my brow hours later, I heard it. The clatter of displaced gravel.

I yanked the bonnet off my hair and ran for the house. My footfalls reverberated on the stairs as I dashed up, and I stumbled in my haste.

Clutching my sack, I raced back out the door. A sturdy mule ambled toward the manor, just a shade lighter than his leather reins. He pulled a crude wooden cart, on which sat a weathered man with lively eyes and a scraggly gray beard.

"Well, there ye are Horace." Mabel wiped her hands on her apron as she emerged from the kitchen. "We feared ye might not make it this day after all."

A raspy chuckle gurgled up from the man's chest. "Now, have ye ever known me to be late? New moon day, rain or shine. But Clyde here's not as spry as he used to be." He gave the mule a pat and climbed down from the cart. "'Tis right good to see ye, Mabel."

"Likewise, good sir. What would ye say to a cup o' coffee?" She beckoned him inside.

"Tea, if ye have it."

I stared after them. He was paying us a social call? My

posture sagged as I dropped my bag in the dirt and followed them inside.

Mabel clutched a towel and lifted a kettle from the fire. "Now, where're my manners? Horace, let me introduce ye to the newest member of our household, Miss Leah Wellstone." She nodded in my direction.

"Pleased to meet ye, Miss Wellstone." Horace removed his straw hat and extended his hand.

My fingers looked childish within his large, calloused palm. "And I, you, Mr. Horace."

"Mister?" Another chuckle rumbled from his lanky frame. "Let's sidestep formalities and be friends, shall we?"

Sister Johanna stepped behind me. "Ah, Horace. Welcome."

"Thank ye, Sister Johanna."

She pulled out a chair across the table from him. "I see Mabel is already attending to you." She inclined her head toward the housekeeper, who rummaged through the cupboard for tea leaves. "I must confess that we have a favor to ask of you."

Horace's grizzled brows furrowed. "Why, o' course, Sister Johanna."

"You've met our new resident?"

I shrank back against the wall as they both glanced in my direction.

"She has need of transport to Glonsel Palace, and we hoped you might allow her to accompany you there."

"Certainly. I'd be glad for the company." He accepted a cup of tea from Mabel and turned back to me with a wink. "What a fine sight I'll be, ridin' through the palace gates with such a pretty young thing at my side."

"I believe she intends to make the return trip as well. Is that right, Leah?"

I forced myself to push away from the comfort of the shadows to take a seat between them. "Yes, that is my hope."

Sister Johanna squeezed my hand. "Horace, when will you next depart Glonsel Palace to travel back up Finnegan's Peak?"

Horace scratched his chin. "Ye're always my last stop on the way down the mountain. I reckon I'll leave 'round the day of the waxing gibbous. Three cycles hence, o' course."

My eyes widened. Two and a half months at the palace. Plenty of time to fulfill my task, plenty of time for my plan to crumble.

"Will that give you enough time, Leah?"

I nodded.

The conversation drifted to other subjects while Horace ate several biscuits and Mabel replenished his tea. My thoughts remained fixed on the journey ahead. If I succeeded in finding proof, would the king and queen consider reversing my banishment? Was there a chance I'd see Rafe once more? Warmth radiated from my core as I envisioned the possibility of a reunion, Rafe no longer engaged...

The decisive *thunk* of Horace's pewter mug on the wooden table jolted me from my reverie. He wiped his beard with a napkin and stood. "Well, what say ye, little lady? We'd best be on our way 'fore we lose the light."

"Of course." I trailed him to the door.

Mabel's hand on my shoulder jerked me back. "Now, Miss Leah, ye didn't think I'd let ye leave here empty handed, did ye?" She offered me a large parcel, her eyes glistening with unshed tears. "This ought to be more than enough to get ye to Glonsel, so there's no need to be stingy with Horace." She clasped my arms in a half-embrace. "Ye hurry back to us, ye hear?"

"I'll do my best. Thank you." Moisture pricked at the corners of my eyes as well.

She shook herself. "Well, I expect Horace is just about ready for ye. We'd best not keep the man waitin'."

My steps faltered at the far side of the garden. With the

exception of Sister Clarice, all the sisters had assembled to bid me farewell. As though I were one of them.

I soaked in their collective strength. These women lived their entire lives in devotion to the Luminate—perhaps I wouldn't be alone on this journey after all.

❧

The mule picked his way down the mountain at a sluggish pace. Impatience wouldn't get us there any faster, so I appreciated the luxury of traveling by cart instead of on horseback or my own two feet. Horace's genial chuckle and endless store of anecdotes never failed to elicit a smile.

Thatched roofs at the edge of the first village came into view. I shrank back and tucked my hair into my cloak. What if someone recognized me?

No one paid us particular notice as we passed through, and I choked back a laugh. Of course no one here knew I was an exile. If anything, I attracted less attention than usual. My red hair was hardly noteworthy in a place where nearly a quarter of the residents possessed hair of a similar shade.

In the next town, Horace took me to a haberdasher to sell the stack of handkerchiefs I'd embroidered. The small pouch of coins I received in return produced an unfamiliar *chink* as I attached it to my belt. No doubt it would empty soon enough. Thank the new moon I didn't need to buy food due to Mabel's generosity.

On the afternoon of the fourth day, the road broadened into a wide, well-maintained thoroughfare. An array of carriages and riders on horseback funneled in from offshoot paths. Pointed turrets took shape above the tree line, menacing as the claws of a giant, rearing bear.

Panic gripped my heart as we approached the thick wall encasing the palace grounds. What now? My rehearsed explanations and inquiries for work dissolved like a hunk of snow in a puddle.

"Horace? Let me get off here."

He flicked the reins to dislodge a fly. "Now why would I do that?"

I glanced at the carriage rattling past. "I don't want anyone in the palace to associate you with me. You've been so kind, and I'd never want to cause you any trouble."

"Trouble?" He barked a laugh. "Fear not, little miss. I promised to deliver ye to the palace, and that's what I intend to do. The guards'll recognize old Horace well 'nough. They know better than to give *me* any grief." He winked and spurred Clyde to a faster pace.

I clung to the seat of the cart. *Please let him be right.*

The palace, cold and majestic, towered over us as we reached the outer wall. I never truly appreciated the welcoming appearance of Dorendyn Castle. Its tall windows, white marble, and wide arches posed a stark contrast to the tight enclosures and dark slate of the structure before us.

Trepidation and homesickness threatened to engulf me. Sam and Ned's taunts about my hair were child's play compared to the challenges I'd face here.

A guard called out to Horace, snapping me to my senses.

"Well, Horace. We thought it was just about time for your return. What does a man need to do to get an introduction to your fair companion?"

My racing pulse propelled a wave of heat to my face.

"Hmm, being such a rare opportunity, I'd best make this good." Horace pulled at the rough ends of his beard. "How 'bout a drink at the tavern?"

The guard bowed his assent with a jovial smile. "It's the least I could do."

Horace cleared his throat to cover a chuckle. "Then without further ado, let me introduce ye to Miss Rachel

Waters," he pronounced, using the pseudonym we'd agreed upon. "Rachel, this here is Vincent Therringer."

"A pleasure to make your acquaintance, Miss Waters."

I balled my hands into fists as he approached the cart. Rafe was the only gentleman who'd ever kissed my hand, and that wasn't about to change.

"What brings you to Glonsel?"

The dryness sheathing my throat made it impossible to swallow. "I seek —"

He leaned closer.

"I seek employment."

Horace gave me an encouraging nudge.

"As a maid."

Vincent's eyebrows rose. "I see. Very good. Mrs. Floram should be able to get you situated." He gestured toward the gate. "Let's proceed, shall we?"

We passed beyond the wall into the bustling courtyard, and my chest deflated in a sigh of relief. Perhaps the Trellans weren't as hostile and cagey as their architecture made them seem.

Vincent drew near once more as the cart came to a halt. "May I help you down, Miss Waters?"

I lightly placed my hand in his, letting go as soon as my feet touched the ground.

Horace scratched behind Clyde's ear as he made his way around his cart to join us.

Vincent clapped him on the back. "Come find me this evening, and we'll have that drink. I trust you know where to make your deliveries."

"Sure do. But first I'd like a word with the lady."

"Of course." Vincent backed away a respectful distance.

"Now, Rachel," Horace began with a wink. "When we've reached the waxin' crescent o' the third cycle, you check right here each morning 'til ye spot me. I always depart just after a good breakfast."

"I will. Thank you." My hands trembled at my sides. I wanted to cling to him rather than be torn from this last bit of familiarity.

He clasped my shoulder. "The Luminate go with ye, little miss. We'll be making our way back up Finnegan's Peak again in no time."

He nodded to Vincent and lifted Clyde's reins.

Vincent marched forward with an eager smile. "May I escort you inside, Miss Waters? I'm certain it'll be no trick at all to secure you work as a maid."

"Um, yes, thank you." I took his offered arm, grateful to have an ally in this strange place.

The memory of standing outside the throne room doors, Rafe radiating warmth and love at my side, overpowered me. How I yearned for him now, to quell my fears with a glance, to still my quaking hands with a touch. If only I could know what he was doing, whether he was safe.

I shifted my gaze to the highest parapets of Glonsel Palace. *I'll endure this and so much more for you, Rafe, if it will keep you alive and well.*

CHAPTER 16

a butler stopped us just inside the narrow doors of a side entrance to the palace.

"Ah, Strom. Good." Vincent inclined his head. "Would you please fetch Mrs. Floram for us?"

The butler—Strom—narrowed his eyes at me. "Who do ye have here?"

Vincent coughed. "Someone who needs to speak with Mrs. Floram." His voice had lost its cheerful lilt.

Strom leveled a glare at each of us before he stomped down the hall, grumbling under his breath.

Vincent turned to me with a grin. "Sorry about old Strom, there. Rather a gloomy chap."

I summoned a half smile. I'd never get a job at Glonsel Palace if Strom had anything to do with it.

Vincent pointed out scenic tapestries depicting lakes and mountains, and a bust of a noteworthy palace adviser. I tried to look in the appropriate directions, but the pulse thundering in my ears drowned out most of his chatter.

His voice trailed off. Strom appeared at the end of the corridor, accompanied by a middle-aged woman with the attire of a housekeeper but the bearing of a queen. Strom motioned to us and trudged out the door.

Vincent gave Mrs. Floram a gallant bow. "Allow me to introduce our new arrival, Miss Rachel Waters. Miss Waters, this is Mrs. Floram, the head of our palace staff."

I dipped into a low curtsy, gritting my teeth. I'd nearly forgotten my fake name already.

"And what brings Miss Waters here?"

"She would like to find a position with us. I trust you'll be of assistance." Vincent flashed her a charming smile before taking my hand. "I'd best return to the front gates. I hope our paths cross again soon."

"Yes, thank you." I bent my trembling knees into a small curtsy as he released my hand.

Mrs. Floram towered over me, hands on her hips. "What kind of work is it ye seek?"

I shifted my feet. "I hoped to find employment as a lady's maid. Perhaps for one of the young princesses?"

Her eyes widened.

"I—I've just come from such a position."

She blinked as though pondering the weight of my statement. "But where're ye from?" A vein tensed in her neck. "Why do you want to work *here*? Did your mistress dismiss you?"

"No, ma'am. She didn't dismiss me. I served a lady of rank in northern Imperia, but I just had to leave." My conscience bristled at the lie I was about to tell, but I swallowed it back. "You see, I was engaged to a gentleman who now prefers another." I lowered my gaze. "I didn't think I could bear to—"

I started as Mrs. Floram grasped my arm.

"Ye poor child! Abandoned by yer fiancé, the scoundrel. Of course ye couldn't stay."

Pleasure and guilt warred for prominence at my story's success. I kept my head down, nodding in silence.

"I'm sure we can do something for ye. Let's head toward

the servants' wing." She steered me along the hall, nodding curtly to everyone we passed. "Princess Sophia came of age just a few months back, so of course her staff's increased exponentially. Perhaps there might still be a place for ye, though I can't make any promises."

"I understand. I'd gratefully accept a more menial position if that's all you have available. I worked as a chambermaid before I had the good fortune to be assigned as a lady's maid."

Mrs. Floram gave my arm an approving pat. "Now there's a healthy attitude. Some of these lady's maids can be a bit uppity, if ye don't mind my saying so. I'm glad ye're not one of them."

"The ball tonight is going to be simply divine." Princess Sophia's ringlets coiled and unfurled as she bounced in her seat. "I cannot wait!"

After a rigorous examination of my skill with a needle and thread, Mrs. Floram had deemed me a suitable lady's maid and assigned me to the staff of the newly-of-age princess. Now, a week later, we were preparing Princess Sophia for the first social event of consequence since my arrival.

"Your Highness will look stunning in this shade of blue." Wilhelmina, one of my fellow lady's maids, parted the gauzy curtains of the princess's canopied bed to lay out a taffeta gown.

Princess Sophia studied the dress with a sigh. "I hope so. Do you think we added enough beads?"

I glanced at Evangeline, another of my fellow maids, and pressed my lips together to hide a smile. Given the proper lighting, the princess's skirt would glimmer as brilliantly as any chandelier.

"I suppose it's too late now, anyway. Rosamund, fix this curl, please." Princess Sophia tugged at the offending strand of hair. "I just want everything to be perfect. I'd like nothing more than to catch the eye of the prince of Lower Flynn. Though he is a younger brother." She selected a tiny pastry from a fluted silver stand on her vanity and popped it into her mouth. "I'm absolutely green with envy every time I think of Pen. Engaged to a crown prince! Even if he is from Imperia. Oldest sisters have all the luck."

I winced and walked to the princess's dresser under the pretense of fetching more hairpins. *Pen* didn't seem to think herself quite so lucky.

Wilhelmina discreetly squeezed my elbow as she walked past with a petticoat draped over her arms. I forced my lips to curve upward out of their frown. Hopefully she thought my sour expression resulted from the princess's derogatory comment regarding Imperia.

"Oh!" Princess Sophia threw her hands up, making Rosamund jump. "Speaking of princes, did I tell you little Dominick took his first steps yesterday? He just gets more precious all the time. I must tell Nurse to stop in tomorrow so he can visit his favorite sister. Vivienne wouldn't agree, of course, but he smiles at me more."

"He must be very strong to walk at such a young age." Rosamund set the curling iron back into the hearth's glowing embers. "He'll make a fine king one day."

"Oh, yes. Papa dotes on him already, and Mama would've been so proud. If only..." Princess Sophia's voice trailed off, and she fell into a rare silence, looping a spiral of hair around her finger.

I knew the queen had passed away within the year. Had she died in childbirth? I looked to Wilhelmina, trying to convey my question.

She glanced at the princess, then back to me, sadness filling her eyes. Her nod was barely perceptible.

Poor Princess Sophia. What a tragic contradiction, to gain a sibling and lose her mother in the same day, and at only four-

teen. I'd try harder not to resent her endless requests for beadwork and embroidery.

∾

The sewing room dedicated to Princess Sophia's maids was laid
out in precisely the same manner as our sitting room at
Dorendyn Castle. A wave of dissonance struck me each time I
entered. Foreign surroundings shouldn't hold such strange
familiarity.

I selected several shades of purple thread and took my
usual seat.

Rosamund peered over my shoulder and giggled. "She
wants ye to embroider her *gloves*?"

"With flower petals," I murmured, pressing the end of the
thread between my lips.

"Ridiculous." She sank into the chair beside mine. "I guess
I'm fortunate to have ribbon duty. What do ye have there,
Evangeline?"

I barely registered Evangeline's response, already lost in
my needlework.

An unnatural hush fell over the room an hour later. My
hands paused, and I glanced up. Wilhelmina regarded something behind me with wide eyes and a slack jaw. Evangeline's
eyes were fixed on the same spot, her brows furrowed.

I turned to follow their line of sight. Vincent leaned against
the doorframe.

My pulse stalled. Had I done something wrong? I
wandered the maze-like corridors of Glonsel Palace every
spare moment, but I had yet to locate Princess Penelope's
chambers, let alone search them.

He grinned, and my heartbeat resumed.

"Miss Waters, there you are." He swept into a graceful
bow. "Pardon the intrusion, but I promised old Horace I'd look
out for you while you settled in. And I can see you're thriving

already, just as I'd hoped. I knew Mrs. Floram would waste no time securing you an excellent position."

"Yes, I'm doing quite well. Thank you. Your introduction made all the difference, and I'm very grateful."

He bent to study the elbow-length gloves laid out on the table before me. "What stunning work. It's no wonder the princess snatched you up as a lady's maid. Such an intricate design must be very difficult."

"Thank you."

His gaze moved to my face. Apparently I was supposed to keep talking.

"Ma—that is, my mother—is an excellent seamstress. She taught me as much as I had the patience to learn." As a girl, I never wanted to sit for sewing lessons. What I wouldn't give to be at her side now.

His laugh blew across my collarbone. "It looks like you learned plenty."

I stared at my lap as heat seared up my neck. It was Sam all over again. The same distressing interactions, the same pinch in my stomach. Only Vincent was too amiable to deflect with irritation or sarcasm.

A faint cough from the other side of the table hurtled my mind back to the present.

Swiveling away from Vincent, I rose and stood on the opposite side of my chair. "Where are my manners? Are you acquainted with my fellow lady's maids?"

"I don't believe I am."

He nodded politely with each introduction. "What a delight to meet you all. I can see Rachel is in good company." He removed his corded hat and tucked it under his arm.

How long did he plan to stay? I picked at a loose strand on my sleeve and surveyed the room. Wilhelmina gaped at Vincent, her lips parted in a rapt expression. She was open and sweet, her oval face and striking hazel eyes framed with thick auburn hair. Perhaps I could do us all a favor...

"You know, Vincent, if you think this embroidery looks challenging, you should see the beading Wilhelmina's working on."

"Is that so?" A question replaced the eagerness in his eyes. "Then I'd be curious to see it."

He followed me to the other side of our broad worktable. I stepped back to let him stand next to Wilhelmina.

Her gaze darted between me and Vincent, clouding with confusion. "It's really nothing."

"Not at all." Vincent leaned closer and pointed to a row of beading. "You've incorporated these pearls with such skill, I wouldn't have known they weren't part of the fabric in the first place."

Pink blossomed in Wilhelmina's cheeks. "Ye're very kind. Thank you."

Vincent turned back to me. I instinctively retreated.

A frown crossed his face before he covered it with a bright smile. "Well, ladies, it's been a pleasure, but I shouldn't detain you from your work any longer. It's lovely to see you again, Rachel. If you ever need anything, don't hesitate to ask."

"Thank you." I bobbed a curtsy.

Indecision teemed in his eyes as he bowed and crossed to the door. "Until next time." He replaced his hat and withdrew into the hall.

Releasing my pent-up breath, I dropped into my seat. Every set of eyes fixed on me.

I sank behind my embroidery.

Evangeline scurried to the door, looked out, and then returned to the table. "Rachel, ye sly thing. Never mentioning ye've already acquired a new gentleman caller."

The heat in my face blazed like a stoked fire. "I haven't. Vincent is very attentive, but there's nothing between us."

"I think there easily could be." Rosamund raised her eyebrows. "He wouldn't need much encouragement."

"And he's so handsome and well-mannered." Wilhelmina clutched a fistful of fabric.

My veins thrummed as though I were caught in a trap. "There's nothing wrong with him, and he does seem fond of me, but I—" I could hardly explain I was in love with a prince and planned to leave in two months.

"Your fiancé, o' course." Evangeline settled back in her chair. "I hope one day ye can give your heart to another, but perhaps it's too soon just yet."

"Yes, exactly." *Bless you, Evangeline.* "It wouldn't be fair to accept Vincent's attentions, when I'm still holding out hope…"

Rosamund patted my hand. "We'll help ye divert his interest." She flicked a glance at Wilhelmina and gave me a covert smile.

~

My fingers fumbled as I edged a hem with crimson ribbon. *Slow down, Leah. Only a few inches left.*

I had at last found Princess Penelope's chambers. If I could finish this trim before the princess returned with a new assignment, I might be able to sneak inside.

I knotted the thread and trimmed the excess. "Would you mind if I step out for a bit?" I held my breath and glanced around the table.

Evangeline shrugged. "Fine by me."

"Take your time." Rosamund flicked her hand in a shooing motion.

I didn't wait for them to change their minds.

I strode down the halls, hoping to appear nonchalant. The tension in my shoulders released when I arrived at Princess Penelope's door.

Unguarded, just like last night.

I slipped inside and eased the door closed behind me.

Gleaming bedposts, perfume bottles lined up neatly on the vanity, a fireplace without a speck of ash.

Princess Penelope's chambers gleamed with eerie spotlessness, indicating they were vacant but cleaned often.

I squinted past plush, brightly-colored fabrics, ornate lanterns, and bejeweled curios to determine the practical use the princess made of these rooms. Where would she hide something she considered invaluable but of the utmost secrecy? I glanced through the doorways leading off her receiving chamber and located her bedroom.

My heart hammered as I sifted through drawers and peered into the deepest corners of shelves. Every dry leaf blown against the window made me flinch as though amplified a hundredfold. I sped up my pace but uncovered nothing. How long dared I stay?

Only one drawer left to try in her dresser. I knelt to lift a pile of stockings, careful to keep them in a neat stack.

A key.

I jumped, and the stockings tumbled to the floor. A curved brass key with a pink ribbon tied on the end was tucked into the far corner. I needed to find the box or chest it belonged to.

I folded the stockings and replaced them in the drawer, my thighs bouncing against my calves. Next, I would...

A loud creak punctured the air, followed by footsteps. *No.*

Should I hide? But I may be discovered, or the intruder might stay longer than I could remain hidden. I'd have to fabricate a reasonable explanation.

I closed the drawer with the key and opened another, my fingers trembling.

"Who's there?" The fear in the young woman's voice matched my own.

Luminate, help me. I peeked around the doorframe. "Just me. I'm a lady's maid for Princess Sophia. She wanted to borrow a pair of her sister's gloves she thought were left behind, but I believe she's mistaken. I can't find them anywhere."

"They told us no one is to enter these chambers. Who gave ye permission?" The girl looked several years my junior, her eyes wide and uncertain.

I hoped my laugh sounded flippant. "I didn't realize I needed permission to open a few drawers in search of a pair of gloves."

She pursed her lips, conflict playing across her features. "Even then, I still think…" She shook her head. "We're under strict orders. No one is to enter Princess Penelope's chambers without express permission. I'll take ye to Strom. He can sort it out."

Strom. The dour butler. My stomach twisted like a wrung dishcloth. I might as well pack my bags now.

CHAPTER 17

*T*he maid dragged me down the hall, maintaining a firm grasp on my wrist. Did she think I'd try to escape? Curious glances from passersby brought warmth crawling up my neck. I looked like a disobedient child on her way to a scolding.

"Hold there. Stay a moment." A voice carried from an adjacent corridor.

She paused, and I stepped forward to close the gap between us.

"Miss Waters? What's going on here?" Amusement and concern warred in Vincent's eyes as he halted before us.

My warden piped up. "I found her in Princess Penelope's private rooms. We're on our way to see Strom."

"I'm sure Miss Waters had a good reason to be there." He turned to me, brows raised.

"I was looking for a pair of gloves for Princess Sophia."

"There, now." The tension left his expression. "Sounds innocent enough."

"But only someone with express permission —"

Vincent nodded. "I understand completely. Why don't you

hand Miss Waters over to me, and I shall investigate the matter further."

The maid chewed on her thumbnail. I almost felt sorry for her.

He patted her shoulder. "Strom is a busy man, and I don't think he'd appreciate being disturbed for such a trivial offense. Do you?"

She scuffed her foot across the floor. "No, I guess not."

"But I know he would appreciate your diligence. As do I."

She bit her lip.

"Now, go back to your duties, and don't give the matter another thought."

"Yes, sir." She glowered at me one last time before taking off down the corridor.

Vincent watched her retreating form, then held out his arm. "Miss Waters, let's take a walk."

I linked my arm with his, not daring to refuse.

"I'll admit, I didn't expect *you* to stir up trouble."

"I didn't mean to cause any trouble, I—"

His laugh rang across the arched ceiling. "Please know I don't suspect you of the least bit of wrongdoing. But I promised the little lady I would investigate, so I'll just make sure your story corroborates with that of your fellow maids."

My heart flailed like a fish trapped in a net. The other maids knew nothing of an expedition to find gloves. What would Vincent do when he discovered I was lying?

We reached the doorway of the sewing room. I tensed. Hopefully he couldn't feel me shaking.

He released me and bowed with a flourish. "Ladies. Lovely to see you again."

They returned his greeting with smiles and words of welcome.

"There's been a little misunderstanding I'm hoping to clear up. A suspicious chambermaid found Rachel in Princess Penelope's rooms. She explained she was merely looking for gloves per Princess Sophia's request. No doubt one of you heard the conversation and can clear her good name?"

Dread lanced my chest like a carving knife. Of course no one overheard a conversation that hadn't taken place.

Vincent scratched his jawline. "No one? Hmm." Glancing at me, he pressed his lips together. "I guess I could ask the—"

"Oh." Evangeline rose from her seat. "Princess Sophia did say this morning that she wished she had a pair of yellow gloves."

"Excellent. Thank you, I won't take any more of your time." He inclined his head. "Miss Waters, if you would join me in the hall for another moment."

"Of course." I rubbed my palms against my skirt, but they remained sticky with sweat.

He paused in the corridor.

"I'll be dismissed, won't I?" I couldn't meet his eye. "Or will I be sent to the dungeons?"

Vincent's chuckle made me look up. "I certainly hope we can avoid punishments as severe as that. But, I'm afraid I do have to ask..." He surveyed the hall. "Did Princess Sophia truly make a request for you to search her sister's rooms? I could ask the princess, and I will, if I must, but—"

"No." I swallowed past the boulder lodged in my throat. "As Evangeline said, this morning Princess Sophia expressed a wish for gloves to match the yellow gown she'll wear to the ball tonight. But we told her it wasn't possible because we don't have fabric in the right color and would have to order some." The truth could take me that far—now I was on my own. "I hated to see her disappointed, and I knew Princess Penelope couldn't have brought her entire wardrobe along to Imperia, at least if she has half as many gowns as her sister. It seemed it wouldn't do any harm to check, and I thought if I could find matching gloves, it would help me stay in her good graces."

Vincent nodded and rubbed his forehead.

"But I see now it was foolish. I'm still so new to Glonsel

Palace, and of course they don't want just anyone snooping in the princess's chambers."

"Don't be too hard on yourself." He grasped my elbow. "Palace life does take some adjustment, and it sounds like an innocent enough mistake."

"Thank you. I…"

Wilhelmina appeared in the doorway. "Oh, I'm so sorry to intrude." She picked an invisible fleck of dirt off her apron. "I'm just going to see if I can scrounge up more cream-colored lace."

Vincent waved his hand. "No intrusion at all. I've heard everything I need to deem Rachel fit to resume her service to the princess. Would you care for an escort? Wilhelmina, was it?"

"You remembered! That is—but everyone calls me Mina."

"Mina. That's very pretty." He held out his arm. "Shall we?"

She accepted as though he offered a treasured artifact.

The memory of Rafe taking my arm to escort me through Dorendyn Castle flashed before my eyes. Would I ever feel the thrill of his touch again? The same butterflies I could almost see chasing each other about in Wilhelmina's ribcage?

Vincent tipped his hat to me. "Good day, Miss Waters. No more poking around in private chambers, understood?" He frowned and shook his finger before breaking into a grin.

All reminiscences vanished as my stomach spiraled into itself like a fist.

I wasn't nearly done poking around in private chambers, and even Vincent couldn't save me a second time.

A visiting royal party departed two days later. In the absence of any banquets or balls to prepare for, Princess Sophia granted us the afternoon off.

Did I dare resume my search? My limbs quaked at the thought. No, better to wait until my nerves settled. And while my fellow lady's maids had been kind enough to overlook the glove-searching incident, I didn't want to give them any further cause for suspicion.

I exited the nearest door and raised my face to the welcoming sunshine. A perfect day to attempt the secondary goal I'd set for myself during my time at Glonsel Palace. I directed my steps to the stables.

Air thick with hay and horsehair embedded in my lungs. The stables were among the few things I *didn't* miss about Dorendyn Castle.

I milled around the perimeter until I spotted a stable hand who appeared to be around Ma's age. Swatting at hovering flies, I ventured closer.

"Excuse me, sir." I cleared my throat. "Have you worked in the stables long?"

He dropped a bag of feed, emitting a puff of powder. "Well, hello, little miss. I didn't see ye there. Aye, I've worked in these here stables since I was a boy. Can I help ye?"

"I was wondering…" I buried my hands in my apron pockets. "Are you familiar with the name Reginald Wellstone?" I'd never spoken my father's name aloud. The words felt strange on my lips.

"Reginald Wellstone." He tapped his foot. "Oh, ye mean Reggie?"

I nodded. An ache pinched my chest. I'd never met my father, and this stranger knew him well enough to call him by a nickname.

"I ain't heard that name in at least a decade. O' course I knew old Reg. These beasts were fond o' him, the like o' which I've never seen." He patted the neck of a bay, who snorted into her empty trough. "He could tame a horse so fast ye'd swear it'd ne'er given ye trouble in the first place."

I tried to memorize his every word. "Do you know what happened to him?"

"Taken by the Gravedigger's Bounty. A real shame it was, too." The man looked down and placed a hand on his chest.

He was dead. The knowledge simultaneously set my mind at rest and extinguished a flicker of hope.

"When things here got so bad the borders closed, the good man up and volunteered to care for the sick. After a time, he caught it too."

"How brave of him." And kind and selfless. No wonder he was a perfect match for Ma.

"Oh, yes, for there weren't no escaping the Gravedigger's Bounty once it got hold of ye." He shook his head. "I consider myself right blessed to have been spared—two o' my little ones were taken."

"I'm so sorry."

"Well, if the Luminate had need of 'em, who was I to tell 'im no?" His voice took on a gruffer tone. "What's yer interest in Reg, if I may ask?"

"He—I believe he was a relation of mine."

One side of his mouth crinkled into a smile. "I'm honored to meet any relation o' Reggie's. A fine man."

"Thank you." I scuffed my boot in the dirt. "I appreciate your taking the time to tell me about him."

"Happy to, little miss. Have yerself a fine day, now."

"You too." I curtsied and hurried away.

I sank against a stump in a secluded copse of trees, curling my knees to my chest. Tears streamed down my cheeks. I let the details about my father swirl in my head until they could sink in and become part of me.

What a comfort it would be to Ma to have such closure. I had to find a way to get back to Imperia.

~

My visit to the stables warmed the chambers of my heart that had numbed during months of exile. Renewed hope and energy invigorated me, giving a fresh sense of purpose to my sojourn at Glonsel Palace. I couldn't leave without searching every inch of Princess Penelope's chambers.

I cringed at the dark, moonless sky that evening. More than one lunar cycle had already passed, and I had little to show for it.

The next day, Princess Sophia assigned me the tedious task of sewing buttons up the bodice of her lavender gown. My needle punctured the silky fabric again and again. The round, lustrous pearls reflected the golden morning sun.

In and out. String a pearl. In and out.

My mind wandered to Princess Penelope's rooms. I needed to go back, but when?

No matter how I weighed the options, I reached the same conclusion. My best chance to search undisturbed would be under the cover of night.

A shiver stole down my spine. If I were discovered this time, I could never talk my way out of it.

I lay in bed for hours that night, until nothing but the gentle breaths and snores of my fellow maids disturbed the quiet. I pulled my black dress from the convent over my nightgown and stepped into my leather-soled slippers. Holding my breath, I eased the door closed behind me.

Tiptoeing through the halls at this late hour was a nightmare come to life. Every shadow terrified me, and the slightest creak made me lurch.

I turned a corner and spotted the pinpoint of a lit candle at the end of the corridor. A patrolling guard. My pulse stuttered, and I slunk back into the adjoining hall. Ducking into a doorframe, I pressed myself against the wall until the echo of the guard's footsteps faded to silence.

The walk took an eternity.

I reached Princess Penelope's chambers at last, struggling

to rally my frayed nerves. *Concentrate, or this entire ordeal will be for naught.* I crouched to the floor to light the taper from her bedside table. Staying low, I resumed my search in the most methodical fashion I could contrive.

I opened a desk drawer, revealing two tidy stacks of letters. My breath caught. Could it be — ?

I eased a letter free from the twine tied around the first stack. Flourishing handwriting. I squinted to survey the contents. Penned by the princess's cousin.

I huffed and rubbed my eyes. The remainder of the stack derived from the same source, with no mention of the duke.

The second pile proved equally disappointing. Childish notes exchanged with a friend.

As the hours ticked by, despair weighed down my shoulders. If I didn't find anything, Rafe would still be at the mercy of the duke and Princess Penelope. I'd have no hope of helping him, no hope of returning home.

Fatigue blurred my sight by the time I finally spotted it. A decorative box tucked in the far corner of a wardrobe in the princess's dressing room. Wood of a deep-red hue, carved with swirling vines and beaconflowers. And sealed with a lock.

Excitement swelled in my veins like a surging river in a storm.

Nearly stumbling on the hem of my dress, I scurried into her bedchamber to retrieve the key from the dresser.

My fingers quivered as I inserted the key into the lock. A *click* released the catch. I lifted the lid, scarcely daring to look. My spirits couldn't withstand yet another disappointment.

I clamped a hand over my mouth. The familiar scripted handwriting. A stack of ten letters or so, all from the duke.

Bowing my head, I pressed my eyes shut. *Thank you, Luminate. Thank you for this chance to make things right.*

I tucked the letters into my waistband. Though frantic to know their contents, I didn't dare tarry any longer. A smile tugged at my lips as I returned the box, key, and candle to their original locations.

My heart continued to pound as I trod silently back through the dark corridors and slipped beneath my covers. This time, with exultation.

CHAPTER 18

I rubbed my eyes again, but the haze wouldn't clear. Stifling a yawn, I pressed a strip of lace against the collar of Princess Sophia's gown and plunged the needle back in.

Blast. Another missed stitch. At this rate, I would rip out at least as many stitches as I'd kept.

I curled my fingers. It had been a week since my midnight trek to Princess Penelope's chambers, and the letters consumed my every thought. Did they contain sufficient evidence to end Rafe's betrothal? To provide me safe passage back to Imperia?

I had to find an opportunity to read them.

"Are ye just about finished with that lace trim, Rachel?"

I jumped and stabbed myself with the needle. "Just —just about."

Wilhelmina winced. "Sorry to startle ye. I don't mean to make ye rush, but the princess asked me to add some beading to that gown before dinner."

Warmth stole up my neck. I'd been working on the dress for hours and barely passed the point of the V-shaped neckline.

"I'm having a little trouble getting the lace to lie flat, but I'll try to hurry."

"Poor thing. How can anyone expect ye to concentrate?" Evangeline patted my arm. "I bet ye're thinking about *him* again, aren't ye?"

My head jerked up. "Who?"

"Why, your fiancé, o' course."

"Oh, yes." The tempo of my heart slowed. "I try not to, but—"

"Anyone can see it's been hard on ye." Evangeline stood to survey the gown laid out before me.

I pretended to smooth the sleeve, hoping to cover my sloppy work.

"If we turn it this way, I think ye could sit over here and do your beading, Mina, without getting in Rachel's way."

"Perfect. I should've thought of that." My chair rocked as I rose and adjusted the gown. I looked at Evangeline and forced my lips into a smile.

I couldn't wait to put this charade behind me.

"Will ye join us at the tournament this afternoon, Rachel?"

Rosamund matched my gait on our way to the kitchen to deposit dishes from Princess Sophia's luncheon.

"Won't we be attending to the princess?"

"No, she said after we dress her, we're free to go." She leaned closer and lowered her voice. "My guess is she's keen to be alone with that young Flynnite prince. Though I couldn't say why—I've never seen a gentleman with so many freckles."

I giggled along with her, but my thoughts strayed elsewhere. "Will *everyone* be at the tournament, do you think?"

"Oh, yes. Trellans are some of the best swordsmen in the land, ye know. So you'll come?"

"I'm not sure." I shifted the heavy ceramic platter under my arm. "I've been waiting for a chance to spend some time in the gardens."

"Save the gardens for later. They'll be here any old time."

"I know." I chewed my cheek. What excuse could I give? "But I'd love to do some sketching. You have a few flowers here I've never seen before. And I can concentrate so much better when there aren't throngs of people walking by."

"Makes sense, I guess. I didn't know ye were an artist."

The familiar coil of remorse snaked up my back. If only this endeavor didn't require so much deceit. "I haven't had many opportunities since my arrival."

Rosamund snorted. "I can certainly believe that. Well, suit yerself." She shrugged. "If ye decide to come, the servants generally sit on the open lawn to the left o' the stands."

"Thank you, I'll think about it. I appreciate the invitation."

Anticipation quavered in my limbs throughout the process of getting Princess Sophia ready for the tournament. I held back sighs of exasperation as she requested one more fix to her hair, one last fluff of her skirt.

At last she departed, leaving the maids free to do their own preparations. I helped Wilhelmina braid a ribbon into her hair and buttoned the back of Evangeline's dress.

When they, too, set out for the tournament, I heaved a pent-up sigh.

I rummaged around our sewing room until I found a pencil and several scraps of paper. I'd best attempt a sketch or two, in case Rosamund asked to see them. Stopping in our bedchamber, I untied the bag hidden under my mattress with trembling fingers. I placed the paper and pencil inside and secured the bag around my waist, tucking it beneath my apron.

The halls were already emptying as I made my way outside. Everyone I passed in the courtyard headed in the opposite direction, toward the mounting clamor on the eastern side of the palace. *This might actually work.*

I scanned the gardens, peering down every row and over

each contoured hedge. As far as I could tell, I was the only living creature aside from the moss squirrels and calling doves.

Choosing the most secluded corner I could find, I perched on a bench. Cylinder-shaped bushes rose behind me, too tall for anyone to see over. If I stayed alert, I'd see someone approaching well before they reached me.

Keeping the satchel close to my side, I uncinched the opening. I placed the pencil and paper on the bench, then removed the top letter from its ribbon. Surveying my surroundings once more, I unfolded the page.

My pulse throbbed in my ears. I willed my hands to steady so I could focus on the text before me.

My Dearest Pen,

It is but a day since I arrived in my home country, but already my heart cries out for you, my eyes long to behold each flawless feature, my arms hunger for your embrace.

I sat with King Frederick in his study last night and proposed our solution for ensuring a lasting peace with Trellich. He expressed surprise, but the idea seemed to please him, though he couldn't guess how the prince might react. With this strong beginning, I have no doubt I will manage to convince their royal majesties within the week of the wisdom of our plan. I rejoice that success on my part will hasten you to my side, though the secret of our love must be preserved now more than ever.

All I ask of you, darling, is to remain true to me, even while convincing your father to wed you to another. The thought of your marriage to Prince Raphael makes my blood boil, but I have a renewed appreciation in the grandeur of this place, taking comfort in the knowledge that one day it will be ours.

Your devoted,

Nicholas

I read the letter again and again. Could I be dreaming? The words of this one note should be enough to provoke suspicion in the king and queen, and the stack contained many more.

Happiness and relief flooded every inch of my body. I could've run and leapt down the garden path, but I contained myself to bouncing on the edge of the bench.

Rafe would be free. Safe. I might even be allowed within Imperia's borders again one day.

I stuffed the letter back into the bag and tried to sketch with shaky hands, hardly seeing the surrounding blossoms. Moments later, I abandoned my pathetic drawing attempt and rushed to my room to hide the key to Rafe's safety once more.

The moon's cycles advanced slower than a pond snail. My eagerness to study the remainder of the letters and post them to Rafe made me jittery, but I kept them secured under my mattress. They contained the proof I needed—everything else could wait for the safety of the manor.

When the waxing crescent of the third cycle arrived at last, I darted to the front window as soon as we'd cleared Princess Sophia's breakfast. Grasping the frame, I strained my eyes against the sunlight.

Horses stomped, carriages came and went, and travelers called greetings to one another. But no mule or cart came into view.

Air expelled from my lungs, fogging the glass. What if I missed him somehow, or he wasn't able to return?

"Rachel, it's time to go. The service starts in fifteen minutes."

I turned to meet the princess's frown. The service? I shook my head. Sunday, of course.

"She's just checking to see if we should bring yer parasol. Right, Rachel?" Evangeline walked to my side and took my elbow.

I swallowed. "Yes. I think you might need it, my lady. In case you decide to take a stroll after Mass." I squeezed Evangeline's arm as we set out, clamping my eyes shut to stifle the pooling tears.

❧

The following morning, I steered clear of the window until Princess Sophia left for a carriage ride and the other maids retired to our sewing room. No need to display further erratic behavior.

I curled up in the window seat, but I couldn't bring myself to peer out. What if he still wasn't there?

Just look.

I directed my gaze to the front lawn. There — Horace's gray cloud of hair drifted above his stooped back. I clapped my hands.

Thank you, Luminate. I slipped out quietly and broke into a run after passing the guards at the front gate. "Horace, you came!"

A grin crinkled the corners of his eyes. "O' course I came, little lady. Missed me, did ye?"

I scratched behind Clyde's ear. "I'm just so relieved. When I didn't see you yesterday, I began to worry…"

"Now, that's hardly fair. It's still the waxin' crescent, ain't it? Just like I told ye. Not much can be said for old Horace, but he is reliable." He clapped me on the back. "Are ye ready? I took care o' my deliveries yesterday, so nothing's keepin' us here."

My hand paused. "No, not quite yet. Do you mind waiting a bit? I'll go as fast as —"

"Take yer time, little miss. I'm not goin' anywhere."

"Thank you." I grasped his arm, willing him to still be there when I got back.

My heart stuttered like a lid on a kettle of boiling water as I ascended the palace steps. For the last time, with any luck. I hastened to the dormitory and donned the velvety traveling cloak the sisters had lent me. Retrieving the satchel beneath my bed, I felt for the parcel of letters at the bottom before folding my dresses on top.

I clutched the bag to my chest and paused at the doorway of our sewing room. Remorse edged the back of my mind. I had lied to the other maids and would now abandon them without warning, leaving extra work.

At least this would be the last chapter of my deceptive tale.

I cleared my throat. "I hate to leave all of you, but I have the most exciting news. My fiancé sent someone after me. He wants to marry me after all." My breathlessness made it easy to appear excited. "You must make my apologies to Princess Sophia."

"How wonderful!" Evangeline ran forward and pulled me into a hug. "That fiancé of yers better be on his best behavior from now on."

"Or he'll have us to answer to." Rosamund threw an arm about my neck.

"I think it will all turn out well, once we're together again." If only I could be sure.

Wilhelmina peeked around Evangeline. "We'll miss ye."

I grasped her hand. "And I shall miss all of you." I couldn't wait to leave the tension of my theft and false identity behind, but I meant it. "You've all become dear friends in my short time here. Thank you for everything."

An indecipherable chorus of congratulations and well wishes followed me down the hall.

I burst through the front entrance into the sunlight once more. There was Horace, just where I'd left him. *I'm free.*

Loud footsteps echoed on the stairs behind me.

"Miss Waters?"

Vincent. Guilt pooled in my stomach. I'd hoped to escape without fabricating an explanation for him.

He halted before me, tugging at his collar. "Is everything all right? Why do you have your bags?"

"I..." I glanced at Horace, who ran a brush over Clyde.

"You can't be leaving."

"I'm afraid I am." I took a deep breath. *Do the right thing, Leah. Look him in the eye.* "I thought I would enjoy this new adventure, and I have, in many ways. But I find I'm very homesick, and Horace has agreed to take me back."

Vincent dragged a hand through his hair. "I see. I'm very sorry to hear that."

"Please know that your kindness and friendship during my time at Glonsel Palace has meant more than I can say."

"It was my pleasure." He looked past me to Horace and raised a hand in greeting. "I guess I'd best not hold you up, then." He clasped my offered hand.

I turned away, but he gripped my shoulder.

"Miss Waters?" Color spread up his neck and into his face. "Wilhelmina, does she...is there any particular gentleman she speaks highly of?"

A grin tugged at the corners of my mouth. "You mean, aside from *you*? Not that I've heard."

"Ah. Well, then..." He cleared his throat and gave a self-conscious smile. "Safe travels, Miss Waters."

"Thank you. And the Luminate bless you, Vincent."

Horace waved to Vincent and stowed the brush in one of his packs. He winked as I drew near. "*Now* are ye ready to depart, Miss Waters?"

"Yes." I took his hand and climbed into the cart.

I'd never spoken a truer word in my life.

Mist blurred my eyes as the manor's brick chimneys emerged on the horizon. *At last.*

I grasped the side of the cart, resisting the urge to jump out and run.

Impatience had been my constant companion over the past five days as Clyde's hooves clomped up the mountainside step by step, interrupted by a social call to every cottage we passed.

A sleepwalking turtle could've made faster progress.

I grinned at Mabel's plump form bent over in the garden. She straightened and held her arms outstretched as she scuttled to meet us. She wrapped me in a tight hug before I'd set both feet on the ground.

"May the Luminate bless ye, Horace, for bringing her back to us in safety." She squeezed again before holding me at arms' length. "Heavens, child! Did they feed ye at all while ye were away? In one piece, though, and there's a blessing."

Horace chuckled as she ushered us inside. "No doubt ye'll 'ave the girl plumped right up in no time."

I soaked in the warmth and familiarity of the kitchen. Mabel heaped food onto our plates, and several of the sisters stopped by to offer their greetings.

Sister Johanna took a seat at my side. "We're so glad to have you back, Leah."

"Thank you. I'm very happy to be back."

"Did you—?" She leaned closer. "Were you able to find anything?"

"Yes. I just hope it'll be enough."

She laid her hand over mine. "Well done, child."

After the sisters dispersed, Mabel shooed me upstairs. "Ye can resume yer work tomorrow. Ye've had a long journey. Why don't ye go lie down?"

"I will. Thank you, Mabel."

I dashed upstairs, clutching my satchel. Rest could wait. The unread letters beckoned.

I pressed the door closed behind me. The bright, cozy room brought a smile to my face. Not my true home, but for now, it was the closest thing to a home I had.

Sinking to the floor, I undid the bag's drawstring and turned it over.

I snatched the letters as they slid into view, and my fingers fumbled to untie the ribbon holding them together.

I laid them out and scanned the entire array before settling in to study each letter in detail. Their contents were similar to the first—expressions of love and devotion followed by updates on the duke's progress arranging the betrothal and securing the services of someone he referenced only as D.L.

Gathering the missives, I moved to my desk. I retrieved a stack of blank paper and began to painstakingly copy each letter word for word. The candle's hot flame coated my fore-head with sweat as it dwindled. By the time I finished, my hand was so cramped I could hardly release the quill from my grasp.

But my spirit soared like a cherry hawk. I didn't even try to distract myself from the scene I'd imagined so many times since my arrival at Glonsel Palace. The look on Rafe's face as our eyes met after such a prolonged separation. The feel of his arms around me, his tender voice assuring me that now all will be well, that we can be together at last...

I dragged my thoughts back to the present. No such reunion could take place until the letters were in Rafe's hands.

I tucked my copies in a drawer and tied the original letters back into a secure parcel. Prying my door open, I peered into the quiet hall. Mabel and the sisters must've long since gone to bed. I tiptoed down the dark stairway to retrieve brown paper and twine from the kitchen.

Back in my room, I began to wrap the parcel, but my hands stilled. Rafe would need some explanation, but what could I write?

The thought of such a direct communication set my nerves abuzz with a pleasant flutter. I yearned to pour my heart out to him, detailing all that had happened since our parting—every joy, fear, and uncertainty. But though he would cherish such an epistle, it might never reach him if the king and queen suspected me as its originator.

After an hour of deliberation and countless rejected drafts, I at last settled on:

Dear Prince Raphael,

 Enclosed you will find all the evidence you should need—I pray it reaches you in time. I am safe and well, and I fervently wish the same for you.

 Yours always,

 Red

I thrust the note within the parcel of letters before I could mar it with tears. After wrapping them in the brown paper, I secured the package with twine and seized the quill one last time to write the direction.

When there was nothing left to do but wait for morning, I lay across my mattress, rubbing my aching hand and watching enchanting visions of home flit through my dreams.

The sun peeked above the horizon hours later, prompting me to scramble out of bed. I snatched the parcel of letters and made my way downstairs.

"Heavens, child! Have ye slept at all?" Mabel gaped at me as I stumbled into the kitchen.

"A little. But it's no matter." I hurried past her to don a traveling cloak at the door. "Will you tell the sisters I've run down to Haverton?"

"Haverton? Ye do realize it's two hours o' walkin' from here. And the sun's hardly up!" She pulled on my arm, coaxing me back into the room. "At least sit 'n have a bite o' breakfast first."

"I'm eager to be off."

The determined glint in her eyes suggested she didn't intend to allow me to skip a meal so easily.

"Can you give me something to take along?"

"Oh, very well." She heaved an exaggerated sigh and turned to slice a loaf of bread.

The scent of currants roused my stomach despite my haste.

"What's yer business in Haverton, anyway?"

"I have a package to deliver to the post office."

"And it can't wait 'til Sister Helen's next visit to the market?" She pressed two generous slices of soft bread into my hands. "One look at ye tells me it can't. All right, then, I'll tell the sisters. Though I hardly know what they'll think o' ye."

"Thank you, Mabel." I bit off a mouthful of crust as I made my way out the door, waving to her with a smile.

I'd only accompanied Sister Helen into Haverton once, but the rough dirt path was easy enough to find. Every sense was on high alert in my sleep-deprived state. The pinks and oranges of the blossoming dawn never appeared so lush, and every lark within miles sang on this glorious morning. I breathed deeply of the fresh mountain air, letting it invigorate my rapid steps.

The townsfolk of Haverton were awake and bustling by the time I arrived. I spotted a butcher's shop, general goods store, and haberdasher, but none of the buildings exhibited the bow and crossed arrows of the Imperian coat of arms.

Tugging the letters tighter to my side, I walked down the street and turned a corner. A pristine, white building displayed a dark shield with a knight on a gray steed hanging above the doorframe. The Trellan coat of arms. Of course.

I swept the hair off my forehead and charged forward. Removing a small pouch from my waistband, I entered and approached the woman at the counter, who scanned the lines of an account book.

"I need a messenger to deliver this to Imperia, please."

She held up a finger. Dipping her quill in ink, she dashed a note in the margin and snapped the book shut. "Certainly. Where in Imperia?"

"Dorendyn Castle."

"Very good." She glanced at the direction on the package and placed it in a wooden crate. "That will be five querets."

I opened my pouch and removed five small coins from the wages I'd earned at Glonsel Palace. "When…how long will the delivery take?"

"That far into Imperia? I'd say two weeks."

"Thank you." I smiled before turning away with a sigh.

Help is coming, Rafe. Just two more weeks.

CHAPTER 19

*S*ix weeks, and still no news. Did the sisters *never* receive word of the outside world? My growing agitation threatened to leech every last fragment of my sanity.

I pounded the dough I was kneading more forcefully than I intended, sending it sliding across the counter in a puff of flour.

"Heavens, child. What did that poor loaf o' bread e'er do to ye?" Mabel set down her paring knife and brushed off her cutting board.

"I'm sorry. I'll try to be more careful."

She squeezed my shoulder on her way to the washbasin. "I know the convent life's quieter than ye're used to. Give yerself time to adjust."

"But don't the sisters want to know what's happening out there?" Another gust of flour accompanied my gesture toward the door. "Do they even care?"

"Oh, child. O' course they care. I'm guessin' ye haven't missed the dark looks passin' between 'em of late. Makes a person right jumpy. But Sister Helen will go to town wearing her habit, which no doubt steers the gossips clear of 'er. And they can't afford too much interest in worldly affairs, ye see. Interferes with their connection to the Luminate. So most of our news comes from old Horace, though his next stop's a month out yet."

An entire month before we'd hear an update. Would I make it that long?

I reshaped the bread dough and draped a towel over it. After wiping my hands on my apron, I grabbed a broom and swept the excess flour through the doorframe. A path in the distance caught my attention. The broom clattered to the floor.

"May I go to town? Instead of Sister Helen?"

Mabel's face crinkled into a grin. "Now, why didn't I think o' that?"

I practically skipped down the hill toward Haverton. The freedom to spend an afternoon outdoors, away from the convent, filled me with a heady feeling. I inhaled deeply of the fresh air and tried to retain the image of each grevel tree and golden beaconflower I passed.

After so much time in the quietude of the manor, the bustling marketplace both exhilarated and overwhelmed me. I walked a circuit around the wide perimeter. Merchants called out to passersby, hens squawked in wire pens, and disheveled children shrieked, chasing each other in and out of the rows of stalls.

I consulted Sister Helen's list before diving into the fray.

After making purchases from a butcher and produce vendor, I lugged my basket to a stand displaying rows of beige eggs, jars of milk, and thick cuts of cheese.

The seller adjusted the bandana covering her hair. "What can I help ye with today, miss?"

I glanced around. All the surrounding patrons were engaged at other stands. "A dozen eggs 'n three quarts o' milk, please." I did my best to shorten my vowels as Mabel and Sister Rochelle did. With any luck, I'd pass as a native of Trellich.

"O' course. Have a big family, do ye?"

"Yes." I cleared my throat. "Though it's been some time since we've made it into town. Do ye know, is our Princess Penelope still goin' to marry that prince in Imperia? I was never quite sure of that alliance."

Her eyes lit up as she tucked a canister of milk into my basket. "Ye haven't heard, then? My, what a to-do it's been."

I held my jaw steady as my pulse hurtled through my veins. "Heard what?"

"Some time ago—maybe a month, give or take—the engagement was broken off." She pressed the lid closed on a carton of eggs and set it before me. "Real mysterious, like there was somethin' fishy about it."

"Is that so? How very strange." I took the eggs, my chest swelling as though a flock of birds soared within. *Thank you, Luminate, for answering my prayers.*

"Ye haven't heard the half of it!"

The birds faltered. What more could there be to the story?

"Everyone thought Princess Penelope would return to Glonsel Palace, but she ne'er did. Then, what do ye think? We hear, just two weeks later, that the engagement is back on."

No. It couldn't be. Black specks distorted my vision.

She leaned forward, eyes wide. "Not only that, but now it seems they're so eager to wed, they've moved up the date o' the wedding."

"What?" The hammering in my chest made her words sound as though we stood at opposite ends of a tunnel.

"To the twelfth day o' March." Three weeks away.

I had to return to Imperia.

~

I shoved through the kitchen door and dropped the heavy basket on the table.

Mabel glanced up from her mixing bowl. "Ah, ye're back. Why don't ye put those cuts o' meat over—"

"I'm sorry, Mabel, but I can't help just yet. I must speak with Sister Johanna."

Her brows arched. "Then be on yer way, by all means."

"Thank you." I dashed for the stairway.

At Sister Johanna's chamber, I made myself pause and knock. I leaned against the wall, gulping deep lungfuls of air.

The doorknob clicked, and I lurched forward. "Oh, Sister Johanna, I—"

She started and gripped the doorframe. "What a state you're in, child. Why don't you come in and sit down?"

She directed me to a faded armchair.

"Now, tell me what's the matter." She pulled out a desk chair and lowered into it. "You've been to town, haven't you? Is there bad news?"

"Yes." I placed my shaky hands on my knees. "But first, I should tell you what I found at Glonsel Palace."

She nodded, no flicker of surprise registering on her face.

I related the specifics I'd never disclosed about the conversation between Princess Penelope and the Duke of Brantley, the burned letters, and my hope of finding letters at Glonsel Palace that hadn't met the same fate.

As I described my search for the letters and their contents, I stole a glance at Sister Johanna. No doubt she would condemn my theft and breach of the princess's privacy. But her gaze remained fixed elsewhere, as though she could see something outside the walls of her bedchamber.

Eager to progress to the end of my story, I continued, "I posted the letters to the prince the day after I returned from the palace, hoping the termination of the engagement would soon follow. But today, in the marketplace..."

Sister Johanna blinked, meeting my eyes. "Yes, what is this distressing news?"

"I was told the engagement broke off for a short time but has since been reinstated. The wedding will take place in three weeks." I wrapped my arms around my waist, shuddering.

Her brows furrowed. "That is strange, indeed. If I only knew how it all fit together." She gave my knee a pat. "But no doubt the Luminate will reveal all in His good time—"

"Please forgive me, Sister Johanna, but I don't think I can wait for the Luminate to act. I need to return to Dorendyn Castle and see the prince for myself. I can't rest until I know what happened." I set my jaw. No argument from Sister Johanna could persuade me otherwise.

But she merely nodded. "Perhaps you're right. Something odd must be transpiring, and time is not on our side." She rose and returned her chair to the writing desk. "I need to pray on this. Go pack your things and help Mabel assemble some packets of food. We leave in the morning."

"We?" I halted in my path to the door. "You mean, you're coming with me?"

"Of course. You've been banished from Imperia—I'd hardly allow you to undertake such a perilous journey alone. I shall issue an invitation to the other sisters as well."

"The other sisters? But I'd hate to cause such a disturbance—"

She raised a hand. "You're not the one causing the disturbance, my dear. And if the forces we're dealing with are as dark as I fear, we'll need as much assistance as we can recruit. Now, we don't have any time to lose. Off with you."

How could having more sisters with us make any difference?

Sister Johanna turned and knelt on her prayer bench. Instead of questioning her further, I slipped from the room.

Soon we would be on our way to Imperia, where I would find my answers.

~

I sat across from Sister Clarice and Sister Johanna the next morning, pushing eggs around my plate. Dark clouds smothered the sunlight as though the heavens themselves were affected by the grim news.

Sister Rochelle and Sister Val entered, conversing in hushed tones. Each held a valise.

My fork clattered to my plate as gratitude constricted my throat.

Mabel offered them steaming mugs with trembling hands. "So many o' ye leavin' at once. I ne'er saw the like. What shall become of us if somethin' should happen to ye?"

Sister Johanna grasped her arm. "We will leave it in the Luminate's hands."

Sister Clarice snorted but didn't glance up from her breakfast.

Humid air pressed on us from all sides as we filed out the door. After several hugs from Mabel, I said goodbye to Sister Marianne and Sister Helen. Guilt churned my empty stomach as I stood to the side and watched the sisters bid each other farewell.

My eyes narrowed. They each took extra time with Sister Clarice. How could anyone be sad to part with *her*?

We embarked on a slow, steady trek down the path. After the manor faded from view, I caught up with Sister Johanna.

"Is Sister Clarice going somewhere?"

"Yes. She has decided to leave us, at least for now, to embrace a solitary life."

"What?" I stumbled and grasped a tree branch.

She held my arm until I steadied. "It's her belief that the Luminate is calling us down separate paths."

"She's leaving because of me? Because you're helping me?"

"There's far more to it than that, child. Our mission has

merely called into question the wisdom of her choice to live in a communal setting."

A burst of anger swept through my remorse. "But why would she oppose what we're doing? How could we stand aside and let a plot proceed against the royal family without at least trying to stop it? She was under no obligation to join us. Why couldn't she stay back with Sister Marianne and Sister Helen and leave it at that?"

Sister Johanna laid a hand on my shoulder. "Sister Clarice is entitled to her own opinion on the subject, Leah. She feels we are being too hasty to interfere, that we should allow the Luminate's plan to develop further until it impacts us more directly." She turned and continued down the path.

I sucked in a breath. "But we don't have time to let—"

"I know. That's why we're on our way as we speak." She lifted her skirt to pick her way down a series of large boulders. "You mustn't be too hard on Clarice. Her life has presented many hardships. The vocation of a—well, a nun—is not an easy one. When Clarice first heard the Luminate's call upon her heart, her family rebuked her and tried to marry her to a cruel man. They forsook her completely after she dedicated her life to the Luminate."

My anger dissipated as quickly as it had come. "That's dreadful. To be disowned for pursuing such a noble calling."

"Yes, it happens more often than you'd think. I believe she sought out communal life hoping to fill the void left by her family. But she has increasingly been plagued by"—she cast me a sidelong glance—"dreams, I guess you might say, of fire, the meaning of which she has not been able to interpret. I believe her aloof behavior masks fear. At times I think she even questions her decision to follow this vocation. It's a heavy burden to bear, and we must pray for her."

"Of course." Though if the other sisters were already praying for her, I doubted my own efforts would have any effect.

We walked in silence until the pointed fence posts surrounding Haverton came into view.

My breath caught in a sudden panic.

"Are we planning to walk all the way to Imperia?" My journey to Trellich with the guards had taken nearly a week, and we were on horseback. How much longer would such a journey take on foot?

Sister Val laughed. "I should hope not, or I would've never signed on to this excursion." She pointed. "We're renting a carriage in town."

A mixture of relief and guilt replaced my anxiety. "That does sound better. But won't it cost a great deal?"

"Don't fret, my child." Sister Johanna paused at my side. "We have a store set aside for such occasions."

I hung my head. I was taking from the meager till of the women who'd already shown me more kindness than I could repay. "Oh. Thank you."

"You're welcome. But remember we're not doing this only for you, but to do good among the Luminate's people. You are not alone in bearing this burden."

I met Sister Johanna's smile. Reassurance washed over me, adding new determination to my steps.

"We're going to need to hide that hair if we want to sneak you back in." Sister Val pulled her bag onto the carriage seat and rummaged inside.

We'd made fast progress, traveling on well-maintained roads after alighting on the base of Finnegan's Peak. Today, we would cross into Imperia.

She emerged with a headpiece matching her own and passed it to me.

Heat inflamed my cheeks. "Won't that make everyone think I'm a nun?"

"Precisely. Hopefully no one will have anticipated such a development."

I accepted the headpiece but held it at a distance. "Isn't it wrong, though, to give such a false impression? Especially to assume the garb of someone who's taken religious vows, when I haven't?"

"The lines of right and wrong get dreadfully blurry at times." She took it back from me and positioned it on my head. Holding the headpiece in place with one hand, she rifled in her bag with the other until she removed a set of hairpins. "Isn't it wrong that you should need a disguise to return to your home country when you're innocent? Besides, we need to get you in somehow, and it's the best we've got." She slid the pins into the hair at my temples.

I looked at Sister Johanna. "But—"

She patted my knee. "It suits you."

It was settled, then. I would return to Imperia dressed as a nun.

The round, stone towers of Dorendyn Castle finally came into view as dusk muted the sky. I could hardly blink, transfixed on the welcome sight.

Home. Not a dream this time. Real, solid, and almost within reach. Every inch forward seemed to stitch together a severed piece of my heart.

My gaze swept over each surface of the walls and roofline, the vines and carefully landscaped trees and bushes. I wanted to re-memorize them all.

As we drew closer, my attention strayed more and more to the North Wing. If only I could see the chambers within. Was Rafe there? I ached to know he was near, what he was thinking and feeling. Why hadn't the letters been enough to end the engagement?

Sister Val pulled me back toward the upholstered carriage seat. "I know you're eager, but we'll be there soon enough." She bent closer to whisper, "Falling out of the carriage would hardly be the way to make a discreet entrance."

Warmth crawled up my neck. I hadn't realized how far forward I was leaning.

I reluctantly settled back. If I wanted to see Rafe or achieve anything with this visit, I needed to be careful.

Fear stole my breath as we neared the palace city. Jedd stood guard, watching us approach. I fixed my eyes on the vibrating floor of the carriage and clasped my hands together.

He called for us to halt before we reached the gate.

"Good afternoon, sisters. What brings you to our palace on this fine day?"

Sister Johanna straightened. "My brother works here in the village, and I'm long overdue for a visit. My friends have never witnessed the grandeur of Dorendyn Castle and were eager to join me."

"Ah. Well then, welcome to all of you."

I gritted my teeth and dipped my chin lower. Why was he hesitating to let us through?

"You, miss." He tapped my arm.

My pulse spiked, and I barely contained my jump. I looked up, setting my lips into a firm line. "Yes, sir?"

Please, Luminate, don't let him recognize me.

He scrutinized my face, his brows furrowed. "You seem familiar. But you say she's never been to the palace before?" His gaze flitted to Sister Johanna.

"Not that I'm aware of." She raised her shoulders in an innocent shrug.

He glanced back at me.

"'Tis true." I widened my eyes. "I've ne'er seen a place such as this."

Sister Rochelle squeezed my wrist under the blanket covering our laps.

He blinked at me once more before stepping back. "Never mind, then. My apologies for detaining you. Please, enjoy your stay." He bowed and waved us ahead.

Sister Rochelle continued to hold my trembling hand as we passed through the gates. No longer eager to look out, I shrank as far into the carriage as I could.

Would I be so lucky next time?

Sister Johanna rented us a room in a small, plain inn at the outskirts of the palace city. My frayed nerves unwound as the door clicked shut behind the innkeeper. Here, at least, I should be safe.

After we unpacked, I joined the sisters for communal prayer before they lapsed into their own silent meditations. Sinking onto one of the beds, I allowed my body to relax as my mind wandered.

Tomorrow, I would find a way to see Rafe.

CHAPTER 20

orning at last. If my heart wrenched any further toward the palace, it would separate from my body.

I splashed water on my face, brushed my hair into a tight knot at the nape of my neck, and donned my black dress and headpiece. Not the wardrobe I'd envisioned for my long-awaited reunion with Rafe, but it would have to do.

Sister Val checked my headpiece one last time on our way to the door. "Not perfect, but it's better than nothing. If you keep your head down, hopefully your hair won't draw any attention."

Sister Johanna placed her hands on my shoulders. "Are you ready, Leah?"

"More than ready."

"Good. Sister Valeria and I will follow your lead."

"Do be careful out there." Sister Rochelle scurried in from the adjoining room. "I'll be praying for you."

I rehearsed my plan as we slipped into the bustling flow of people making their way to the palace. It was Saturday, and the weather was fair. If Rafe was still allowed any measure of freedom, he'd spend the day outdoors. The best chance to catch him would be on his way to or from the stables.

Once inside the palace grounds, I clenched my jaw and tucked my chin to my chest. Sister Johanna and Sister Val shuffled along behind me. Just before cresting the hill near the pastures, we veered off into a quiet corner of shrubbery. I couldn't venture closer without risking a run-in with Sam or Ned.

I found a dry patch of grass and knelt. The sisters followed my example. Removing their rosaries from their waistbands, they began a series of murmured prayers. I bowed my head and folded my hands, my attention fixed on the path behind us.

Before long my knees were damp and sore, and I'd begun to fidget. Passersby came and went, but none bore the face I ached to see.

Another set of footsteps tromped below. I froze, recognizing the cadence of his gait. There, striding up the hill, was Rafe.

My heart did a series of pirouettes. Dearest Rafe, who I thought I might never see again. I clamped a hand over my mouth to stop myself from crying out to him.

His hair was longer than when I'd left, the ends curling in the humid air. The set of his jaw indicated determination, though I couldn't place the expression in his eyes. He radiated strength and assurance, so different from the gawky boy who had first stumbled into my closet so many years ago.

I could've gaped at him all afternoon, memorizing his every feature.

Sister Johanna stiffened at my side. I nodded to her and rose, trying to swallow past the parched wasteland at the back of my throat.

I reached him and tapped his arm with unsteady fingers. "Excuse me, Your Highness? Might I have a word with you?"

He jerked away with a start. "I—er, certainly."

I motioned to him, and he followed me into the relative privacy of the flower garden on the far side of the hedgerow.

Inhaling deeply, I raised my face to him. The moment I'd dreamed of so many times. An entire colony of butterflies stirred in my chest.

His gaze met mine, but with no jolt of recognition. "Can I help you?" Kindness and impatience vied for prevalence in his expression.

Tears rimmed my eyelids. He didn't recognize me?

I glanced back to the path and quieted to a whisper. "Rafe, it's me. Leah."

He regarded me with a blank, confused stare. Something about his eyes looked unfocused, almost hazy. "Well, it's nice to meet you, Leah. But please, it would be best if you address me as Prince Raphael. And if there's nothing I can help you with, then I really must—"

"Rafe!" I hissed, grabbing his elbow before he could turn away. "Listen to me, look at me! I'm *Leah*. See?" I folded the edge of the headpiece up to reveal more of my hair.

Still, no sign of recognition eased his frown. Instead, he receded from my grasp. "Please, miss. I have the utmost respect for those such as yourself who have taken religious vows, but I must ask you to unhand me. Tell me what I can do for you so I may be on my way."

Despair suffocated my last flicker of hope. Could I just let him go? Every fiber of my being revolted at the thought, but if he didn't know me by now, he never would. "I'll not detain you any further. I'm sorry to have taken up your time."

Shaking his head, he bowed and stalked away.

My illusions of a poignant reunion crashed and shattered like a dropped mirror. The shards gouged at every turn as I tried to piece them back together. Even if he no longer loved me, Rafe couldn't have forgotten me entirely. If he feigned lack of recognition for my protection, he couldn't keep his eyes so cold, his expression so blank.

What was wrong with him?

A tap on my shoulder made me jump.

"Is everything all right, child?" Sister Johanna's brows knit as she searched my face.

The gathering tears spilled down my cheeks. I shook my head.

Sister Val took my arm. "Let's get you back to the inn." She lowered her voice. "We'll be safer there."

They steered me out the gates, down the road, and through the inn to our chambers. I saw only the ground at my feet, as though blinders restricted my view.

Sister Johanna guided me to sit on a bed, and Sister Val latched the door behind us.

Sister Rochelle did a hasty sign of the cross and rose to meet us. "I didn't expect you back so soon. Were you able to speak with the prince?"

Renewed tears streaked my face.

She sat beside me and placed an arm about my shoulders. "There, there, my dear. Whatever it is, the Luminate must have a plan."

"Now, tell us what happened, Leah." Sister Johanna settled on my other side.

I sucked in deep gulps of air until my sobs subsided enough to answer. "The prince, he—he didn't recognize me."

Sister Rochelle handed me her handkerchief.

Sister Val shrugged and took a chair across from us. "That is a setback, no question, but surely there are other ways we can find out more about the engagement. Would any of your family members or friends be likely to have useful information? At least your disguise was effective."

My entire body trembled with the effort to restrain my weeping. "No, you don't understand. He should've known me."

Sister Rochelle rubbed my arm. "I know it's a blow to your pride, my dear, but recall that it's been many months since you've stepped foot in Dorendyn Castle, and the prince has a great deal on his mind with the wedding coming up so soon."

I shook my head. "Something is wrong. Rafe—Prince Raphael—would always recognize me, even dressed as a nun."

"But Leah, were you not a chambermaid? It may not be right, but you shouldn't be so surprised that the royal family takes less notice of their servants than the servants do of them."

"No, I wasn't just a servant to him." I sniffled into Sister Rochelle's handkerchief. "I know this will sound hard to believe, but Prince Raphael was my friend. One of my dearest friends."

The sisters regarded me with a mix of skepticism and concern.

"We've spent hours and hours together. He was the one who taught me to read. He even…there was a time when he declared he was in love with me."

I could practically read Sister Rochelle's exact thoughts as she puckered her face and removed her arm from my shoulder.

"No, nothing like that. We never fell into sin. He truly loved me—he wanted to marry me." I took another gasping breath. "But when I spoke with him today, he showed no trace of recognition, even when I told him my name and called him by the nickname only I ever used."

"How did he look?" Sister Johanna's frown didn't seem to be directed at me. "Was there anything unusual in his appearance?"

I reviewed my mental image of him. "Nothing except his eyes. They seemed clouded, or unfocused. Almost as though he'd been drinking heavily, but that's not like him at all. And he didn't stagger or slur his speech."

The sisters exchanged glances heavy with meaning.

My stomach clenched to the size of a pebble. "You know something, don't you?"

"I think it's time we tell you." Sister Johanna looked to the others, who nodded. "Though I'm sure Sister Clarice wouldn't approve."

"There is a great deal Sister Clarice doesn't approve of." Sister Val's eyes lit with mischief. "That's never stopped us before."

Sister Johanna arched an eyebrow at her before turning back to me. "You know us as a collection of nuns, living in a convent, though an unusual one. While that's not untrue, we're not what one would think of as ordinary nuns." She shifted to face me more fully. "You see, Leah, we're mystics."

"Mystics?" The word felt foreign on my tongue.

"Never even heard the term." Sister Val massaged her temples. "My, how things in Imperia have changed."

Sister Johanna ignored her. "Yes. A mystic is typically a nun who, in the midst of her life of reflection and prayer, receives visions from the Luminate."

My fingers curled around the edge of the bed. "Visions? You mean, of the future?"

"Sometimes. We're given whatever vision the Luminate wants us to see at that particular time—of the past, present, or future. Perhaps even something out of time entirely, something not of this world. The visions may be given for inspiration, personal or for a larger community, or informational, such as when Sister Marianne saw you on the mountainside in need of aid. On occasion, they're given as instructions. A mystic may even receive the supreme blessing of hearing the Luminate's voice speak through a vision." She smoothed her skirt over her knees. "Mystics also have the power to perform mighty deeds in the Luminate's name. Miracles, you might say."

I lived among miracle workers. The knowledge was both awe inspiring and humbling. "Are all of you mystics? All the nuns?"

Sister Rochelle chimed in. "Not all nuns are mystics, but yes, each of us, along with the sisters we left at the manor, are mystics."

What incredible things might have taken place behind their closed doors while I polished silver or darned socks?

"But"—I focused on Sister Val—"you seemed surprised I hadn't heard of mystics. Are there any in Imperia?"

Sister Val barked a harsh laugh. "None who would own up to it."

"Who would want to hide such a thing?"

"We have a complex history in Imperia, I'm afraid." Sister Johanna crossed her arms. "No doubt you've heard of the Gravedigger's Bounty that afflicted Trellich. Though perhaps you weren't even born yet."

"Yes, I've heard of it. That's how my father died."

Sister Rochelle patted my back.

"Well," continued Sister Johanna, "King Frederick and Queen Beatrice, who had only taken the throne some two or three years before, were terrified the outbreak would spread to Imperia despite the closed borders. They placed their trust in a powerful sorcerer, Lord Damien Lessox, to keep the country safe. But his power was derived from a very dark magic. It only took a year for his relations with the royal family to sour as they came to understand the nature of the demonic beings he called upon."

Palace gossip crowded back into my mind. "He's the one who cursed the king and queen. The one who made them barren."

Sister Johanna raised her shoulders. "I don't know whether that part of the story is based on fact, though it wouldn't surprise me. But as I was saying, in their eagerness to be rid of Lord Lessox, the king and queen made another impulsive decision. They enacted an edict banning all magic from the kingdom, with capital punishment to be doled out to any who dared disobey."

The influx of new information swirled in my head, making me dizzy. "But what does that have to do with mystics? You don't practice magic, do you?"

Sister Val scoffed. "No, certainly not the kind King Frederick and Queen Beatrice were trying to eradicate. But their edict was so all-encompassing that the miracles performed by mystics fell within its scope."

"Couldn't they just amend the edict?"

"Perhaps." Sister Johanna sighed. "But the king and queen's hatred of magic had turned so vehement, no one dared reveal herself or approach them with such a request."

"So that's how you all ended up in Trellich."

"Yes, though several mystics remain in Imperia. They maintain a life of solitude, hidden away from the king and queen and any who might turn them in." Sister Johanna patted Sister Rochelle's knee. "But we were fortunate enough to be taken in by Sister Rochelle, who inherited the manor in which we reside."

My encounter with Rafe still lingered in my mind. "But why are you telling me now? Did you have a vision concerning Prince Raphael or the plot against the royal family?"

A significant look passed between them. Apprehension pulsed through me and seemed to pour in every direction, setting the air abuzz.

"For some time now, a number of us have received visions that seem to relate, but we've struggled to interpret them." Sister Val moved to the window and lifted the shade. "A darkness is encroaching, but we do not yet comprehend its source."

"We tell you this now because of your disturbing report regarding the prince," Sister Johanna added. "We think your Rafe may be under a spell."

Bile rose in my throat. "What can we do?"

Sister Val snapped the shade back into place. "It seems the duke and princess have an accomplice."

"Indeed, if only we could discover who it is." Sister Johanna rose and began to pace. "We must be vigilant in our prayers and hope the Luminate will provide answers."

"What if...?"

"Yes, Leah?" Sister Rochelle tapped my arm.

"I transcribed the letters from the duke I found in Princess Penelope's chambers. They referred to a set of initials several times. I assumed they hired an assassin of some sort, but what if it's a sorcerer?"

"Yes!" Sister Val grasped the back of a chair. "What were they?"

"I don't recall. They didn't mean anything to me. But I packed the letters with my other things."

"Very good, Leah." Sister Johanna pulled me to my feet. "Find the letters. We can divide them between us and search for useful information."

Soon we sat in silence, each scouring a pile of transcribed notes.

An exclamation from Sister Val shattered the quiet. "No. It can't be—"

"What is it?" Sister Johanna set an open letter in her lap.

"I found the initials. D.L."

Sister Johanna and Sister Rochelle gasped in unison.

"Damien Lessox," Sister Johanna whispered under her breath.

Damien Lessox, the powerful sorcerer who'd fallen out of favor with the king and queen. My insides coiled as though trapped in an instrument of torture.

"How could it be him?" But before the question was out, Rafe's words resounded in my ears. *They say he was never found.*

"No one knew what happened to him." Sister Val's brows creased. "Everyone assumed he fled the country, but..."

"Perhaps he was an even better deceiver than any of us gave him credit for." Sister Johanna wrung her hands. "Rochelle, Valeria, it is high time we returned to prayer. We must be fervent in our pleas for the Luminate's guidance and hope He grants us visions accordingly."

My thoughts took a different route. How far did Damien's magic reach? Was Ma safe? "I need to go back to the castle."

"No." Sister Johanna gripped my sleeve.

"But what if others are under the spell? Shouldn't we find out—"

"I'm sorry, Leah, but it's too dangerous. We can't take any chances when it comes to Lord Lessox."

Her grasp loosened as my posture slumped.

"If it's any consolation, I doubt he could extend such a robust spell beyond Prince Raphael and the king and queen. Maybe to a few additional courtiers at most. Besides, would it change our course whether one person was ensorcelled or twenty?"

"I guess not." *Please, let Ma be unharmed.* "But there must be some way I can help."

"There is. Please review the remainder of the letters for any additional clues. And after that, your prayers would certainly be appreciated as well. Even if you don't receive a vision in return, they will be heard just as readily as ours."

Always prayers—first Ma, now the sisters. But with Rafe's life threatened by a vengeful sorcerer, I was willing to try anything.

CHAPTER 21

We gathered our belongings and headed downstairs, huddling together while Sister Val called to a stable boy to ready our horse and carriage.

My eyelids chafed against eyes puffy from crying and lack of sleep. The sisters had spent the entire night on their knees in prayer. It was a wonder they could even walk.

Sister Val rejoined us, pulling her cloak tighter around her shoulders. Sister Johanna murmured to her and hurried off, clutching a stack of papers.

I stepped beside Sister Val. "Am I allowed to know where Sister Johanna's going?"

"She's off to hire an express messenger to deliver a few letters." She grinned. "We're calling for reinforcements."

Reinforcements. I tried to think back to Sister Johanna's stack of letters. How many mystics were there? She must've thought at least a few would join us if she was taking the trouble to contact them. *Please let them be closer than Sister Marianne and Sister Helen in Trellich.*

After breakfast, our carriage rumbled back through the palace city gates. The angle of the sun indicated we were traveling north, but I couldn't guess what the sisters had chosen as our destination. Had the Luminate revealed Damien Lessox's location, or would we have to search for him?

My heart compressed as though bricks piled on my chest. The wedding would take place in just over two weeks, a pitifully inadequate amount of time to track down a sorcerer who'd evaded detection for the past seventeen years.

I sat up and arranged the blanket over my legs. "Where are we heading?"

Sister Johanna opened her eyes, which held a somber expression. "Just to Cyndale, a little north of here. We thought it best to leave the confines of the palace city as soon as possible for your protection. For the protection of us all."

Sister Val added, "We've surmised that Lord Lessox can't be too far from the palace if he's exerting such powerful magic there. The presence of a growing number of mystics may not escape his detection."

The damper on my spirits lifted. "Do you know where he is?"

"Not precisely, but I have seen where the confrontation will take place."

My head jerked toward Sister Johanna, and Sister Rochelle stiffened beside me. Dread trickled down my spine. What else might Sister Johanna have seen? What wasn't she sharing with us?

Sister Johanna folded her hands in her lap. "The clues from that ought to be enough to bring us close, and from there, I doubt we'll have any difficulty tracing his magic. His perception of us may even draw him out."

"How long must we wait at Cyndale?" Sister Val perched on the edge of her seat.

"Not more than six days, I imagine."

I clamped my jaw shut. Six days? It would seem an eternity, holed up in an inn with nothing to do but pray with the sisters and wonder how Rafe was faring. At least his physical health seemed unchanged, but what damage might the spell be imparting on his mind, his spirits?

Taking a deep breath, I resigned myself to wait. If we needed reinforcements to confront Damien, I couldn't argue. Better to delay and face him with a full force than go in unprepared and risk defeat.

I shivered. No, defeat wasn't an option. We were Rafe's only hope.

I tied a satchel closed and hung my head. We'd spent three days in almost perpetual silence, praying. Waiting. Packing and repacking the food for our upcoming journey a dozen times grew tiresome. I needed something to do, something more I could contribute toward helping Rafe.

Something to pass the time.

Sister Val tiptoed out of the chamber the sisters were using for uninterrupted prayer and pressed the door closed behind her. "Why, Leah, you look awfully glum. Is something the matter?"

Aside from Rafe being under a spell and not knowing whether Ma was all right? I wiped my forehead. "Is there anything else I can do? I know Sister Johanna wants us to pray, and I have, but…"

"You want something a little more active?" Sympathy softened her eyes. "I understand. You must be worried sick about your prince." She tapped her chin. "Actually, there is something. Wait here."

Grinning, she disappeared into the other room. She returned, wielding a long, wide knife.

I lurched back. "What is that?"

"A dirk. Or dagger, if you prefer."

"But why — ?"

"Why would a nun have a weapon?" She tossed it to her

other hand, making me flinch. "It was a gift from my father. The idea of my living in a convent made him very nervous. In his opinion, a group of unarmed nuns would be an easy target. So he taught me to defend myself."

These women would never cease to amaze me.

"I planned to lend this to you when we set out to find Lord Lessox. You ought to have some sort of protection, in case…" She eyed the tip of the blade. "This is even better. Now you'll have a chance to practice with it."

She held out the hilt to me.

I took it in both hands, keeping it far from my body. "Even with a few days to practice, I'm not sure I could…"

"I know." She tweaked my nose. "But it can't hurt to get a feel for it, strengthen your wrist a bit. Besides, it'll give you something to do."

I didn't know what I expected her to come up with, but this wasn't it. Still, it couldn't hurt to try. Unless I sliced off my finger.

She removed a black, gilt-edged sheath from her apron pocket and slipped it over the blade. "We can practice with it like this, if you'd prefer." She took the hilt back and wrapped her fingers around it. Squaring her shoulders, she receded a step. "Now, in order to execute an effective thrust, you need to—"

A rap at the door scattered my tense nerves like beads bouncing across a polished floor.

The rap sounded again. My eyes locked with Sister Val's. She nodded, lowering her arm.

I held my breath and pulled open the door.

In bustled a lively woman, her round face framed by a black-and-white headpiece. Her bulging carpet bag dropped to the floor with a thud.

Sister Val rushed forward to embrace her. "Eleanor! I knew you wouldn't let us down."

"Well, of course. How could I let you take on such an adventure without me?"

"I suspected that's how you'd feel."

Eleanor raised Sister Val's wrist to examine her weapon. Her brows arched. "Who, exactly, were you expecting?"

"It never hurts to be prepared."

Sister Johanna and Sister Rochelle emerged from the adjoining room.

"Sister Eleanor, how good of you to join us." Sister Johanna grasped her hand. "I'm sure you remember Sister Rochelle. And you've met Leah?"

"Not yet." Sister Eleanor turned to appraise me. "I'm thrilled to make your acquaintance, Leah. Once a frail exile, now a brave rescuer. What a fascinating story you have to tell!"

My cheeks warmed as I dipped into a small curtsy.

"You and I shall have to get to know one another better." Sister Eleanor picked up the bag she'd deposited on the floor. "Give me a moment to get my things situated, and we'll take a walk. How does that sound?"

"Lovely." My lungs expanded at the very idea of sunshine and fresh air.

"Would anyone else care to join us?" Sister Eleanor resembled a shadowlark, dark and inquisitive, as she surveyed the room with rapid movements.

"Oh, no thank you." Sister Rochelle waved her hand.

Sister Johanna shook her head and retreated to the other chamber.

A frown crossed Sister Val's face before she replaced it with a broad smile. "Excellent idea, Eleanor. Why don't you get settled right over here?" She directed her to a bed and nightstand, then they joined me near the door.

"Sister Eleanor and I were trained together at a convent here in Imperia, ages ago by this time," Sister Val explained as we donned our cloaks. "She decided to stay on, quietly, after the edict, while I jumped ship and fled north..."

"I had hoped we'd be joined by a few more, but I don't know how much longer we can wait." Sister Johanna leaned forward at the small table where we'd convened for breakfast.

"Others may yet be led to us, even if we depart now." Sister Rochelle glanced around at each of us.

Sister Johanna set her jaw and nodded. "You're right. It's time we move on."

The sisters rose and began to assemble their things.

I remained pinned to my chair, immobile. I was so eager to depart, but now...

We were about to challenge the most powerful dark sorcerer in the kingdom, with less help than we'd been counting on.

The dagger attached to my waistband prodded my hip. Sister Val had resumed her instruction, and I'd spent the past few days in a clumsy, solitary dance of thrusts, strikes, and parries. But years of practice couldn't prepare me for what lay ahead.

Sister Rochelle paused by my side. Shifting her pile of freshly-laundered aprons to balance on one arm, she placed the other about my shoulders. "I understand, child." Her face radiated compassion. "Pray."

I bobbed my head as she shuffled away. *Pray.* Letting my chin sink against my chest, I prayed the only words my mind could formulate. *Help me, Luminate. Be with us.*

A rivulet of peace seeped into my heart, enough to break through my terror. I straightened and moved toward my bed, meeting a few of the sisters' reassuring smiles on the way.

Rafe needed me. I couldn't let him down.

~

One foot in front of the other. Blisters inflamed my toes, but I pressed on. We had deposited our carriage at a stable yard the day before for safekeeping for the return journey.

If there was to be a return journey.

Now we traversed a thin path winding through dense, damp forest. I'd fallen into the last position, trying not to wince with every step.

Leaves thrashed behind me. I clutched the nearest tree trunk, poised to break into a run.

Sister Val scampered to my side and peered into the thick foliage.

A small, stout woman pushed through the greenery, her chest heaving.

"There you are at last." Her gray bun bobbled as she plucked off stray leaves. "I've been chasing you nigh since breakfast."

Sister Val's face relaxed into a smile. "Myrna, you found us. I'm afraid we'd quite given up on you."

More cries of greeting arose as the other sisters gathered.

"Thought I could fly my way to the palace, did you? I'm not as young as I used to be, and even then I was never very agile on these stubby legs." She acknowledged the others, and then turned to me with a wink. "You must be Leah. Gotten this lot into more trouble than they've seen in years, from what I hear."

Heat seared my cheeks. I opened my mouth, but words deserted me.

She tapped my chin with a chuckle. "I'm not laying any blame, mind you. It's good for these ladies to get stirred up a bit. I'm Myrna, and I'm tickled to meet you."

"It's nice to meet you, too, Sister Myrna."

The wrinkles in her face multiplied as she grinned. "None

of that 'sister' business with me, deary. Just plain Myrna, if you please."

"Oh, certainly." I pursed my lips to forestall a frown. Why had the sisters summoned this petite, aged woman if she wasn't a mystic? She wore a dress of dark gray but lacked the apron and headpiece worn by the others.

"Let's keep walking," Myrna called to Sister Johanna and Sister Rochelle, who were at the head of our small procession. "I ought to be able to keep up now that I've caught you. You can fill me in on the details later." She fell into step next to me as we resumed our trek. "I'm a mystic, right enough. But never in a convent setting, so I don't feel the need to adopt the formalities."

I sometimes wondered if mystic abilities included mind reading.

She lifted her skirt to avoid a puddle. "I've lived alone for some fifty years, long before the edict, before Frederick and Beatrice even took the throne."

She conversed very naturally for someone who had lived in solitude for so long. "I guess I have much to learn regarding mystics. I thought the Luminate only called those who had taken religious vows."

"And so I have, in my own way." Her chuckle sounded like she'd swallowed a mouthful of gravel. "Nuns are certainly the most common, but the Luminate calls whomever He chooses, whether or not she's wearing a habit."

"Are only women mystics, then?"

"Perhaps not, but the only ones I've heard of are women. We females are the superior listeners, you know." She nudged me with her elbow.

"Have you ever performed a miracle?" I bit my lip. Perhaps such information was meant to be confidential.

"A few over the years." She turned her gaze to the side of the path as though she could see far beyond the mingled greens and browns. "We are supremely blessed to have the opportunity to perform the Luminate's work, though He often asks things of us that are beyond our ability to understand. He once instructed me to find a couple who were staying in a nearby village. A tailor, I believe, and his wife. They were having a dreadful time trying to conceive a child, poor dears, and had come to consult a local physician. There was nothing the physician could do, of course, but the Luminate sent me to them, and using His words, I placed a blessing on her womb. The Luminate later conveyed to me that they now have two beautiful daughters."

Myrna's story took my mind off our destination, at least for a moment. A warm, comforting blanket seemed to wrap around my soul. If the Luminate sent Myrna all the way to this couple to give them a miracle, how much more might He accomplish through so many mystics for the sake of an entire country?

Our progress slowed when the sun descended below the tree line. Conversation fell silent, and the sisters' movements became tense and wary. If only I could find out what had them on high alert. But I didn't dare make a sound.

Sister Johanna motioned us off the path. The scent of wet leaves thickened as we sidled through trees to dodge an endless assault of low-hanging branches. Soon the darkness penetrated so deeply I had to rely solely on my sense of touch to edge past rough trunks and outstretched limbs. At last, we came to a stop in a little clearing illuminated by starlight.

"We ought to be safe here for the night, but we'll set a watch just in case." Sister Johanna sank against the base of a wide tree. "Tomorrow, we'll retrace our steps and find Lord Lessox."

The sisters murmured their assent.

I tucked my knees to my chest and gnawed at my thumbnail. We'd already passed Damien's hideout? So near, we could no longer travel safely on the path.

Fear and anticipation sent a tremor through my entire body. *Tomorrow.*

The sisters debated and planned in muted tones well into the night. Sister Johanna instructed me to lie down and rest, but my mind jolted about, processing the tidbits of conversation I overheard and my own anxious thoughts.

Why weren't they including me in the planning?

I braced my back against the hard earth and lost myself in the endless abyss of black above, lit only by tiny pinpoints of light. I was so small. So insignificant. Of course they wouldn't involve me in the planning. I could cook, clean, and sew. Skills made laughable by a threat from a powerful sorcerer, the plight of the rulers of a kingdom.

I couldn't even stand up to the servant boys who teased me about my hair.

The contrast between myself and the surrounding women who the Luminate had called to be His miracle workers struck me more forcefully than ever. Who was I to think I could contribute anything of consequence in the upcoming battle? I was a common servant—they didn't need me in the slightest.

I rolled to my side and curled into a ball, letting my tears saturate the cloak folded beneath my head.

CHAPTER 22

"*L*eah? Wake up, child."

I rolled over and rubbed my eyes, grimacing at the grit coating my hands.

"It's time." Sister Johanna crouched before me.

It's time. Panic galloped through my veins like a spooked stallion. I jumped up, nearly knocking Sister Johanna off her feet.

"Steady." She grasped my shoulders. "There's something I need to speak with you about."

I couldn't read her expression. Pity?

"You don't need to accompany us today if you don't want to. We would all like to keep you safe." She gestured around the clearing, where the other sisters tied up bedrolls and shrugged packs onto their shoulders. "And we wouldn't think any less of you if you chose to stay behind."

I turned to gather my belongings, hiding my face from those eyes that saw too easily into my soul.

Did I want to stay behind? I'd be little help to the sisters against Damien, and this way at least one of us would remain unharmed.

Objections raged through my cowardice. There was a chance I could contribute in some small way. Would I send the sisters to their deaths on a mission I initiated? Back out of helping Rafe at the most critical moment?

Clutching my bag and cloak, I faced Sister Johanna. "I don't want to be left behind. I'll try not to be a hindrance."

Her brow creased. "No one fears you will be a hindrance, Leah. I just wanted you to know you have a choice. I'm glad you're coming." She patted my arm. "Grab a bite to eat—we'll clear out in a few minutes."

Daylight streaming through the tree cover eased our trek back to the path, but it bore more resemblance to a funeral march than a stroll through the woods. A chill breeze sent shivers through the leaf buds. No one spoke above a whisper, until soon even the murmurs fell silent.

Myrna stopped and brandished her hand. My feet skidded on mud as I halted just behind her, narrowly avoiding a collision.

She lowered her satchel to the ground. "Our need for secrecy is at an end. He knows we're here."

My breath stalled, and gooseflesh prickled my arms. There was no turning back now.

We piled the remainder of our bags to the side of the path. Sister Johanna motioned us ahead, her lips set in a grim line.

Our pace quickened, and every rustling footstep and snapping branch made me flinch. The light filtering through the trees increased, and we broke into a wide glade. A gaunt man in a worn, gray cloak strode out from the opposite end.

My pulse thundered like drenching rain battering a roof. The sisters stilled at my sides.

He paused in the center of the clearing. "Well, well, ladies. Here you are at last!" His voice was deep and smooth, each syllable flowing into the next like a song. "I've sensed you for some time, and no wonder, with such an assembly as this." He pushed his hood back, revealing scraggly brown hair etched with white. "To what do I owe the pleasure?"

He swept his gaze over us, pausing on each face as though memorizing us one by one.

The temptation to cower bombarded my every instinct. I stiffened my spine.

"You know why we're here, Lord Lessox." Sister Johanna stepped forward. "We've come on behalf of the Imperian royal family."

"Surely there's no need for such formality." He spread his hands in a peaceful gesture. "Do call me Damien. As for the royal family, I'm simply giving them what they deserve. You can hardly fault me for that."

"For bewitching them and plotting their deaths?" Myrna planted her hands on her hips. "I see plenty to fault."

"But what of their sins?" His lips dipped into a snarl. "Their betrayal? My only fault is not finding a way to exact revenge sooner. Good thing that mollycoddle of a duke didn't have the nerve to complete his coup without assistance." He continued his path toward us, rubbing his palms together.

"The Luminate judges all in His own time." Sister Johanna's voice exhibited the utmost serenity. "Even when we are wronged, it is not for us to—"

A half-laugh, half-screech erupted from Damien's throat. "Listen to yourself—a well-behaved, mindless drudge. They betrayed you, too." He threw his arm in a sweeping motion. "All of you! You're no more welcome in this cursed kingdom than I. Think of all the lives you could've saved if King Frederick and Queen Beatrice allowed you to use your gifts. All the good they prevented you from doing. Yet what judgment has the Luminate taken upon our noble king and queen?"

Fury mounted in my chest. Rafe didn't deserve to pay for his parents' faults. I stormed past Sister Johanna, shaking her hand off my shoulder. "What about the prince?"

Damien froze. He turned to me, his expression relaxing

into a smirk. "Not one of *them*, are you? From a distance I wasn't sure, but now it's obvious." He stalked forward and wrenched the headpiece from my hair.

Sister Val ran to my side and pulled me back a step. I trembled with alternating surges of anger and terror.

"Despite your deceptive garb"—he clenched the headpiece, then threw it to the ground—"commonality emanates from your being." He glowered at me with bloodshot eyes. "You must be the snitch, then. The one who almost unraveled my plans. Think you're so clever, do you?"

"You—you never answered my question." I squared my shoulders, centering every thought and feeling on Rafe. "The prince has done you no wrong, yet you've enslaved him by a spell."

He snorted. "You're one to speak up for the royal family, young lady. Did they not banish you with hardly a thought? Would you call *that* justified?"

"But the prince—"

"Yes, yes, the prince! Quite fixated on him, aren't you, my dear? It seems the handsome young prince has you under a spell of his own. Unfortunately, he must fall to make my plans succeed. No, leaving the son of Frederick and Beatrice on the throne would hardly provide the satisfaction I seek. Their entire line must be cut short and replaced by someone who will respect me, respect us..." He addressed the entire group. "Now, ladies, I've a proposition for you. Are you ready to stop living in the shadows? Will you join me? After all, you too will be welcomed back to Imperia upon the demise of Frederick and Bea—"

Sister Val slapped him.

Damien grabbed her wrist, a scowl twisting his features.

She gritted her teeth. "How dare you imply we could ever consider allying ourselves with the likes of you?"

"I see this is not to be a friendly meeting of the minds, then. Disappointing. Our joined forces would've been the most powerful this kingdom has ever seen. So be it." He threw Sister Val's hand down. Black sparks spewed from his fingers toward her.

She cried out and fell.

The other sisters lurched ahead as a unit. Damien ran back to the center of the clearing, then closed his eyes, murmuring strange words. He splayed his fingers, and a glowing red line appeared before him.

The sisters halted.

"So you know what this is. Very good." Damien began to pace beside the line, which crossed the entire glade, suspended midair at the level of his hip. "You see, though you underestimate me, I do not underestimate you." He fixed his gaze on me. "I suppose I should explain for the simple little maid. I have conjured a Line of No Return. Cross it, and you will die."

I couldn't contain the tremor jarring my limbs.

His grin held an edge of madness. "So has your Luminate ordained any miracles to overcome an obstacle such as this?" He faced the group, raising his eyebrows. "No? Pity."

Damien raised his hands above the Line. He flexed his fingers, and showers of sparks exploded in every direction.

I bolted for the trees. Diving into the shrubs, I looked back to the sisters. They stood across from Damien, clutching each others' hands. A gleaming white light arced out before them, deflecting the assault.

My breathing resumed. The Luminate was protecting them, at least for now.

Sister Val still lay crumpled where Damien had struck her. I crawled through the grass, each blade grazing my palms. When I reached her feet, I gripped her ankles and dragged her farther from the supernatural combat. Huffing, I knelt and leaned near her face.

Breath warmed my cheek. *Thank you, Luminate.*

A hasty examination indicated no outward injuries, so I tucked my cloak around her and folded my apron beneath her head. Hopefully she would at least be comfortable when she woke.

If she woke.

Shuddering, I focused on the battle. Damien brought a deluge of streaks of black lightning crackling against the sisters' protective barrier. A beam of light radiated from Sister Eleanor's palm, but he deflected it with a flick of his wrist.

Myrna's taut arms dipped low. Even with the Luminate's support, the sisters couldn't keep this up indefinitely.

How could Damien be defeated?

A vial contains the demon that is the source of his power. It must be destroyed.

I gasped. My gaze instinctively moved to Sister Val, but she lay as still as before. The voice had come from within.

Had the Luminate answered my question? Spoken to *me*? The thought was both heartening and overwhelming.

We needed to destroy a vial containing a demon. Where was it?

Nothing on Damien's person bore any resemblance to a vial, though I couldn't tell what might be hidden under the folds of his cloak. For the first time, I noticed some items in a far corner of the clearing—a cauldron slung over a fire, and a crude table and stool. I narrowed my eyes and scanned his meager belongings.

My gaze felt pulled to a particular tree against which he had erected a small canvas tent. A faint green glow emanated from a hollow among its lower branches.

Nerves quaking, I crept to the edge of the glade. Once surrounded by trees, I stood and ran, keeping the Line of No Return in my sight. It had to end somewhere.

After several minutes, I slowed to a jog. The Line still stretched as far as I could see, almost as if it were lengthening as I went.

I stopped, my posture sagging. *Blast*. It would be useless to keep running if the Line could follow.

I retraced the Line back to the clearing, ignoring the twigs snagging on my hair and skirt. The trees thinned to reveal Damien sending rows of fire through the grass, separating the sisters. Sister Rochelle was on her knees, her head lowered. A vise clamped around my throat. Was she — ?

Raising her arms, she lifted her face to the sky. A cascade of cool rain poured down, extinguishing the flames.

Damien grunted. He made a beckoning motion to a tree, and its branches flailed. Rocking from side to side, it wrenched its roots from the ground and clomped forward. The sisters scattered.

I had to get that demon vial. But how, if I couldn't get around the Line of No Return?

The spell does not result in immediate death.

I sank against a tree under the weight of the revelation. I could cross and survive long enough to retrieve the demon. But then...

Fear threatened to wrench my stomach in two. The Luminate was calling me to die. To sacrifice myself to defeat Damien.

Moisture crowded my eyes. I'd never see Rafe or Ma again. *Luminate, please, is there another way?*

My plea was met with silence.

Gulping, I located the demon vial once more. After I crossed, I would need to sprint past Damien to reach it.

I sidled through branches until the Line was close enough to touch. It quivered with a muffled hum.

My death waited on the other side of that red blur. Would it hurt? I closed my eyes, releasing streams of tears. I wanted more time to think, to *live*. But if I were to perish, it had to be in time to help the sisters. In time to save Rafe.

Taking one last shaky breath, I opened my eyes and lunged forward.

The line had disappeared.

I halted, sorrow and confusion sweeping my insides into a whirlwind. Where was it? Had I crossed without noticing?

Damien's cry of rage drew my attention to the area of combat. The sisters surged forward several steps ahead of me with Sister Johanna at the lead, clasping her midsection.

Horror congealed my mind with an icy chill.

Sister Johanna had crossed the Line of No Return first. She would die in my place.

I fumbled onward. I had to stop Damien before my hesitation cost any more lives. Breaking out of the tree cover, I raced to the far end of the clearing.

Damien's voice boomed as he turned in my direction. He hurled a spray of sparks at me, and I dove forward. Behind me, a bush burst into flame.

I charged ahead, my throat constricting around my gasps for air.

He ran toward me. I ducked behind his table just as more black sparks flew over my hair and set a tree alight.

Hoping to catch him by surprise, I leapt into a full sprint. Damien yelled something incoherent, and three trees at my side began to thrash. I screamed, raising a hand to shield my face as I groped past his tent.

Myrna and Sister Eleanor called out in unison. A thick, iridescent rope coiled around the trees, and they stumbled. I scrambled out of the way as they hurtled to the ground, writhing in a deafening onslaught of scrapes and creaks.

The demon vial glowed emerald just above me. Disgust and trepidation swirled in my chest as I reached up and grasped it. It was more of a cylinder than a vial, encased by engraved metal at the top and bottom. Smoke churned within, emanating a pulsing heat.

"Put that down, wretch." Damien's growl came from the other side of the tent. He staggered toward me, eyes wild. Behind him, the sisters blocked a series of fiery orbs plummeting from the sky.

I was on my own.

I seized the vial in both hands and smashed it against the tree, creating a web of cracks in the glass.

Damien roared and lunged at me. He pressed his thumb and forefinger to the front of my neck, shoving the back of my head against the tree trunk. With the other hand, he immobilized my wrist that held the demon vessel.

"Little meddler! Didn't they teach you not to touch things that aren't yours?" He tightened his grip. "Give me that vial, or I swear the pain of my next spell will make your worst nightmares feel like fantasies."

I shook my head. Black spots swam across my vision.

"No?" He leaned closer and stroked his thumb across my forearm. "You do have a bit of spirit, pretty maid. Such a pity you got in way over your head."

I shifted my weight, struggling to stay upright. Sister Val's dagger nudged my thigh. I slipped my free hand under my apron and fumbled for it.

"Do you think anyone will even notice when you're gone? That anyone will—"

Freeing the blade, I swiped at his leg.

He staggered back, cursing. Curving his fingers, he generated an ever-widening vortex that smoldered with glowing blue embers.

My hair whipped across my face as he hurled it toward me.

For Rafe. I threw the vial to the ground, steadied it with my foot, and drove the dirk into the glass.

CHAPTER 23

The vial splintered into a hundred fragments. Black smoke poured out with a loud hiss, spreading in every direction as the vortex rose into the air and dissipated.

I released the dagger and stumbled back.

Damien made a gagging sound, followed by an anguished cry. He dropped to the grass, writhing against an invisible assailant.

Nausea curdled my stomach. I gained my footing and ran toward the sisters.

Myrna and Sister Eleanor met me with open arms. All traces of the flaming orbs had vanished.

"You've done it. Praise be to the Luminate." Myrna's breath came in rapid pants. "It's over."

It's over. The tension gripping me slackened, leaving me limp.

"Thank heavens you're unharmed." Sister Eleanor smoothed back my hair. "Let us take care of him from here. Without his demon, he shouldn't be much trouble."

She took Myrna's arm and headed toward Damien's prone form, which now lay still.

Someone grasped my shoulder.

I turned with a jolt. "Sister Val, you're all right!"

"I am now. I believe this is yours." She fastened my cloak around my neck. "I'll be stiff for a few days, I imagine, but it could've been much worse. What did I miss?"

"Damien's fallen at last." My voice grated against my dry throat like sandpaper. "I—I used your dagger to break the demon vial."

"Did you really?" She looked to where Sister Eleanor was binding Damien's feet with a thick rope. "Luminate be praised. Well done, Leah. We ought to be safe now, even your prince." She prodded me with her elbow. "But how disappointing that I missed all the action."

My smile faded. We wouldn't *all* be safe. Mist shrouded my vision as Sister Johanna's sacrifice replayed itself in my mind. How could I tell Sister Val what my hesitance had cost?

"Is everything all right, child? Are you hurt?"

I shook my head. The words wouldn't come.

She squeezed my shoulders. "Now, Leah, surely it can't be that bad. Damien has been defeated, and no one has fallen—"

"Not yet."

Her eyes sought mine, wide with apprehension. "What do you mean?"

"He made a Line of No Return. I was going to cross it, but I waited. And then Sister Johanna..." I searched the clearing. She sat propped against a tree, her head in her hands. Sister Rochelle knelt beside her, rubbing her back.

"Sister Johanna?" Sister Val followed my gaze, her jaw slackening. "No. She can't...we must go to her."

I nodded. Clutching each others' arms, we crossed the glade.

Sister Val sank to her knees at Sister Johanna's side. "Johanna. Can it be true? You—you're..."

Sister Johanna met her gaze, her eyes already so much more aged than before.

"You knew, didn't you?" Sister Val leaned closer. "Why didn't you tell me?"

A shadow of a smile crossed Sister Johanna's lips. "Would you have accepted it?"

"No." Sister Val's head drooped. "What shall we do without you?"

"You were born to be a leader, Valeria. I know you won't let them down."

I watched from a distance, numb. Empty. I caused this. If I had acted faster, the sisters would've remained whole. Sister Johanna wouldn't have to bear the suffering meant for me.

"Leah. Come here, my child." Sister Johanna's whisper drew me out of the deep, black cavern of my regret.

I approached and lowered to the ground. "Sister Johanna, I—"

She touched Sister Val's wrist. "I'd like to speak with Leah for a moment. Alone, please."

"Of course." Sister Val sniffed and wiped her hand under her nose. She rose and joined the others, who regarded us with red-rimmed eyes.

I encased Sister Johanna's hand in both of mine. Cold. As though the life had already drained from it. "I'm so, so sorry. This is all my fault. The Luminate called *me* to cross the spell line and sacrifice myself, but I—I hesitated. And now you'll die, when it should've been me." The words poured forth in an unrelenting tide, as though they could alter the events of the battle, undo the consequences of my cowardice.

Her fingers tightened in my grasp. "Leah, you must listen to me. It was not the Luminate's intent that you sacrifice yourself."

"But I heard Him. He told me to get the vial, that crossing the Line—"

"Yes, but you were not meant to die." A cough sent a tremor through her entire body. "I've known for some time that the Luminate would use this confrontation to bring me home. I am honored to be chosen."

Shock clattered through me like a stone in a quarry. She came into this mission knowing she was going to die. The Luminate had informed her of her coming death, and she still loved Him, trusted Him...

"When I saw that you were about to cross the Line, I ran forward. I had to ensure the sacrifice played out as the Luminate intended."

Gratitude swirled with my remorse, making me woozy. "After everything you've already done for me, you—you saved my life."

"You saved many more lives today with your bravery." She winced and swayed.

I sprang forward to hold her upright.

"Perhaps you'd better summon the sisters. I should—I'd best lie down."

Choking back tears, I motioned to Sister Val.

"But, Leah?" Sister Johanna tugged at my sleeve. "The Luminate spared your life for a reason. He has an important future planned for you, grander than you've ever imagined. Don't be afraid to embrace it."

I bowed my head. How could the Luminate intend for me to live if it meant Sister Johanna had to die?

Sister Val crouched at my side. Together, we helped Sister Johanna lie down. Sister Rochelle hurried over to position a cloak as a pillow, and Myrna followed with a blanket. Sister Eleanor offered her a drink from her waterskin, dabbing a trickle off her chin with a handkerchief.

I couldn't bear the sight. Sister Johanna, my beacon of calm strength. Now stretched on the ground, trembling, the color fading from her pallid face.

Her eyelids fluttered closed.

No. "Isn't there something you can do?" My gaze darted

among the sisters, latching on to Sister Rochelle. "You made it *rain*. Can't you heal her?"

Sister Rochelle shook her head, pressing her lips together. "Only if it's the Luminate's intent. I'm sorry, child."

"But we can't just—"

Sister Val drew me against her as sobs convulsed my chest.

I looked back to Sister Johanna. She had stopped shaking, her expression serene. My heart folded inward like a flower closing its petals in the absence of sunlight.

Sister Johanna had breathed her last.

"How are you faring, child?"

I pulled my gaze from the passing trees and sprawling wooden fences to Sister Rochelle, seated beside me in the carriage.

"Fine." I kept my voice low, glancing to where Sister Val dozed on the opposite seat. We'd parted ways with Myrna and Sister Eleanor after breakfast and now headed toward Dorendyn Castle.

"I know it's hard. We all miss her." She adjusted the blanket over her lap. "I thought the priest did a lovely job with the funeral rites yesterday. But what a shame we couldn't bury her at the manor. I know the others would've liked to be there."

I nodded, fiddling with the corner of my apron. My tears had run dry by the time we took Sister Johanna's remains to the nearest village church. A tiny flicker in my soul assured me she had reached the fulfillment of her union with the Luminate, but the remainder held only emptiness and disbelief.

The price of my survival had been too steep.

"Did Sister Val tell you we blessed the bush she planted at the grave site? It should bloom year round."

I attempted a smile. "She would've liked that."

"Oh, yes. But just think how it pales in comparison with the wonders she must be experiencing in paradise."

"I suppose." I shifted against the thin cushion.

"Yes, dear Sister Johanna is past any shadow of earthly pain and sorrow. But Lord Lessox, now, I'm afraid his pain has just begun." A line creased her forehead. "I almost feel sorry for the man. Separating from a demon is nasty business."

Damien had roused several times after the destruction of the vial, but his mumblings were incoherent, his movements erratic. The local sheriff vowed to deliver him to the palace straightaway. The king and queen would not deal with him lightly, but perhaps his loss of sanity might elicit a small token of mercy.

Sister Rochelle nudged my side. "Speaking of Lord Lessox, I believe I heard you tell Sister Johanna that the Luminate spoke to you in the midst of the battle."

I winced at the reminder. "Yes. At least, I believe so. He told me we needed to destroy the demon vial."

She nodded, her brows raised. "You know, Leah, now that the Luminate has spoken to you once, it wouldn't surprise me if He'd be willing to do so again. In fact, you may have it in you to become a mystic yourself."

I gripped the seat. Me, a mystic? I was just beginning to sort out what the Luminate meant to me. Surely He'd prefer to call someone much more established in her faith.

Sister Johanna's words whispered through my mind. *An important future...grander than you've ever imagined.* I inhaled sharply. Was *this* the grand future she had in mind?

My soul shriveled like a blade of parched grass. As much as I respected the sisters and their vocation, could I embrace a life of solitude? A life cut off from Ma, a future with Rafe impossible?

I glanced back to Sister Rochelle.

"Just something to think about." She squeezed my knee. "You will always be welcome to live with us, regardless of whether the Luminate is calling you to be a mystic or Mabel's trusted assistant."

~

The tall spires of Dorendyn Castle pierced the horizon, gradually dispersing the haze that had settled on my mind in the days since Damien's defeat.

Rafe must be on the palace grounds, somewhere. Was he free of the spell? Did the duke have a secondary plan if Damien failed him? Goosebumps swarmed my arms. Rafe might still be in danger if the duke continued to roam free.

I stared out, hardly daring to blink. But to all outward appearances, daily life in Imperia had suffered no disruption. The wedding date was less than a week away. Would they be in the midst of preparations if it was going forward as planned?

Sighing, I sat back and rubbed my temples. The view contributed nothing toward answering the flurry of questions threatening to make my head implode.

I needed to see Rafe as soon as possible. My stomach crumpled into a tight wad. What if it hadn't worked? What if he still didn't recognize me?

What if he *did* recognize me? A pleasant shiver prickled my spine.

I'd hear his laugh again, feel his arms around me as if he never wanted to let go. Freed from his engagement to the princess, he would take me to his parents, proclaiming me as one of their brave rescuers. Then they…

My hopes splintered like a tree struck by lightning. Was I so naive? To the king and queen, I would always be a chambermaid. Lowborn. Common. I could save them from a dozen would-be assassins before their very eyes, and they'd never welcome me as a daughter-in-law. Even with proof of my innocence, they wouldn't risk allowing me back into Imperia when

I might distract their son or cause him to reject the young noblewomen they wanted him to marry.

Months' worth of dreams of my joyful return home faded into oblivion. I would see Rafe and Ma but not to be reunited. Only to say goodbye again.

This time, forever.

CHAPTER 24

$\mathcal{T}$he main thoroughfare to the palace bustled with people scurrying to reach home before evening fell. I'd left Sister Val and Sister Rochelle at the inn, where they would spend the night, and now drifted through the throng, keeping my gaze fixed on the dusty street.

I grasped the rosary beads affixed to my belt, murmuring snatches of prayers to discourage prying onlookers. Would I ever resume a life free from concealment and disguise?

My fingers strangled the beads as the enormous palace doors drew me into their shadows, but the guards merely returned my nod as I passed through.

My heart tugged toward Rafe, desperate to scour the halls until I was at his side. But the only place he might spend the evening alone would be his private chambers, and I couldn't risk another encounter with his valet.

A breeze swirled in my chest. There was one other room where he could be alone.

I strove to adopt a meditative stance as I meandered the familiar corridors, hoping no one could see my vigorous steps under the thick folds of my skirt.

At last I arrived in front of our closet. My breaths came quick and shallow. Rafe might be on the other side of that door.

In one swift movement, I opened it and swept inside.

The closet appeared frozen in time. Cobwebs hung in every corner, the air dusty and stagnant. Disappointment punctured my heart like a pincushion.

Even the note I'd left for Rafe in the sand lingered, untouched. My eyes watered at the words. *All will be well. I love you.* Had he ever seen the message?

Memories of Rafe crashed over me in unrelenting waves. A lanky boy with a tear in his pants bursting through the door to evade his governess. My patient instructor tracing letters in the sand again and again until I had mastered them. The reluctant scholar frowning at his textbook, devising any excuse to put off his reading assignments. The grin of my dearest friend as he presented me with the emerald pendant for my birthday. My comforter holding me against his chest as I cried. The man I loved declaring he wanted to spend his life with me.

I lost myself in bittersweet nostalgia until the last light from the window faded to darkest blue.

Rafe wasn't coming.

Tomorrow, I'd trail him as long as it took to catch him alone. But for tonight, there was another chamber I might visit in safety.

After surveying the closet one last time, I set out into the quiet halls. I edged my way to the Eastern corridor, straining to hear any hint of a guard.

I tapped on the door of our bedroom, then pressed my ear against the coarse wood.

Sorrow settled in the deepest chamber of my heart. *Not ours anymore, just Ma's.*

Feet shuffled within before the door cracked open. I flinched back.

"Who is it? The hour is late."

I could only stand and stare. *Ma.*

She gaped at me. "Leah? I must be dreaming. It can't really be…"

"It's me, Ma. You're not dreaming." Tears flowed down my cheeks as she pulled me into the room, grasping me in a tight hug as soon as the door closed behind us.

I stepped back, keeping a tight hold on her shoulders. Her hair looked grayer, her face more lined, but she didn't stoop any worse than before or seem to be in any pain. I started to resume our embrace, but froze, sensing movement in the corner. Panic smothered my breath.

We weren't alone.

The vise on my throat loosened as I recognized Anne standing near the bed. She beamed at me, her face wet with tears.

Ma followed my gaze. "Can you believe it? She's come back." She motioned Anne to join us. "Anne was kind enough to offer to live here and look after me when —"

I nodded. I didn't want to hear the completion of her thought any more than she wanted to voice it.

"She has been a great help." Ma lowered herself onto the edge of the bed.

A cyclone of emotions overwhelmed me into silence. My gratitude to Anne for taking care of Ma was tinged with sadness, even a hint of jealousy.

Ma needed someone to take my place.

Anne approached as though facing an apparition. "Leah, it really is you." She grasped my arms. "Praise be to the Luminate that you're safe. Your ma has missed you so. It's a blessing to see such a joyous smile on her face again."

"Thank you for watching over her."

Her brows arched. "Are you able to stay?"

I shook my head just enough to be perceptible to Anne, but hopefully not Ma.

Anne nodded and bit her lip. "I know the girls in my

former dormitory would be more than happy to take me in for the night. I'll let the two of you have some privacy."

"I don't want to put you out."

"Not at all." She waved off my weak protest. "I shall return in the morning."

"Thank you. I wish I had more time." I swallowed back the new surge of threatening tears. "May the Luminate bless you."

She pressed my hand. "And you. Goodnight."

"Anne? Please—don't tell anyone."

"Of course." She nodded, then crossed the room and disappeared into the dark hall.

Ma stared at me as though trying to reconcile her mental image with the figure standing before her. "My Leah. I still can't believe it's really you."

I sat beside her on the bed. "I have so much to tell you. But first, how are you? Your back and your joints—have there been any changes?"

"You've had enough to concern yourself with, my poor child. I hope you haven't been anxious about me."

"Of course I've been concerned for you. To have to leave, not knowing—"

"I understand, my darling, believe me." She folded her arms across her waist. "My condition is stable. From what we can tell, my physical decline has reached a plateau, at least for the time being. Please don't fret for me. My spirits haven't been high, I'll admit, but seeing you safe and well has restored them a hundred times over."

My insides wound like thread on a spool. "Ma, before you allow yourself to hope too much, I must tell you. I'm not sure I can stay. As far as I know, my order of banishment has not been lifted. So unless that changes, I must depart again as soon as possible, and no one must know I was here. I wish..." I shook my head. "The risk would be too great, for both of us."

Ma's posture slumped. "Well, I have you here now, which is already better than I'd dared hope for." She patted my knee, her brows furrowed. "But why have you returned? Do you think they would spare your life if you're caught?"

"The royal family was in grave danger. Worse than I initially thought. And I needed to stop Rafe's—the prince's—wedding, if I could." I reached up to my headpiece. "I've done my best to disguise myself."

Her eyes crinkled into a smile. "That does explain some things." The light in her expression faded. "But what of the royal family?"

"I hope the worst of the threat has passed." My pulse surged, producing a rush of lightheadedness. "Have you heard anything of the prince and princess? Has the wedding been called off?"

"It has. Just yesterday I heard talk of an uncomfortable confrontation between Prince Raphael and Princess Penelope. And it seems the Duke of Brantley has been stripped of his title and lands and sent to the dungeons."

I clasped my hands in my lap. *Thank you, Luminate.*

Ma narrowed her eyes. "Has this all been your doing?"

"I was involved—indirectly. After the guards left me in Trellich, a set of nuns took me in." I described my journey into Trellich, glossing over the near-starvation, and my life among the sisters. When my narrative reached my time at Glonsel Palace, I paused. "Ma, I spoke to someone there. I hope you don't mind."

"Why would I mind?"

I took a long, deep breath. "I asked one of the stable hands about Father."

"Oh, I see." Ma plucked the edge of her shawl. "What did he say?"

"Father died of the Gravedigger's Bounty." I watched Ma's face. *Please let my words be a source of comfort instead of further pain.* "Once the borders were closed, he volunteered to care for the sick and eventually took ill himself."

Ma blinked, sending a tear sliding along her jawline. "That

sounds just like Reginald." She leaned forward, covering her mouth with her hand. "To be sure, after all these years. You don't know what this means to me, Leah."

Now I was crying again, too. "I couldn't wait to tell you. I so hoped this knowledge would ease your mind."

"It has, my darling, it has." She sniffed, dabbing her nose with a handkerchief. "But tell me, did you ever find those letters?"

I launched into the rest of my story, omitting the details of our battle against Damien.

Ma gripped my shoulder. "Heavens, what you've been through! How good the Luminate is, keeping you safe through it all. But don't you think you could stay, now that Princess Penelope and the duke have been exposed?"

"I wish it were so simple. But I fear the king and queen may suspect an attachment between me and the prince and wouldn't welcome me back. I'm so sorry."

"Say no more. There's nothing to be sorry for."

I hugged her, pressing my cheek against her soft night-dress. Dear, selfless Ma, who gave so much but required so little. I never wanted to take her goodness for granted again.

"Sister Rochelle and the others have offered me a home with them. I'll miss you terribly, but—"

She jerked back. "You'll be living with the sisters? Do you think they might offer me a home there as well?"

Ma could come to Trellich. I tried to quell my hope before it cultivated permanent roots. "I'm sure they would. But it would mean leaving your work, your friends."

"I know." She shrugged. "They're small sacrifices to make if I could spend my last years with my daughter."

I struggled to think logically. We couldn't overlook any potential obstacles. "We have a hired carriage. Do you think you could tolerate the journey?"

"I'll manage somehow." Her lips curved into a grin. "Now, tell me more about this manor. I'll pack my things tomorrow."

She was coming. A portion of the despair weighing down my chest lifted.

The manor would feel so much more like home with Ma there.

∾

Ma bustled about the room, seemingly in a hurry to get dressed.

"Are you going somewhere?" I tried to rub the bleariness out of my eyes.

"Just down the hall. I'll be right back."

Where could she be off to so early in the morning, and with such an air of secrecy?

A knock sounded at the door just as I fastened the last button on my nun's frock. I jumped back, searching for a place to hide.

Ma's bright face appeared in the doorframe. At her side was Gretchen.

"It is you! When your ma came, I was hoping, but I didn't know..." Her hug nearly sent me tumbling onto the bed.

Ma tapped my arm. "I'm going to head to the sewing room so no one comes looking for me. I'll meet you at the inn this afternoon."

I nodded. Ma winked at us before closing the door behind her.

"The inn?" Gretchen stepped back. "Why is she meeting you there?"

"She's coming with me when I return to Trellich."

"Oh, so you're not staying." Her melancholy expression was fleeting. "At least we have you here for a little while. Your ma is such a dear, giving us a chance to talk."

"Yes, I should've known she'd gone to fetch you. How are you? What have you been doing all this time?"

"I'm very well. I've still been working for Princess Penelope, at least until the engagement broke off again. She sure left in a hurry, but she almost seemed relieved about it. Remember how jumpy she could be? It got a hundred times worse. The poor thing seemed on the verge of a nervous spell at every moment by the end."

"I hope she's happy to be home." *And that she stays there.*

"I should think so. Anyway, now I've been taken on as a lady's maid for the Earl of Shrempton's eldest daughter, who just reached her Maturity. Harriet, too! But speaking of engagements—"

I gasped. "You and Ned?"

She nodded, a smile lighting her entire face. "He asked me just a few weeks ago. Got down on one knee and everything. Who would've guessed he'd be such a romantic? We're to be married at the next full moon."

"Oh, Gretchen, how wonderful! I hope he makes you very happy." If only I could see her walk down the aisle of the chapel in her white dress.

"He will, if he knows what's good for him." Her mischievous grin slipped away. "But Sam..." She huffed. "You'd scarcely been gone a week when he started making eyes at one of the kitchen maids. Do you remember Olive? Ugh, I just about slapped him."

I laughed and shook my head. "That news doesn't bother me in the least, I assure you. In fact, I'm very glad to hear Sam's found a new prospect. He never had a chance with me, even if I had stayed." I threaded my fingers together. "I have so much to tell you."

She bounced forward. "About the time you've been away? Have you met someone?"

I bit my lip. She deserved to finally hear the truth. "The story starts much earlier than that. You've long accused me of disappearing, and you're right. There's a particular spot I'd go to, a closet. But I wasn't always alone..."

Starting at the beginning, I told her my entire history with Rafe. She listened with wide eyes.

"You know how to read? And I can't believe you call him Rafe!"

I took her hands. "I know. I should've told you long ago."

She shook me off with a giggle. "Keep going! I'm dying to know whether things between you and the prince got more interesting than reading lessons."

Bracing myself, I jumped ahead to my birthday and the events leading up to Rafe's declaration.

"Leah!" Gretchen's whisper managed to sound like a squeal. "Prince Raphael kissed you? He wanted to run away with you? That is far and away the most romantic thing I've ever heard. It's no wonder poor Sam couldn't get you to bat an eye at him. And here I thought I was teaching my innocent friend about love when it turns out you were meeting the *prince* for secret liaisons."

The mischief in her eyes faded.

"But I'm not sure Prince Raphael has been well. He did nothing but scowl after you were sent away. I guess now I know why. Then the engagement broke off, and Princess Penelope skulked around for a week. But when they announced the betrothal was back on, the prince acted so—different. All politeness and gallantry, as though he'd never had reason to be upset in the first place. We thought it was because they'd mended their quarrel, but his smiles never seemed genuine after that." She raised her shoulders. "Listen to me, spouting nonsense like a confused old hag."

Poor Rafe. Miserable, then forced into acquiescence with dark magic. "It's not nonsense."

"Anyway, he's not engaged anymore." She waggled her eyebrows. "Have you seen him yet? Since you've been back?"

"Not yet." My insides churned with anticipation. "I hope to find him later today. But I'm still banished, and I'm sure the king and queen will be dead set on keeping us apart."

"All the more reason to take full advantage of this short time together." She folded her hands over her heart, gazing off with a dreamy expression.

I cleared my throat. "Now, would you like to hear about how I accompanied a group of nuns to vanquish a sorcerer?"

Gretchen blinked. "You realize this conversation is making my life feel terribly dull. Who would've guessed our timid Leah would go on to have such romance and adventure? I'm positively green with envy."

"Don't be. If I never have this much excitement again, I'll be perfectly satisfied."

She surveyed me, scrunching up a corner of her mouth. "Banished or not, I have a feeling this story isn't over for you yet."

I hoped she was right.

CHAPTER 25

*W*here *is he going?*
              I'd been trailing Rafe at a distance ever since
he emerged from the breakfast room hours before. After a brief
sojourn outside for a bout of fencing with the guards, rain had
driven him indoors. Now he adopted a brisk pace, avoiding
conversation with those he passed and casting about furtive
glances. Hopefully wherever he was headed next, he intended
to be alone.

He turned a corner, and I followed. Large, imposing doors
at the end of the corridor drew my gaze. My steps slowed to
a halt.

The throne room. The very room where my banishment
had been declared.

Rafe was heading straight for it, his boots clunking against
the polished marble floor. Did I dare go after him?

He entered, and I darted forward, grabbing hold of the
door just before it would've latched shut. I opened it a crack
and peered through. Rafe strode toward the three thrones
occupying the dais at the far end of the room. Around him, all
lay still and quiet. Vacant.

My veins thrummed as though set ablaze. This was my chance.

I heaved the door open just enough to slip through. Letting it ease closed behind me, I ducked into a shadow to survey the room more fully.

Rafe jerked and dropped the book he'd just picked up. He pivoted to face me, his breath releasing in a huff. "Ah, good morning, Sister. You startled me. I wasn't expecting anyone."

I moved forward without meaning to, drawn to him like a compass needle finding north. My eyes traced his every feature, desperate for a hint of recognition.

He jogged down the dais steps, pulling at his collar. "The king and queen aren't holding a public audience at this time, but if I can help in any—" His jaw went slack.

My feet continued their path, my gaze locked on his. The hammering in my head drowned out every other sound. I stopped before him, unable to remember how to breathe.

His voice crept out in a whisper. "Leah? It can't be."

"You recognize me." Tears blurred my vision. He was back. *My* Rafe was back.

He closed the remaining gap between us. "Of course I recognize you. I haven't forgotten a single contour of your face." He reached toward my cheek, then hesitated, frowning. "But have you really taken vows?"

I laughed and shook my head, pulling out the pins near my temples to remove my headpiece. "No, but I've been living with a group of nuns. They let me borrow this as a disguise."

"Thank the new moon for that." He reached for me again, and I nestled against him, clinging to the solid warmth of his chest. It didn't seem possible, to be surrounded by the comfort of his arms after dreaming of him for so long.

"I can't believe it's really you," he murmured into my hair. "Alive, safe, and—*here*."

My shoulders tingled as he tightened his hold.

"You must never leave again."

Thoughts of my imminent departure wouldn't mar the joy of this reunion.

Rafe pulled back to look at me, his brows drawn. "I desperately wanted to search for you. You believe that, don't you?"

I nodded, rubbing my thumb across the smooth silk covering his shoulder.

His hands tensed at my waist. "My parents kept me locked in my chambers for a full week after your exile, heavily guarded anytime I was allowed into the halls. By the time they eased up..." He shook his head, transferring his gaze to the floor. "I didn't know where they'd taken you or where you might've gone from there. I had no idea how I'd ever find you, assuming I could even manage to escape the palace."

I wrapped my arms around his neck once more. "I never blamed you. I know you would've come for me if you could've."

His chest rose and fell, his cheek resting against the top of my head.

I reluctantly leaned back. "But, Rafe, what happened with the princess? Is she really gone, the betrothal ended once and for all?"

Rafe gave an emphatic nod. "Yes."

I nearly collapsed with relief.

He took my arm and led me to sit on one of the steps leading up to the dais. "But you wouldn't believe the strange events of the past few days," he continued as we walked. "And now that you're here, I'm starting to doubt my senses entirely."

"What events?"

He left no space between us as he settled beside me. "Well, my engagement to Penelope was broken off straightaway after I received your package. My father recognized the duke's handwriting, and even my parents couldn't contradict letters filled with such culpable statements." He narrowed his eyes. "Where did you get those, anyway?"

I shrugged, a smile playing at the corners of my mouth. "I

got a job at Glonsel Palace and searched through Princess Penelope's rooms in the middle of the night."

"Did you, truly?" Astonishment and a trace of amusement crossed Rafe's face. "I never would've imagined my sweet little Leah would turn into a spy." He stroked a finger across my cheek before his expression turned serious. "But Penelope certainly deserved it. The engagement was broken off, thanks to you, and she was to return to Trellich. But then, just three days ago, I found her still here. Making wedding plans, no less! I had apparently collapsed and woke in the infirmary with the most dreadful headache. Mistress Donna said I must've hit my head exceptionally hard—I couldn't recall a thing from the previous several weeks. Then to have to face *her* again." He massaged his forehead. "She spoke to me as though the betrothal had never been called off."

I chewed the inside of my cheek. How much should I explain?

"And just as we finished dealing with her and the duke—who will spend the remainder of his pitiful life in the dungeon, by the way, because my parents don't trust him enough to send him into exile—you'll never guess who showed up next. A sheriff insisted on speaking with my parents, declaring the prisoner he had in tow was none other than Damien Lessox. Do you remember the story I told you about the sorcerer who cursed my parents after they dismissed him? He's been found at last, though the poor man does nothing but thrash and rave like a lunatic." He shook his head, brows raised, before leaning close to my face. "But if this is all a dream, now that you're here, I hope never to wake." The fire in his eyes sent my stomach into a series of somersaults.

"Rafe, there's so much I need to tell you."

"Yes?" He kept his face close.

"You've been under the influence of an enchantment. That's why Princess Penelope took you by surprise the other day. She's been here all along. Damien was aiding the duke and put you under a spell so you would go through with the wedding. The problem with your memory wasn't from hitting your head."

He started back, blinking. "A spell? But — "

We both froze as footsteps echoed in the hall.

Rafe took my arm and led me behind a purple, velvet curtain hanging in the back corner of the dais. He bent close to my ear. "We're less exposed here."

I hardly dared to draw breath as the minutes passed, but all remained quiet.

Rafe's iron hold loosened.

"Do you really think we're safe?"

He nodded, squinting around the curtain toward the door. After another moment of silence, he turned back to me. "They must be gone."

"What were you doing in here, anyway?"

He grasped my hand, grazing his fingers across my palm. "I couldn't bear the thought of going back to our closet after your banishment. So now I come here to be alone. Though the memories are no less painful."

"You come *here* to be alone?"

His shoulder lifted in a half-shrug. "I know it seems odd, being such a large room. But it's only used for scheduled audiences and ceremonies, and no one else dares enter at other times aside from a few designated servants. But this is all beside the point. How do you know about Damien Lessox and this spell?"

My breath faltered. "After I sent the letters, I heard that your engagement to Princess Penelope was broken off, then reinstated. I returned to Imperia to find out why."

"You came back here without finding a way to see me?" The reproach darkening his eyes made me cringe.

"I did come to see you, but — " I lowered my gaze. "You had no idea who I was."

He shuddered. "That's not possible."

I glanced back up to see emotion roiling in his eyes.

"How could they?" A vein throbbed in his neck. "Oh, Leah, I'm so sorry."

Gripping his hand, I raised it to my lips. "It wasn't your fault, Rafe. There's nothing to be sorry for. I knew something must be wrong, and when I told the sisters about it—the nuns who came with me—they thought you must've been under a spell."

He gaped at me as I narrated our journey, the expansion of our party, and the subsequent confrontation with Damien. My description of nearly crossing the Line of No Return made his fingers tense, and he caressed my hand when my voice caught relating Sister Johanna's sacrifice and death.

At the completion of my story, Rafe leaned his forehead against mine. "You've been in such grave danger, and all for me. It should've been the other way around. I should've been out there risking my life for you instead of trapped here in this blasted palace." He pressed my hands more fervently, moving his head back just enough to look deeply into my eyes. "I'm free from the spell—I'm *alive*—because of you."

The rate of my pulse doubled in an instant.

"But you're safe now. And I'll keep you safe at my side forevermore. Oh, how I've missed you." His gaze shifted to my lips as he reached out to cup the back of my head.

The feel of his mouth gently moving against mine was even more mesmerizing than I remembered. I savored every sensation, trying to wordlessly communicate the love I'd kept locked away for so many months.

His grip tightened, his kiss deepening.

He wants me to stay at his side forever. But is it possible? A trace of unease wove through my stomach, setting the dancing butterflies to quaking.

Summoning every fiber of my willpower, I stepped back and turned away.

His footsteps shuffled behind me. "Forgive me, Leah. Please. I didn't mean to push you, I just…"

I faced him, adopting what I hoped was a reassuring smile. "No, it's not that. And I've missed you too, Rafe. More than I can express." I swallowed, willing myself to say the dreaded words. "But I don't see how I can stay."

"What do you mean? You must stay. The duke and princess's plot has been exposed!"

A stream of hope wended into my mind. "Has my banishment been revoked?"

"Not yet." Determination flooded his eyes. "But how could they possibly deny you citizenship now? When you've been proven innocent?"

The hatred in the queen's face as she pronounced my exile flashed before me, cutting off the hope at its source. "Knowing your parents, they'll find a way. Even in the absence of treason, they'll be as eager as ever to keep me away from you."

"They can't. I won't allow it. Even if we have to share your story with every one of their subjects to provoke an uprising…"

I couldn't help but laugh every time Rafe reverted from the confident man I'd fallen in love with to the headstrong boy who'd been my dearest friend. "You're free to carry out whatever harebrained schemes you wish on my behalf, as long as you don't put yourself in any danger." Every trace of laughter faded as a boulder settled in my chest. "In the meantime, it's probably best if I return to Trellich. The sisters have offered me a home with them, and we can at least write to each other." I ran my hands up the length of his arms. "If circumstances change, know that I will return as quickly as my feet can carry me, if no other means of transport is available."

His jaw remained set. "I can't let you leave again. Even if we stayed in touch, Trellich is so far." He cradled my face in his hand. "I don't think I'd survive another separation, Leah. Please, don't ask it of me. And if you did stay, surely my parents couldn't bring themselves to put our country's brave rescuer to death."

"Couldn't they?" Tears spilled down my cheeks as I clutched his shoulder. "I'm so sorry, but what else can I do? I know it would break my ma's heart, and yours, if I were imprisoned...or worse. And I've already been to see Ma. What if by staying I put her in danger?"

"Then I'll come with you."

"But you can't, Rafe. You know that as well as I. After all this turmoil, Imperia needs you more than ever. Your stability, your leadership. And Ma will be with me, so I won't be alone."

Rafe's head slumped forward. "I still can't manage to win an argument, even after all this time." His lips quirked into a lopsided grin as he used his free hand to wipe the tears from my face. He wrapped his arms tightly around me, and I basked in his closeness one last time, listening to the steady beats of his heart.

Too soon, he drew back. "Promise me you'll write every day." He tweaked my nose. "You know if you don't, I'll come thundering up there to check on you."

"Wouldn't that give the sisters a start?" My smile dissipated. "But, Rafe, if they never revoke my banishment..."

He put a finger to my lips. "Hush, we won't even speak of that."

"We must. If I can't return, then I beg you—please, find someone else and be happy with her."

Rafe's eyes darkened almost to black. "You know I could never be happy with someone else."

"Don't say that." I couldn't withstand the intensity of his gaze. "You may need to, and you would have my blessing."

He shook his head, sending waves of hair sweeping across his forehead.

I reached up to smooth them away. "Fine. We will discuss it no more at present. But I..." I swallowed, hating the words before they were even spoken. "I have to go. You'll be missed soon, if not already."

He grasped my elbows, bending down until his face was within an inch of mine. "You're truly going to leave me?"

"I must. I'm sorry." I lowered my head as fresh tears drenched my cheeks. "You see that, don't you?"

Rafe's heavy breath warmed my forehead. "Yes, though it kills me to admit it." He raised my chin with his finger, then cupped my face as he leaned forward to place a soft kiss on my lips. "No matter what happens, I will love you until I die," he whispered as he released me.

"My heart is with you, always." Sobs choked my words. "I'll write the moment I arrive at the manor in safety." I placed one last tear-soaked kiss on his cheek before turning to run in the opposite direction, pausing only to retrieve my discarded headpiece.

"Goodbye," I murmured when I reached the door. Rafe had collapsed onto his throne, his head in his hands. How I longed to comfort him, but this was my last moment to be strong.

The latch clicked behind me, severing a piece of my soul with its finality.

CHAPTER 26

I turned blindly from the throne room, fleeing to where the sisters waited for me at the inn.

My steps faltered at the rustle of crinoline. I collided with the wide, stiff skirt of a taffeta gown.

Its owner was none other than the queen.

Shrouding my face, I dipped into a low curtsy. My headpiece hung limp in my fingers, useless. "I beg your pardon, Your Majesty. Pray, excuse me." Keeping my head down, I shuffled to the side.

She grasped my sleeve. "Not so fast. Stay a moment."

My mind screamed at me to run, but my feet stayed rooted to the ground. I held my breath, staring at the floor. *Please, Luminate, don't let her recognize me.*

"Leah Wellstone, isn't it?"

My stomach wove into a rigid knot. There was nowhere to hide now.

I peeked at her grim face. "Yes, Your Majesty."

"Or should I say, *Sister* Leah?" She raised her brows.

I coughed. "No, Your Highness. These clothes are merely borrowed." I tried not to gape at the change in the queen's appearance. The silver streaks in her hair had widened and multiplied, and her eyes reflected weariness where once there had been fire. Most disconcerting was the alteration in her posture. She'd always carried herself with a haughtiness that set her apart. Now I hardly would've recognized her, if not for her lavish attire.

"A disguise. I see."

I twisted the headpiece in my hands as she studied me.

"You were banished from Imperia for treason."

My throat closed in on itself like shear blades. "Yes, Your Majesty. My return was occasioned by unfinished business of the utmost urgency. It has been completed, and I was just now setting off to depart once more, if you could find it in your infinite mercy to spare me." I lowered into another curtsy. "I shall never cross the border into Imperia again. You have my word." My voice trailed off until it was barely audible. The grief I'd tried to delay in leaving Rafe again pressed down on me with full force. I almost didn't care if the queen did order my execution, if Rafe and Ma could be spared finding out about it.

"Yes, so you told my son."

Her words shook me out of my reverie. How much of our conversation had she overheard? The footsteps...my insides stirred like a wind-whipped willow. So much had been said beyond that point. What had I revealed that might incriminate me further?

The queen's laugh startled me with its authenticity. "Yes, I'm afraid I've been standing at this door for some time now. Eavesdropping is a paltry practice for one such as myself, it's true. But I found I was quite riveted by what I heard."

I shrank under her appraisal. What new charges might she level against me?

"Assuming my interpretation is correct, I believe thanks are in order."

What? I must've succumbed to a panicked delusion.

The queen's eyes took on a dour expression. "It seems I owe you my life, in addition to that of my husband and son."

My mouth opened and closed several times. "I'm just happy I was able to help and that I wasn't too late."

"Not half as happy as I." She paced away from me, her hands folded behind her back. "It was very reckless of you—though also brave, I'll admit—to come back here to put a stop to the duke and princess after being accused of treason." She faced me with a heavy sigh. "I apologize for that."

An apology from the *queen*? Hope and disbelief collided with my fear, like arms tugging at me from every direction. "Thank you, Your Majesty."

"Now, the question remains: What's to be done with you?"

I held my arms tight to my sides, trying to subdue my shaking. Here came the point I dreaded.

She raised a brow into a perfect arch. "I understand that my son, or *Rafe*, as you so flippantly call your crown prince, is in love with you."

I gulped. How could I respond truthfully without provoking her anger? "I—he—he has given me to understand that it is so. Your Highness."

The corners of her mouth quirked upward. "A very diplomatic response. You may do well, with the proper training." She straightened, regaining some degree of her customary royal bearing. "Miss Wellstone, since you have been instrumental in preventing the overthrow of our family's reign, and since my foolish boy can't seem to do without you, I must concede defeat in this matter. The two of you shall enter into an immediate betrothal."

My pulse skipped so many beats I feared it had stopped entirely. Could it be possible?

"You're surprised, yes. I know I am reputed to have no respect for servants such as yourself. I suppose it is justified. I have long thought that only a princess, or at the very least a noblewoman of the highest breeding, could make a proper wife for my son. But we were betrayed by so many, our nearest advisers…"

. A hint of sorrow, even uncertainty, flickered in her eyes as she glanced away. Setting her jaw, she returned her gaze to mine.

"You can well imagine what a blow it's been to our confidence in the members of our aristocracy. Perhaps Raphael has chosen better for himself than we chose for him, after all. You have demonstrated acumen, integrity, and courage in your exploits, attributes that ought to make you a suitable princess, and one day, queen. That may be just what Imperia needs at present to restore its faith in the royal family."

My spirits should've soared at such a declaration, but something held me back. Her plan would make my wildest dreams a reality—I could marry Rafe and live out the rest of my days with my love. But I was so weak, so ordinary, how could I be a fit ruler for a country?

A familiar voice seeped into my doubts. *You are worthy, my child. Take the happiness being offered to you.*

Certainty and trust took root in the deepest recesses of my soul, radiating peace. Everything I'd been through—the pain, fear, loneliness—was preparing me for this calling. The Luminate had set me on this path with this destination in mind all along.

Amusement played across the queen's expression at my lengthy silence. "I trust in time you won't appear so dimwitted. Shall we inform my son?"

I nodded, and she marched through the doors of the throne room with me trailing behind.

Rafe raised his head and jumped up. "Mother! No, wait. Before you do anything rash, you must hear me out. You don't understand—" He ran to us, panic blazing in his eyes.

The queen gave him a demure smile. "Actually, this time I think I do understand. Enough, at least, to be of the opinion that we owe a great debt to this young woman." She motioned me to stand next to her. "A debt so great, in fact, that I think it can only be repaid by making her part of the royal family. As your wife. Would that arrangement please you?"

Rafe took a step back, staring between us. "Do you really mean it, Mother? This isn't some kind of joke?"

She folded her arms. "No, Raphael. I hope even I am not so cruel to joke about such a serious matter."

My heart melted right through to my stomach as a wide grin lit Rafe's every feature.

"Then yes, that arrangement would suit me very, very well." He was looking at me now, his eyes brimming with so much emotion, it was hard to keep my distance.

The queen turned to me. "And you, Miss Wellstone. I suppose I never officially obtained your consent to this marriage. Will you accept my son as your future husband, along with all the responsibilities that go along with becoming a princess of Imperia?"

Tears spilled down my cheeks. "Yes, I will. Thank you, Your Majesty."

"Good. Well then, that's settled. Now, I'd best inform my husband of what has transpired here. He wouldn't like to be left in the dark regarding news of his only son's upcoming nuptials."

I detected a sly glint in the queen's eyes as she headed for the door. Perhaps she and I might get along after all.

Rafe remained frozen in place as she retreated from the room. But as soon as the door clicked shut, his full attention turned to me. He moved toward me as though in a daze, putting one arm around my back and slipping the fingers of his other hand into my hair. "Now I'm certain of it. This has to be a dream."

I caressed his cheek. "I sincerely hope not."

His face was so close I could see every detail, relish every breath.

"But Leah, are you sure this is truly what you want? To be

the future queen? I know you prefer a quiet life, and you haven't had any time to think this through…"

I silenced his doubts with a kiss. "This is exactly what I want, to be with you for the rest of my life."

"Then you will be my queen. My wife." A tremor passed through him. "The Luminate is so good."

He placed kisses all over my face, increasing in fervency until his lips met mine. At last, I could return all his love and affection with no hesitation, no guilt or regret, no shadow of future separation. Rafe and I would be joined together forever, in friendship and in love.

The Luminate *was* so good. Though I never believed it possible, He had made a way.

EPILOGUE

*D*ear Sister Val,

    A thousand apologies for being such a lax correspondent. How could I let six months pass since the wedding without writing? It was an absolute joy to see all of you there and introduce you to "my prince," as you like to call him. Please convey my love and regards to Mabel and the other sisters and let me know how everyone is faring.

    Sister Eleanor has made a flawless transition into her role as a palace adviser. The king and queen still regard her with some degree of wariness, but I'm certain her charm and wisdom will win them over before long. And Myrna came to visit last month, sneaking in with no warning just like when she joined us in the forest. She kept us amply entertained, as you can well imagine, though some of the nobles hardly knew what to make of her.

    We at last convinced Ma to retire from being a seamstress and move to a room down the hall from us in the royal chambers. She's a bit scared to touch anything in her new apartment, but her sweetness has endeared her even to the queen. On days she has the energy, she spends her time making dolls for the servants' children. I couldn't say whether the enjoyment is greater on her side or theirs.

    I know you get little news there—did you hear Princess Penelope is engaged to an emperor's son and will be moving halfway across the world? I wish her well, though I must confess I'm relieved we'll see little of her in our future relations with Trellich.

I am settling in as an Imperian princess, though I doubt I will ever get used to people bowing and curtsying just because I happen to walk down the hall. The queen keeps me busy with lessons on etiquette, poise, dancing, and foreign affairs. It seems my progress during the year of wedding preparations was merely a foundation for the real work to be done. There's so much to learn, but she insists she'll get me to a high level of proficiency. Knowing her will of iron, I'm sure she'll succeed! In spare moments, I've been allowed to continue holding reading classes for any servant who wants to attend. What a delight to be able to pass on such knowledge!

You may remember Gretchen, my bridesmaid. She and Ned were blessed with their firstborn a few months back—a delightful, strong boy with a grin just like Gretchen's. Along those lines, if you or the other sisters have any visions concerning the tired, queasy feeling I've been experiencing the past few mornings, please let me know. Our healer suspects a new little royal may be on the way, but I don't want to get my hopes up quite yet. At the very least, prayers would be appreciated.

And I mustn't forget Rafe, but where do I begin? His love and constancy fill my entire existence with light and life. He raises my spirits when I question my merit as a future ruler, and he values my thoughts and opinions as a true equal. After so much uncertainty and time apart, we cherish each moment we have together. Even if more diffi-cult times lie ahead, I could never ask for more than to be married to my dearest friend. He is my perfect partner in life in every way, and I thank the Luminate daily for bringing us together.

I miss you all and pray this letter finds you well.

All my love,

Leah, Princess of Imperia

THE END

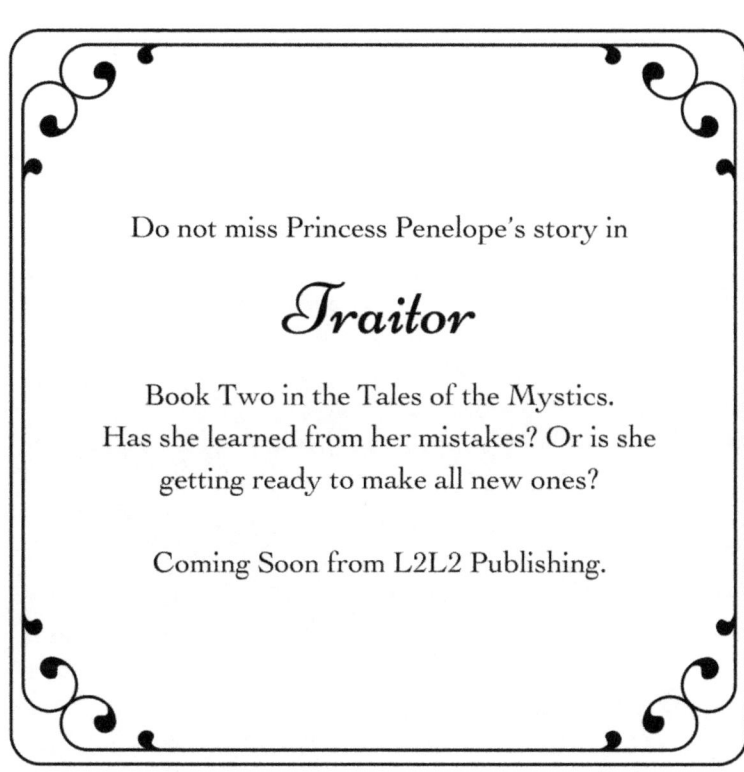

Do not miss Princess Penelope's story in

Traitor

Book Two in the Tales of the Mystics.
Has she learned from her mistakes? Or is she
getting ready to make all new ones?

Coming Soon from L2L2 Publishing.

ACKNOWLEDGMENTS

This book has been years in the making, and I'm so grateful to the many, many people who have made a difference along the way. The call to be an author isn't easy, and I couldn't walk this journey alone!

First, I need to thank my amazing family, especially my husband, sons, parents, sister, and in-laws, for believing in my dream right along with me and accommodating the countless hours I dedicated to reading, writing, and editing. I never would've made it this far without your love and support!

A thousand thank yous to the Love2ReadLove2Write Publishing team, who welcomed me with open arms and worked tirelessly to make this book the best it could possibly be. My manuscript and I could not have found a better publishing home.

I owe so much to my incredible critique group, The Ever Afters, for seeing past my stiff, clumsy first draft to the gem it could become and gently providing the perspective and insight I needed to refine my story to its full potential. (And for being the world's greatest cheerleaders!)

Many thanks to the Minnesota NICE Chapter of ACFW

for becoming my local writing home, teaching me so much, and inspiring me to take my writing and author outreach to the next level. Realm Makers, both in person and online, has become another home-away-from-home, and I'm thrilled to have found such an engaged community of like-minded authors.

My Luminaries have truly been a light and inspiration, blessing me with so much enthusiasm and friendship—virtual hugs and chocolate all around! I'm also so indebted to my fellow contributors at *Lands Uncharted*, both past and current, who helped develop my vague ideas for a group blog into a wonderful reality. Blogging with friends is so much more fun!

I can't begin to express my appreciation to the countless family members, friends, and fellow writers who have offered invaluable prayers, hugs, advice, support, and encouragement at every step along this exciting, emotional journey. I don't want to add an extra chapter by listing you each by name, but know that you all mean the world to me. I'll do my best to pay it forward!

Thank YOU, dear reader, for taking an interest in my book! It still feels unreal to me that anyone might want to invest their precious time and money into a book I've written, but YOU did, and for that I'm eternally grateful.

And last, but never least, all praise and honor to the God who inspires me to enter into co-creation with Him in a way I'd never imagined. If my words touch anyone, it's because God chose to do His work through me—a fact that never fails to fill me with awe.

~Laurie Lucking

ABOUT THE AUTHOR

*L*aurie **Lucking** has always loved diving into imaginary worlds through books, but she didn't start writing her own stories until she left her career as an attorney to become a stay-at-home mom.

After growing up in Wisconsin, she hopped the border into Minnesota to attend St. Olaf College and the University of Minnesota Law School. A Midwestern girl through and through, she continues to make Minnesota her home with her husband and two young sons.

Laurie is the secretary of her local ACFW chapter and a co-founder of **www.landsuncharted.com**, a blog for fans of clean young adult speculative fiction.

Laurie now spends her days driving cars and monster trucks with her sons (in addition to answering their hundreds of questions), relaxing with her amazing husband, and writing during nap times and late at night.

When she gets a break from playing superheroes and driving wind-up cars, Laurie enjoys reading, singing, connecting with other moms, and writing young adult fantasy, always with a central love story to satisfy her inner romantic.

Find out more about Laurie and her writing adventures by visiting **www.LaurieLucking.com**.

Laurie loves to hear from her readers! Follow her on social media, check out her website, or drop her a line to let her know what you thought of Common. *Happy reading!*

www.LaurieLucking.com
Facebook: @AuthorLaurieLucking
Twitter: @LaurieLucking
Instagram: @LaurieLucking

REVIEWS

Did you know reviews can skyrocket a book's career? Instead of fizzling into nothing, a book will be suggested by Amazon, shared by Goodreads, or showcased by Barnes & Noble. Plus, authors treasure reviews! (And read them over and over and over...)

If you enjoyed this book, would you consider leaving a review on:

- Amazon
- Barnes & Noble
- Goodreads

...or perhaps even your personal blog? Thank you so much!

—The L2L2 Publishing Team

More from L2L2 Publishing

If you enjoyed this book, you may also enjoy:

Brenna James wants three things for her sixteenth birthday: to find her history notes before the test, to have her mother return from her business trip, and to stop creating fire with her bare hands. Yeah, that's so not happening. Unfortunately. When Brenna learns her mother is missing in an alternate reality called Linneah, she travels through a portal to find her. Against her will. Who knew portals even existed? But Brenna's arrival in Linneah begins the fulfillment of an ancient prophecy, including a royal murder and the theft of Linneah's most powerful relic: the Sacred Veil. Hold up. Can everything just slow down for a sec? Left with no other choice, Brenna and her new friend Baldwin pursue the thief into the dangerous woods of Silvastamen. When they spy an army marching toward Linneah, Brenna is horrified. Can she find the veil, save her mother, and warn Linneah in time?

Jocelyn washes up on the shore of eighteenth century
Ireland, alone, naked, and missing all of her memories. Taken
in by a lonely old woman full of plots and schemes for the
lovely yet enigmatic creature, Jocelyn knows only one thing.
She longs for the sea with every ounce of her being. Yet it
tried to kill her. Aidan Boyd loves two things. His ship and
the sea. When Jocelyn is thrust upon his vessel in the midst
of his superstitious crew, he finds himself intoxicated by her
—willing to give up everything for her. He soon finds he
cannot live without her. But something holds Jocelyn back.
The whisper of another's love. The embrace of water.
Does she belong to this world? Or could Jocelyn
possibly be from the sea?

More from L2L2 Publishing

If you enjoyed this book, you may also enjoy:

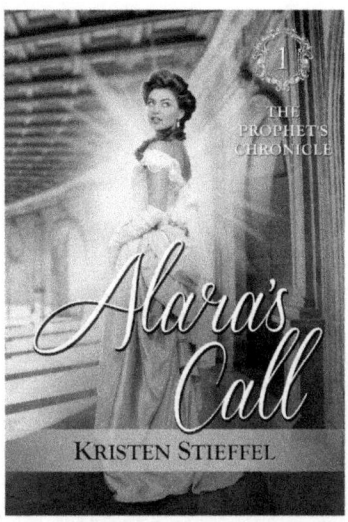

Tales are often told of heroes who fulfill ancient prophecies.
Alara's Call is the tale of a woman who gives new ones.
A young clergywoman with a fiery passion for her Telshan
faith, Alara has been assigned to a mission abroad but longs
to lead a congregation in her homeland. Her father, the
prime minister, jeopardizes her dream and her safety when
he coerces her into what he calls a diplomatic mission. But
it's a ruse. The trip is meant to end with her marriage to the
crown prince of a foreign nation, where members of Alara's
faith are persecuted and women oppressed. All for a trade
agreement her father is desperate to enact. Her mentor
intervenes and takes Alara to Dorrel, the suitor she left
behind. They believe they are safe, but foreign soldiers
are under orders to bring Alara to the king's
palace . . . by any means necessary.

More from L2L2 Publishing

If you enjoyed this book, you may also enjoy:

Ro remembers the castle before. Before the gates closed. Before silence overtook the kingdom. Before the castle disappeared. Now it shimmers to life one night a year, seen by her alone. Once a lady, now a huntress, Ro does what it takes to survive, just like the rest of the kingdom plunged into despair never before known. But a beast has overtaken the castle; a beast that killed the prince and holds the castle and kingdom captive in his cruel power. A beast Ro has been hired to kill. Thankful the mystery of the prince's disappearance has been solved, furious the magical creature has killed her hero, Ro eagerly accepts the job to end him. But things are not as they seem. Trapped in the castle, a prisoner alongside the beast, Ro wonders what she should fear most: the beast, the magic that holds them both captive, or the one who hired her to kill the beast.

WHERE WILL WE TAKE YOU NEXT?

Discover *Spark,*
Read *Ending Fear,*
Drift into *Sinking,*
Buy *Alara's Call,*
and Enjoy *Kill the Beast.*

(*Kill the Beast* coming soon)

All at
www.love2readlove2writepublishing.com/bookstore
or your local or online retailer.

Happy Reading!
~The L2L2 Publishing Team

ABOUT L2L2 PUBLISHING

Love2ReadLove2Write Publishing, LLC is a small traditional press, dedicated to clean or Christian speculative fiction.

Speculative genres include but are not limited to: Fantasy, Science Fiction, Fairy Tales, Magical Realism, Time Travel, Spiritual Warfare, Alternate History, Chillers (such as vampires, zombies, werewolves, or light horror), Superhero Fiction, Steampunk, Supernatural, Paranormal, etc., or a mixture of any of the previous.

We seek stunning tales masterfully told, and we strive to create an exquisite publishing experience for our authors and to produce quality fiction for our readers.

Common is at the heart of what we publish: a heartwarming tale with speculative elements that will delight our readers.

Visit www.L2L2Publishing.com to view our submissions guidelines, find our other titles, or learn more about us.

Happy Reading!

~The L2L2 Publishing Team

CPSIA information can be obtained
at www.ICGtesting.com
Printed in the USA
BVHW03s0538080218
507566BV00001B/62/P